ALSO BY RON LIEBMAN

Shark Tales
Grand Jury

DEATH BY RODRIGO

A NOVEL

Ron Liebman

Simon & Schuster

NEW YORK   LONDON   TORONTO   SYDNEY

SIMON & SCHUSTER
Rockefeller Center
1230 Avenue of the Americas
New York, NY 10020

SIMON & SCHUSTER and colophon are registered
trademarks of Simon & Schuster, Inc.

For information about special discounts for bulk purchases,
please contact Simon & Schuster Special Sales at
1-800-456-6798 or business@simonandschuster.com

Text design by Paul Dippolito

Manufactured in the United States of America

1   3   5   7   9   10   8   6   4   2

Library of Congress Cataloging-in-Publication Data

Liebman, Ronald S.
Death by Rodrigo : a novel / by Ron Liebman
p. cm.
I. Title
PS3612.I33526D43 2007
813'6—dc22   2006100166
ISBN-13: 978-1-4165-3527-0
ISBN-10:   1-4165-3527-6

For Simma

CHAPTER ONE

"That's it? That's all you can say?"

"Oh, give me a fucking break."

"Great. He wants us dead and you want a fucking break."

Mickie looks at me, his cagey eyes searching. If I had something, he'd see it. I'm the open book he can read. But I don't have anything. We are in the shit. Full fucking stop.

Silence. Except for the background din from the few others in the café. The usual prelunch crowd from the Camden, New Jersey, Federal Courthouse directly across the street. A smattering of court clerks on break, a table of past-their-sell-by-date, court-appointed defense lawyers huddling over coffee, gossiping before crossing the street to pick up some small-time offender too inept at his thievery or thuggery to afford even a bad lawyer on his own. That's not us. Nope, Mickie and me take only the occasional court appointments. When we have to. Meaning, when one of the judges makes us. They do. But only from time to time. We are retained lawyers. Our clients might be the scum of the earth: drug dealers, pimps, whores. The occasional low-level Mafia thug. But we are paid. Mostly.

Mickie keeps his eyes on me, then shakes his head.

"Great. Just great," he repeats, his voice thick with sarcasm.

"Somethin' else?" Tamara asks, holding the coffeepot at the ready, her ebony forearm previewing the luxurious tint that covers her fine body head to toe. The top two buttons of her waitress uniform are, as always, unbuttoned so her sizable breasts can bulge. Tamara makes it a point to lean just a little too close when pouring or serving, letting those at the table get a glimpse of what lies beneath, really nice boobs with an indigo tattoo saying "Tamara" in homemade letters. Both Mickie and I shake our heads no, taking in Tamara on display. Smiles exchanged all the way around. The three of us enjoying this even though Tamara's off-limits. No moves are made on her in here. This café is Switzerland. Even the perps are welcome here. Sometimes seated directly across the narrow aisle from their arresting cops. Eating a sandwich before their court hearing, drinking coffee, evil-eye mumbling, How you doin'? at the cops at the other table. Still, our delight with Tamara's feigned come-on momentarily interrupts the problem facing us.

"Okay, guys," Tamara says, turning and giving us a nice long view of her excellent ass and legs.

"Not a white girl alive got an ass like that," Mickie says for the umpteenth time.

With her disappearance behind the swinging kitchen doors our situation reappears like fire ants at a summer picnic.

"This is bad," Mickie says, shaking his head. He stares at me. What am I supposed to say?

"No shit, Sherlock," is the best I can come up with.

He looks away. This is, after all, as serious as it gets.

"I told you we should of stayed out of this," Mickie tells me. "Told that shitbag client of yours to get other lawyers. But no. The fucker waves some money under your nose and that's it. You know what? You carry your brains same place as your wallet."

"Hey," I say, as angry as I'm scared. "Client of *mine*? You were there. I didn't hear a peep from you. Or am I missing something here?"

Mickie shrugs. We are in this together, no question about that.

Mickie and I have been practicing law together since the beginning. But we go further back than that. Sixth grade, to be exact. Both from immigrant Italian families, our fathers carpenters. Like their fathers in the old country. But we were born Americans. Public high school. Protestant girlfriends. Football. Then college. Sure, neither of us were what you'd call scholars. Our skill on the athletic field helped. Mickie did Temple in Philly. Did it straight through. Finished seriously below the middle of his class, but he finished. Me? Well, it took me three schools, if you need to know, but I finally finished up at U Conn. Then we both did military, then became cops. Mickie went into the force in Philadelphia, across the river, first as a uniform, then with vice. Me, I became one of Camden, New Jersey's finest. You know, I actually did pretty well. Went from uniform to homicide detective in less time than anyone else had. I seem to have some sort of knack for crime. Probably would have made a halfway decent crook.

It was Mickie's idea. Law school. At night.

Rutgers' actually took us. Probably because of our law enforcement backgrounds. Both of us older guys, married at the time. But that's another story. Anyway, we did it. Graduated. Okay, it took us more than once to pass the bar exam. Mickie made it the second time. It took me three shots. And if truth be told, without Mickie's help, I'd probably still be taking that fucking test. But you know what? I have to say this. Both of us—yeah, me included—are pretty good at what we do.

I guess you'd call us street crime lawyers. We try cases, negotiate plea bargains, all for a certain kind of client. The people we represent are all guilty. Sometimes not of what they've been charged with. But they're all crooks of one kind or another. Like I said, dopers, bikers, whores, even stone-cold killers.

Mickie and me aren't brief writers—our court motions are store-bought, right out of the form books or "borrowed" from what other lawyers have filed with the court in other cases. You won't ever see too many business letters with our names on them. But juries like us. We're Everyman in lawyer suits. In a way, I guess we're tradesmen, like our fathers were. They were craftsmen. Talented. So are we. Italian genes, right?

And these cases aren't rocket science; one's pretty much like the other. We deal with witness identification. Now tell me, ma'am, how far away was the man you say held up your store brandishing a loaded sawed-off shotgun right in your face? You were scared out of your wits, right? You were shaking? Didn't really see him all that well, did you? Not a hundred percent sure, right? Or search-and-seizure issues. Did the cops really have probable cause, or did they make up stuff and put it in the warrant application for the judge to sign? Cops lie. They want to take their perp down, and to do it they follow the cop way, which, I am sorry to say, isn't always the court way. I mean, who should know better than a couple of ex-cops who did it too. Right?

And I'll take our kind of clients any day over some fancy corporate suit. Telling me he's innocent, what he did technically complied with generally accepted accounting standards when he bled his company dry and cheated his shareholders out of their retirement money. And by the way, Counselor, they will say, what actually are your hourly rates and can we put a cap on what you'll charge? Bullshit to that. No, our clients have no illusions what they are. Who we are. They know they're likely to go down. Whatever Mickie and me can do, we will do. Sometimes that means an acquittal. Not so much because they didn't actually do it, but because we poked some holes in the prosecution's case, or the jury liked us better than some arrogant young Harvard Law graduate stopping off at the United States Attorney's Office long enough to put another notch on his/her résumé before joining some big white-shoe law firm and getting rich. Juries can smell arrogance like that.

Like I said, our clients understand what we are. We don't judge them: they pay, we play. We do what we can do. In most cases pretty damn well. Sure, some of the judges look down their noses at us. To them we're blue-collar lawyers. So what? In criminal it's almost all about the juries. No street-crime lawyer with even half a brain will waive his client's constitutional right to a jury and let his case be tried before the court alone. Nope. Rule of thumb in what we do? Never trust a judge. Never.

There are exceptions, sure, but most judges are out to help the prosecution convict your client. Most play by the rules, give you procedural due process. They don't flagrantly screw you, they're too smart for that, need to have what we lawyers call a clean court record, in case of an appeal, but you've got to watch them. They'll screw you by the rules if you let them.

Look, everyone in the damn courtroom, except maybe the jury, knows your guy's guilty. Like I said, if not what he's there for that particular time, then of something else. Some judges are friendly enough, though a lot of them—especially the federal judges—hate guys like me and Mickie. Sure, that bothers me. Though I never show it. These are more of the "Havvad" crowd. Mostly they made it to the big silk-stocking firms but failed there. What happens? They're smart, sure, but they just don't know how to lawyer. Book-smart doesn't always mean actual-smart. They start screwing up, messing up their firm's big-ticket corporate client cases. Their law partners start getting worried.

The big corporation's big fees are what keep the firm in big revenue. Which in turn pays for the partners' big homes, fancy clubs, Ivy League tuition for their legacy-admittance kids. So these screw-up partners, for all their fancy résumé entries, are jeopardizing the bottom line. That cannot be tolerated. The law firm's exit strategy? Get these bozos on the bench and out of the firm. Departure with honor. And these men and women who couldn't convince a jury that day follows night? They become the judges and, to them, guys like Mickey and me are bumblers, low-rent advocates whose briefs suck, whose educational backgrounds are barrel-bottom low. Sure, we're tolerated in the courtroom, but often barely. Sometimes through clenched teeth. That's why I love it when the jury foreman reads out "not guilty" for some scumbag sitting beside me in the courtroom. I always look up at the judge. My eyes saying, See? That's how you lawyer.

But at the moment the judges aren't our problem. *We* are our problem.

"So, what do we do?" Mickie asks.

Mickie is Michael Carmine Mezzonatti. His father was Carmine Alphonso Mezzonatti. Mickie got an American first name. His mother, Sophia, insisted, told Carmine her husband, We are in America, your son needs to be called like an American. Michael became Mickie on the street, in the neighborhood. Me? Well, everyone calls me Junne (spelled "Junne," pronounced like the girl's name but not spelled that way). To my family and those who go way back I'm sometimes Junnie. My dad was Salvatore Salerno. I have two younger brothers. Giancarlo, called Johnny, and, of course, an Anthony, called Tony. Of course. I was christened Salvatore Salerno, Jr. To my parents, America schamerica, what was good enough in old-country names for my old man was good enough for his sons. For me, Salvatore never stuck. From birth I became Junior. But Junior quickly morphed into Junnie, then, as I got older, Junne.

Mickie's getting a little dumpy-looking these days. I started noticing that a while ago. It's not something you tell a friend. Even your best friend. I mean, neither of us are jocks anymore. Yeah, we both still work out. But truth be told, it's like the guy I once heard that said he got it on with his babe "weekly"—very "weakly." That pretty much sums up our exercise regimen. We do it, but it's harder and harder to maintain. Know what I mean?

So Mickie's getting a little dumpy. To the ladies, he's not what you'd call a head-turner. He's not a bad-looking guy. Still got that high-school-jock-walking-the-halls-before-football-practice gleam in his eyes the girls used to like. His face hasn't sagged or anything like that. He's just getting older. We both are. His hair's still got it, though. Budding flecks of gray just recently making their appearance, but he's got a head of hair just as thick and full like when he was twenty-five. Wears it just a little shaggy. On purpose. Mickie's suits aren't well fitting, his go-to-court ties the kind guys pick without wives standing next to them at the glass-topped counter telling them, No, no, honey, not that one. This one. And the man's got shoes. Spare-no-expense Guccis. Ferragamos. A collection of other high-end brands. His wop-kicks, he calls them.

7

Like I said, he may not be a head-turner, but the thing of it is? With all that, the women still like him. Beats me what it is, but they do. Mickie's been through two wives, though no kids. Shooting blanks, is how he put it after the doctor told him the news. And yet he always—always—has someone nice—at least nice enough—to share his bed. And his current? Okay, not a wife, but really—I mean really—nice. And with a Ph.D. Go figure. Mickie the Italian stallion.

So Mickie's question was the right one. What the hell do we do now?

Maybe the shit we were in was my fault.

You see, about this time last year I represented this little Salvadoran weasel named Hector. He was some low-level drug ring guy. His place got busted just after he takes delivery of five kilos. Really good stuff, not yet stepped on, ready for processing, then distribution. And he's got all the paraphernalia laid out. Scales, bags. You name it. Oh yeah, and an arsenal of guns. It's his third pop, so he's going down hard. That puts a lot of pressure on him to roll over on the guys above him. But that's hard too. Because those guys are not too forgiving. Give them up and they not only kill you while you're doing your time, but they take out your whole family to boot. Business is business.

So Little Hector's resigned to his fate. But he's figured out who set him up. Him he'll give up, but not to the cops. To his bosses. Like a kind of peace offering, letting them know he's straight with them. He may be headed for twenty years' hard time, but what are his options? That or slaughter of his mama, his sisters, his baby brother. And, of course, him too while he's in the can doing his twenty.

But I have a better idea. Give me the name of the guy, I tell him when we visit while he's in lockup. Keep him alive. Let me go after the probable cause for the warrant and the search. Let me take a shot at it. Put the guy on the stand at the preliminary hearing.

Little Hector shrugs. What's he got to lose? If I lose in court and the judge rules the search and seizure's good, he'll see to it—like the Beatles said, with a little help from his friends—that the snitch goes down later.

Lightning strikes. I cross-examine the snitch. Then the cops. I argue the motion to quash the warrant. I win. The judge says I'm right that the snitch told the cops only hearsay and that they lied to the magistrate who signed the warrant when they said all the information in the affidavit that supported the warrant application was based on sworn direct—not hearsay—evidence. Judge throws the case out. Blasts the cops for lying.

No evidence. No case. Little Hector walks.

Once out, he tells his bosses he's got a fucking genius for a lawyer. A few months later one of the bosses gets popped. Rodrigo Gonzáles. Seems he was in Camden, New Jersey, all the way from San Salvador for some big meet. He snuck into town because he's a wanted man. There's a warrant out for him. Little Hector tells him I'm the man. Mickie and me go to see Rodrigo in lockup. He tells us all he wants is for us to get him bail. After that he's good. Because he's not sticking around to prove his innocence. He's out of here and back to San Salvador. Passport or no passport, he's gone. Our job: bail. I say, Rodrigo, this will cost you big-time. In broken English he says, How much? I tell him. He shrugs, says the money will be wired to us. Then he looks at us, hard. Doesn't say anything more. Doesn't have to. Big fee. Bail. That's it. No excuses, no explanation. He delivers. We deliver.

Rodrigo's sitting next to me and Mickie in court, orange jumpsuit, shaved head. The judge says, Bail? What are you smoking, Mr. Salerno? Bail for this Salvadoran drug kingpin? Next case.

Rodrigo just stares up at Mickie and me. Keeps staring at me and

Mickie as the marshals reshackle him and shove him and his orange jumpsuit, "Prisoner" stenciled on the back like there was some doubt, out of the courtroom.

Next day we get a visitor.

Not what I expected. Not some Spanish-looking guy in a flowered shirt, gold neck chain embedded in a forest of thick black chest hair. No. This guy's wearing a nice suit and tie. Hair's trimmed. He's all polite and nice manners. And no accent.

Mickie and me share a small office space we rent from another law firm. What it is, is a room for each of us right in the other law office. They're plaintiffs' lawyers, meaning they're a bunch of Jewish guys who do slip and falls, car crashes, mostly small-time. But they seem to make about four times what Mickie and I do. We get to use their law library. Which we don't. And we get the use of their receptionist. Janice. Pronounced "Janiese" because she's Jamaican and that's how she says it. Our name's on the front door in smaller print. There's "Bernstein, Smulkin, Abramowitz & Wolf." Big print. Under it, like I said, in smaller print: "Law Offices Mezzonatti and Salerno."

So this guy asks Janice pronounced Janiese, can he please see Mr. Mezzonatti and Mr. Salerno. Together? she asks. If that isn't too much trouble, he says. Do you have an appointment? she asks, like she's supposed to. No, no appointment, he says. But if you tell them I am here on behalf of Mr. Rodrigo Gonzáles, that might do the trick. She calls us. It does the trick.

We meet in Mickie's room. It's bigger than mine. Mickie's behind the desk. Me and Mr. Well-Dressed occupy the two visitor chairs. He thanks us graciously for taking time out of our busy schedules to see him. Mickie and me nod, Yeah, sure, no problem. Behind this guy's calm is trouble. I mean, who's kidding who here? He crosses his legs, flicks some imaginary dust from the crease of his trousers.

"Mr. Gonzáles is quite unhappy," he says, still studying his trousers.

Mickie and me exchange glances. Oh boy. Here it comes.

"Yeah, well—" Mickie starts to say, about to add that we—meaning me, I guess—really did our best to get Rodrigo bail. What can you do? Mickie's about to say when Mr. Well-Dressed holds up his hand. Mickie stops about midword.

"I need to make a point here," Mr. Well-Dressed says.

His eyes have left the crease in his pants and slowly—like an enemy sub rising from the depths of the cold North Atlantic—they periscope on me. Then they shift to Mickie, where they stay, boring in on him. The temperature in Mickie's room drops. There's a chill. I can feel it.

Mickie's still as a deer in the woods.

"Your client, Mr. Gonzáles," he says, still sighted on Mickie.

Now, like I said, I have known Mickie almost my whole life. I know his every move. He's thinking, Can I make a joke out of this? Cut the tension here? Say, Whoa, pal—hey, don't look at me. Junne over there argued this, took the case. Heh, heh. You got a beef here, it's with Junne. Chuckle, chuckle. Roll those shoulders, pantomime-punch Mr. Well-Dressed's arm.

Nope. Mickie stays frozen. His self-preservation instincts override his let's-make-light-of-this escape response. Now I know exactly what he's thinking. Same as me.

Shit.

"Mr. Gonzáles wants you to know that he has every confidence that you . . ." Now Mr. Well-Dressed looks at me and Mickie both.

Double shit.

"That you gentlemen," he continues, "will secure bail for your client. He knows that you will make this your highest priority. And that you will not fail."

He doesn't add the word "again." Doesn't have to. And he doesn't say, And if you don't, and Rodrigo has to remain in jail in his orange prison-issue jumpsuit, and not be able to jump bail instead and escape back to his mansion hacienda in the forests of San Salvador, where he can resume living like a king and not like some two-bit convict with a shaved head with some big brutish African-American murderer or Aryan Brotherhood blockhead cell mate, he will see to it—since you took his money to get him out and you didn't—that, not only will he have you killed, he will have your entire family killed, your office torched, and while his men are at it, the killing part that is, not the torching part, they will kill you really, really slowly. Got it?

Am I rambling? Fucking-A I am. Oh my. Shit. (I know, I've said that already. But believe me, you were sitting here with us? In this fix? Prey with an *e*, like us? Believe me, *Shit* is what you'd be thinking. I damn well guarantee it.)

Mickie opens his mouth. Nothing comes out. I watch him staring across his desk. Our eyes meet briefly. I see Mickie nod his head at Mr. Well-Dressed, trying, I guess, to portray some kind of gravity. Message received, he seems to be saying. We will take care of it.

"How long?" we are asked. Mr. WD looking first at Mickie and then over at me seated beside him.

How long what? I am thinking. How long will Rodrigo have to remain in jail before he gets bail? Or: How long do we think we will live if we fail to spring our client? Answer to question number one: Forever and a day. Answer to question number two: Triple shit.

Never underestimate the survival instinct. Finally, Mickie comes to life.

Mickie leans forward on his desk, elbows on his blotter. Looks professional, but my guess is he needs those elbows fastened to something sturdy and hard to prevent his visibly shaking.

"In my estimation . . ." Mickie says, all senatorial in his tone of voice. "In my estimation," he repeats with a quick eye flicker over to me. (Either to wrap me in here or to ask, How am I doing? Who knows which?)

". . . my colleague and I . . ." (Quick wave of the hand over in my direction.)

". . . believe that we will have our papers . . ." (Like I said, the last time Mickie actually wrote a legal brief, as opposed to cribbing something off another lawyer or the form books, he was in law school.)

". . . in to the court within a week. Then I estimate . . ." (Now, when Mickie uses words like "estimate" the bullshit meter is in double digits. This is a guy who uses "fuck" as a major figure of speech: noun, adjective, verb. You name it.)

". . . that the court will allow full briefing between the defense . . ." (Mickie smiles indulgently at Mr. WD, as if to say, That would be us.)

". . . and the prosecution. Then the court will consider the briefs and schedule a hearing on our renewed application for bail in, say . . ." (I can't believe it! Mickie's actually rubbing his chin like he needs to consider this question of when the judge will hear from us. Like there is some leeway here. Listen. The judge is going to get our renewed motion and he isn't even going to require the prosecutor to respond. He will deny the motion the minute his eyes light on it. Bang will go the stamp. Denied! Next case. What the hell is Mickie up to? I ask myself.)

"Well, Mr. . . ." Mickie asks our guest since he has not actually favored us with a name.

"Smith," Mr. WD responds, recrossing his legs, his gaze telling Mickie, You dumb schmuck, you think I'm gonna give you my name now if I haven't yet? What kind of idiots has Rodrigo chosen for lawyers? he's thinking.

"Smith," Mickie repeats as if to say, Yeah, okay, I buy it. If you tell me your name is Smith, I fully without reservation accept that as gospel truth. No problem, why would I question you, nice fellow that you obviously are and, by the way, nice suit and tie, really.

Rubbing his chin again. Oh boy.

"From three weeks to three months," Mickie says, adding, "Mr. Smith, you know how the courts are. Busy docket. Lots of cases competing for the judge's attention." Mickie shrugs. What can you do? he is saying to Mr. WD Smith.

WD Smith rises.

"Do it fast," he says, then turns and leaves.

The door closes behind him, and as it does, all air is sucked from the room. It's hard to breathe. For about a second or two neither Mickie nor I can look at each other. And then.

"Jesus fucking Christ," Mickie explodes. I wince, thinking, Is Mr. WD Smith out of earshot? Mickie doesn't appear to care. He is so distraught—so scared, he's just losing it. Of course, what I should do is calm Mickie down, keep the situation from spinning out of control. What I do instead, of course, is scream right back at him.

"What the fuck is the matter with you?" I shout in Mickie's face.

Now both of us are out of our seats, screaming and pointing and leaning at each other like a couple of completely around-the-bend, screaming—well, okay . . . idiots. Our voices are doubtlessly permeating the hallway and the rest of Bernstein, Smulkin, Abramowitz & Wolf is probably cringing as Mickie and I go at our simultaneous shouting, voice over top of voice. Then Janice pronounced Janiese knocks on the door, which Mickie and I can't hear in our hysteria. So she opens it, slowly at first, in case anything might come flying her way. When we notice her standing there we both stop in midsentence and look at her. She looks back at us, and if I didn't know better I would think she was actually smirking.

"Two of your G-note ladies are here," she says, looking first at Mickie, then at me.

All right, let me explain.

Rosco Jones, aka Buffalo Reds, is a pimp. He's called what he's called because he's originally from Buffalo and because he's got a kind of light coffee-colored, almost red-tinctured skin. He's one handsome guy, sort of dignified-looking—if you don't count the big gold tooth and the outlandish hip-hop clothes he favors, which, if you ask me, really belong on a younger guy—black or white, doesn't matter. What I'm saying is that Buffalo Reds is his street name. Mickie and I address him as Mr. Jones or Rosco depending on how he decides to address us, meaning by our Mr.'s or by our first names. He alternates. Like clockwork, never seems to miss sequence. Don't know why, but it's almost like he's keeping track. Anyway.

Buffalo Reds's girls are all white, every last one of them. It's part of his stock-in-trade, his signature. And the veneer of the street has been removed from them. See, when Reds picks a girl, he invests in her. Gone are the leaning into a car window, micro-mini up-the-crack-of-her-ass skirt, the halter top bulging with fleshy tits spilling into the car. He has a professional dresser he pays to re-outfit his girls. Saks, Neiman Marcus, strictly Fifth Avenue style. The hair is redone. Then come diction lessons. When he's finished with them, Reds's girls straddle that fine line between high-society girl and intimate cocktail lounge slut. It's a work of art, I have to say.

At first glance, if you didn't know better, you'd think you had paid for some good-looking corporate secretary or sexy female executive. But, undressed, the girls sport those whore tattoos they got before they hooked up with Reds. You know, the scrolled wings spread on their lower backs just above their unbelievable asses, the little heart northeast of their shaved you-know-whats. And so on. And if a john gets them angry, treats them with any disrespect, in a flash they can—and will—revert to their former selves and threaten to slice off balls and stuff them down throats.

How do I know? Reds constantly laments to me and Mickie how difficult it is to take the street out of the girl. Needless to say, threatened genital dismemberment does not advance Reds's illegitimate business interests. But one thing Reds's girls do not do. Ever. Is mess with him. One did, as Mickie and I heard it. She dissed him in front of the other girls on the let's-turn-all-our-hard-earned-money-over-to-Reds part of the evening.

As we heard it, Reds listened to this girl rant and rave, telling him she wasn't going to give up everything she made that night to his light-skinned black ass. She told him—scolded him, was how Mickie and me heard it—that she worked too hard for it and, by the way, while she was at it, she was fucking sick and tired of this let's pretend we're some kind of college-educated-bullshit sophisticated bitches who can't speak the way we do and don't know, by the way, what the johns want: like, Hey, baby, you wanna fuck me, don'tcha? As we heard it, this girl stood there, in front of the other girls in Reds's apartment in downtown Philly—where Reds lives since downtown Camden is . . . well, downtown Camden—glaring at Reds, her arm resting on, you should pardon the expression, her cocked hip.

Reds nods at her in front of the other girls, letting her know, Sure, baby, I can see your point of view, you being one of my best girls, a big earner, you looking fine all the damn time. He gently lets his hand with its long tapered fingers, manicured nails always clear high gloss, gently stroke her cheek. Then he lovingly turns the girl around so she's now facing the other girls. He's standing behind her. He puts his arms around her, affectionately pecks her on the cheek from the back. You my best girl, he tells her, but Reds is now looking at the other girls. Those not too dim-witted can see something bad in his eyes.

You my best earner, Reds is telling the girl, nuzzling her ear, almost whispering to her now, as his right hand slips away from her and goes to his pocket. The girl's still mad, but she's getting placated, thinking, Maybe now the man going to give me some respect—and more of my hard-earned money too.

In a flash Reds's hand reappears. He's holding his razor knife, something he's had made for him, shiny knife handle, razor-sharp embedded blade, and with lightning speed he slashes the girl's throat wide open. She hasn't made a sound, her eyes wide with shock and horror. The other girls gasp, but they don't move, frozen by pure animal instinct. Reds holds the girl up, her legs dangling to the floor, her throat now a huge hole, blood streaming down the front of her stylish clothes. She's gurgling, her eyes rolling back in her head.

We heard that Reds then sliced the girl's head straight off and tossed it at the other girls, asking them did any of them have a complaint *they* wanted to make. Mickie and I aren't sure that last part actually happened, but who knows? The girl's body was never found.

Reds's management style seems to have been effective. No more personnel problems from his G-noters.

Oh right. G-noters. They're called that because that's what they cost. You want to avail yourself of the services of Reds's high-class-looking—and -speaking—white girls, it will cost you a G-note: $1,000. She's yours for an hour, or the night. Your call, but the cost: a G-note. So, as you can imagine, the clientele is pretty fancy. Some of Camden's and Philadelphia's finest citizens are repeat customers.

And rarely, if ever, do they see Buffalo Reds. He is strictly a behind-the-scenes man.

But Reds takes care of his girls. If they get arrested, and that does happen from time to time, he sends them to us. Reds never complains about the fee. Says to us, Just take care of it. He also helps them invest some of their hard-earned money in stocks and bonds. He uses other lawyers for that. Mickie and me are strictly criminal. We've heard, though, that Reds takes fifty cents of every dollar of return on investment his girls make from their stock portfolios. After what happened to that other girl, I guess they're more than happy to comply. And, after all, if it wasn't for Reds's insistence on their investing some of their money, they wouldn't likely be doing it in the first place. Right?

Anyway, Janice pronounced Janiese is standing in the doorway. Me and Mickie are now silent, our voice-over-voice screamfest silenced by her presence. She's waiting. Okay, guys, she's signaling, we got these two well-dressed whores in the Bernstein waiting room, what you going to do?

"Okay, thanks, Janice," Mickie tells her. "Bring them back here to my office. Junne and I will see them here."

Janice nods sure, if that's what you want. But that look in her eyes. Something midway between amusement and pity. She's kind of hiding it, at least trying to, but I see it. Well, to hell with her, I'm thinking defensively, but at the same time, gnawing at my insides is an awareness that maybe Mickie and me aren't handling things here in the best way possible.

Janice closes the door. I look over at Mickie. Now it's his eyes I'm seeing. And he's doing the same. Looking straight at me.

Just like at the café across from the federal courthouse where Mickie and me are sitting, Mickie having just asked me, "So, what do we do?" Meaning about Rodrigo.

I don't know. Mickie doesn't know.

Tamara walks by, coffeepot in hand, doing a round of refills. Mickie signals for our check. Tamara nods yeah, sure, still walking by, not breaking stride, as she moves down the café corridor between the tables. She flashes us her trademark pantomime lascivious smile. Want some of this, don't you, boys? Both Mickie and I do what we always do, pretend we're dying for it. But right now our hearts just are not in it. We're doing a bad job of faking it. Tamara sees this. She still doesn't break stride, but her look tells me even she can see that Mickie and me have a problem. That we are sick with worry. Tamara the waitress can see this without even stopping at our table, without even one little inquiry. Without asking, Something wrong, guys?

My heart sinks.

CHAPTER TWO

I live in Camden. Not in the old neighborhood. Nope. Don't live there and wouldn't even if I could. I am a part of decaying Camden, New Jersey's anti-decay redevelopment plan. Look, I'll admit it's not much. Not yet anyway. And it was started by a bunch of those tree-hugging, let's-all-hold-hands-and-sing-"Kumbaya" people. ("Kumbaya," for you non-earth-shoe readers: originally from Angola, Africa, meaning sort of like "Come by here," expropriated by Peter, Paul & Mary types, used mainly while strumming an out-of-tune acoustic guitar, eyes gazing upward.) But you got to start somewhere, right? And now there's developers involved, and people of color who are as tired as the few remaining white folks of the shit hole Camden has become. So yeah, it's a start.

Lots of my friends from here, from the old neighborhood, now live in Philadelphia, across the river. Or else in the Jersey suburbs, in or near the green-grass town of Cherry Hill. You know, in the Land of the Mall. The look-alike house with the circular driveway, the surround-sound system hanging on whitewashed walls guarding the new flat-screen like a band of soldiers on night watch in enemy territory. (That was Mickie's suburban house I just described, which, I freely admit, sees me no less than twice a week—not including weekends—seated on the brushed leather couch, ninety-degree angle in front of the flat-screen. Beer can on low table, bags of salt-fat disguised as munchies within easy reach.)

But I live in Camden. The city fathers—maybe I should say mothers, since the mayor's a woman. A black woman. Anyway, the city whatevers got some urban renewal going, down by the waterfront, at the Delaware River, the revitalized Philadelphia waterfront on the other side. I'm in a building called the Victor on account of it was once a cabinet factory for those old RCA Victor phonographs. You know, the stupid dog looking into that big funnel while the old record player plays "his master's voice," the dog thinking, What the . . . ? It's kind of a loft place with apartments, a "promenade" out front along the river for "leisurely strolls or maybe a spring morning jog," like the brochure says. Well, maybe someday. Right now, you want to take a spring morning jog, you better run like the wind, or else carry a Glock nine with you, 'cause you're gonna get robbed, or worse. But, it's getting there. Where I live it's mostly singles living. Families? No, not yet.

Yeah. Revitalized Camden. The city of Walt Whitman, poet of *Leaves of Grass*. Visited here during his nineteenth-century lifetime by the great Irish playwright Oscar Wilde. Rugged, handsome, bearded Walt Whitman, a big influence on one of America's major twentieth-century poets Allen Ginsberg. Three great men of letters. And what did they all have in common?

Great men of letters, like I said, you say. Ding! Wrong! Three fags. All three faggots. I'm being a little insensitive here, you're maybe thinking? I've got my reasons. Believe me. All in good time.

All right. Why wait, right? It's going to come out sooner or later. This isn't easy for me. I'm not sure you need to know. I mean, what's it got to do with anything? But I'm . . . well, I'm sort of, you know, one of them. I really don't want to talk about it.

I may live in Camden, but nightlife, if you want it, stills lives across the river in Philly. That's where I am now, sitting at the bar at a place called the City Tavern, where Mickie's current squeeze works. I'm waiting for Mickie, who'll be here any minute so he, me, and Cynthia, that's her name, who gets off soon, can go someplace else for dinner. Mickie's been down in Atlantic City, where he's doing a sentencing for some guy who tried cheating the casinos with some stupid scam or other. These slobs never learn that the house is not beatable. Period. Anyway, Cynthia passes me, a tray of drinks held high, nodding my attention to the woman seated one barstool away. I see the woman, nice-looking. Well, nice-enough-looking, glancing at me, not too obvious, but seeing am I interested.

Here's where this gets tricky. Mickie knows about me. I mean, Mick's my best friend. (Not like that. He's like my brother.) We've got history together. I think it may have been the hardest thing for him to take. You know, accept my you-know-what. Thing is (and I know what you're going to think), I am attracted only to heterosexual men. Calling Dr. Freud, you're thinking, right? But not Mickie. Not him. I mean it.

I know I'm a good-looking guy. Not in some faggy hairdresser limp-wristed way. I'm in shape. I work out, like I said. All right, I'm sort of in shape. And you know what? You can always tell the fags at the health club. They're the ones with the sculpted bodies who al-ways—and I mean always—wear a towel tight around their waists to

and from the showers. Not the straight guys. See, they may be checking out some guy's pickle, but they're thinking, Am I as big as him?
You know, like in a comparative kind of way. What they're not thinking is, Oh, look at that, wouldn't it be nice if? The fags wear that
tightly wrapped towel 'cause they're worried they're gonna look at
some guy's dork who's in the buff passing on the way to the showers.
The fags are worried they're thinking what they're thinking and then
Mr. Happy's gonna start flagpoling on them. Me? I never wear a
towel in the locker room. I don't look at nobody. And I don't talk to
nobody. Period.

So, I'm not too bad-looking. Kind of dark-complexioned, with
that olive skin Italians from the lower boot have. My hair's dark too,
and curly. But, unlike Mickie's, mine is starting to thin. What can you
do? My features are what girls like. You know, my eyes are soft, my
nose small, and my lips not too thin. Yeah, I said what girls like. I was
married, you know. Yes, to a girl. It didn't last. Six months, that was
it. And I still date women. And I have slept with some of them. I
admit, I date when I've got to. Like when there's a family thing. My
dad's no longer with us. But my mother's still alive and my brothers
all got families of their own. Sundays we visit. Sometimes I bring a
girl. It just makes things easier. None of them know. I think my dad
did. We never talked about it. Never. And I was your typical kid.
Sports. Neighborhood fights. All the boy things. But I think I could
see it in his eyes. I think he knew.

Where does it come from? This condition. No, that's not fair. It's
not a condition. There's plenty of, okay, gays, not fags, who are con-
tent with their condition. There, I said it again. For me it's . . . I don't
know what. What it's like is this unwanted traveling companion sitting in the seat next to you. Always. Never leaving you alone even
though you're like sending signals, Leave me alone, for Christ sake.

I started knowing in junior high. It was a torment. Believe me. I wanted—no, make that want—to be like the other guys. I know there's something somewhere. This thing I've got about heterosexual men. Something you want but can't have. Maybe some repressed experience as a kid. Or maybe it's just as simple as I want—deep down in my soul—to be like all those men I have known. Not tormented. With girlfriends. Wives. Okay, for Italian men, sometimes both at the same time. But with families. Kids. Not these urges.

I take out women. So nobody around here's whispering. And if I occasionally sleep with one? Well, it gets around. Yeah, I can do it. Look, with Viagra you can fuck a horse if you need to. You take the blue pill, then you go out. What you're thinking when you're in bed with her's your business. Right? You don't have to announce what you need in your head to get that woody. You just need the woody.

And I don't, you know, see guys around here. Never.

Not that you need to know, but occasionally I do go out with someone. Out of town. Always out of town. Once or twice in Atlantic City, though that's too close, really. Scares me that I will bump into someone from around here. I don't go to gay bars. I mean, why? Those guys don't do anything for me. And too risky. What if someone sees you going in? Or leaving? Even alone. No, porno on the Web's about as risky as I go. I mean, that's anonymous, right?

And, like I said, Mickie knows. But only Mickie.

Not like I care. But please don't think bad of me. I mean, you got your own demons, don't you? I mean, I function. I have a life. It's just this unwanted traveling companion I got.

So, the woman one barstool away's still clocking me. Giving me that I-wouldn't-mind-if-you-slid-onto-the-stool-between-you-and-me look. I smile back. "How you doin'?" I say to her. "Hi," she says.

Okay, so. Mickie's due any minute. Cynthia doesn't know. Only

Mickie. He says he doesn't tell his babes. He swears that to me. And I believe him. Like I said, it was hard for Mickie to deal with this. When I told him, it was years ago. First he thought I was like joking. Then when he saw I meant it, he got really mad. Punched me. Called me names. Threw me out of his house. Said, Get the fuck out of here. But then, I don't know. He came around. Told me it was the hardest thing he'd ever done. Said, Just don't talk about it, okay? Yeah, I said. Sure, no problem.

Now I'm thinking. I slide over to this woman. We talk. Mickie gets here. I tell her, Want to join my friend and his girlfriend for dinner? Make it a foursome? She's up for that. Makes the evening maybe less awkward. Cynthia's got another woman along. Someone to go to the ladies' with. Joke at the table. These guys, honestly, can you believe them? So I'm thinking, Why not? when Mickie blows in.

He comes over to the bar. Tells me, "This fuckin' guy"—meaning the client. "We're standing there front of the judge. All this mope's got to do is look hangdog, tell the court he's so goddamned embarrassed on account of what he did, trying to cheat the casino with his bullshit scam. What's he do when the judge says to him—after I make my speech how this slob deserves probation, if not for him, then for the clinically depressed wife and kids he's disappointed? The judge says to him, Anything you want to say before I pass sentence?" Here Mickie rolls his eyes. Wait till you hear this, he's signaling.

Right then he catches the eye of the girl on the barstool. She's been listening in. Mickie smiles at her. "Hi," he says. "Hi," she says. And now what I see is that this woman's clocking Mickie. Like I said, Mick's looking kind of dumpy these days. And, you know, he's been in the car for over an hour. A three-year-old Mercedes S-Class we took off a doper as a legal fee. But Mickie's got this something that just magnets the girls. The barstool woman's shifted all her attention from me to Mickie, her eyes flirting, letting him know, him she'll take. Right then Cynthia walks by on her way to one of the tables she's serving. Right up to Mick at the bar. Plants a big fat one mouth-to-mouth on him. "Hey, baby," she says, completely oblivious to the other girl's attentions. "Hey, sweetie," Mickie says. That other girl's no longer existing in Mickie's universe. He knows what's what here.

"So the guy looks up at the judge," Mickie continues, eyeing Cynthia's ass as she goes to deliver her drinks. "He says, Judge. Another twenty minutes and I would of beat 'em. And those goons the casino had grab me? Judge. They manhandled me. Hurt my neck. My arm. When this case here's over, my lawyer—now the schmuck's pointing at me, like I'm a part of this bullshit he's saying—my lawyer here's gonna sue them. Casino too. For millions. Anything else? the judge says down to him, the judge's face now fucking Mount Rushmore. Stone. Letting the guy—who misses it, of course—know, this fuck's going down. Nope, the client says, real smug-like 'cause he's satisfied he's done one hell of a good job here. Judge, I interject, you know, trying to see can I salvage anything here. Mr. Mezzonatti, the judge says, cutting me off, I heard enough."

Mickie stops, still ignoring the girl eavesdropping because to him there is no girl there anymore. He catches the bartender on his way by, who we both know by name. Says, Billy, Dewar's rocks. Billy nods you got it.

Billy's got the scotch in front of Mickie in like two seconds flat. Mickie swirls the ice around, then takes a long pull. He's shaking his head, still into the case, the client now back in lockup, bail revoked, on his way to Mid-State Correctional. The only bone the judge threw Mickie, not putting the mope in Rahway, where, after about three seconds, he'd be corn-holed by the really bad boys. The Bloods. The

Aryan Brotherhood. Standing in black-white lines waiting their new-fresh-meat turns.

Now I see the barstool babe's back into me. Mickie's taken, she sees. I'm backup here. Her eyes telling me, It's you. Not him. Never was him. I smile at her, but my eyes are signaling back at her. Printed there, and she reads it: Dinner tonight's for three. I see her disengage. Now she's clocking the rest of the bar, seeing maybe dinner's sitting on one of the other stools. Give her credit—no harm, no foul. She's not mad, just making the best of her situation.

I don't reconsider, though. I'm going to leave dinner before dessert and coffee. I've got a trial tomorrow. It's only a one-day—two, max—thing. And then after court I'm going to see Professor Mumbles.

Okay, first about the trial. Then Professor Mumbles.

This is another mope. But this one's a bad kid. Came to us through a major thug. The thug controls a big share of the west side ghetto. Drugs galore, I'm telling you. Big, I mean his operation's big. Thug's been around too. Unlike so many others, he hasn't gone down. His name is Williams. The street and the cops both call him Slippery Williams. On account of nothing sticks to him. A kind of underworld gangster Reagan with that Teflon thing they used to say about him. Anyway, the kid's his nephew. Some hip-hop jive-ass punk with shit for brains. What happened was the kid's got a small crew. His uncle Slippery says, Be careful, know who you're dealing with. You got questions, come to me. But no. The kid's thinking he's an entrepreneur. He's going to show some initiative. Fuck his uncle. Come the day, he's going to take the motherfucker out, anyway. Take over the business.

So the kid and his crew meet this guy, says he's from New York and he's looking for some new supply lines. Can the kid produce enough good-quality H? Then be one of his steady suppliers. Got ya good, the kid says. Follow me in that fancy Lexus you drivin', looking fine and all with them New York plates.

See, the nephew figures he knows one of his uncle's new temporary supply houses. It's run by a lieutenant the kid's figuring is going to work for him once he offs his uncle, soon as the kid amasses the war chest he's going to build through side deals like this one. With the New York guy following in the Lexus, he and his two-man crew drive to the house. Wait here in the car, the kid says to him. Be right out with what you need. Flashing his gold-tooth grin at him. Just be a minute.

So this is where it gets interesting.

Inside the house the lieutenant tells the kid no. Slippery's shit is Slippery's shit. No fucking way is the lieutenant going to side-deal any of it. Nephew or no nephew. Forget about it. The kid's real disappointed, figures to himself, The day comes, the lieutenant gets offed along with his uncle. But now there's a more immediate problem. The guy's sitting down there in the Lexus waiting. Big pile of cash with him, expecting to exchange it for drugs he can take back to New York and retail on the street. The lieutenant says, Tell you what, take this sawed-off. You take it down there, relieve the motherfucker of his money. I'll take twenty percent as rent. Ten, the kid says. Fifteen, the lieutenant says. Deal's made.

Now we're down on the street. The kid's standing at the Lexus. Driver's side, window's rolled down. The kid's wearing a jacket the lieutenant threw in, so the sawed-off's momentarily hidden. The guy in the Lexus says, "So? We in business?" The kid rips the sawed-off out from his jacket, presses it right in the guy's cheek, cocks it. "Blink too loud, motherfucker, and I'll blow your head across the passenger side this here fine car."

Now the kid's hot and his two-man crew are standing there beside him gleeful, seeing is the kid going to take the money and pull the trigger anyway, or just take the money?

"The money, bitch," the kid tells the guy.

"Okay, okay," the guy says, reaching down under his seat for the bag with the cash.

He hands it to the kid. This is the moment. The kid's thinking. What's he going to do? He doesn't know himself. He presses the sawed-off harder into the guy's cheek.

"Let's go," he tells his crew, and they run for their own car. The guy in the Lexus speaks. "I'm okay," he says into the mic hidden in his shirt collar, because he's an undercover and all around the neighborhood are plainclothes parked, waiting. The kid and his crew take off, now under hot pursuit by the cops.

So, when we are called in to the case, the kid and his crew have been apprehended, as the cops say. I show up for the arraignment, meet the kid first time in the courtroom, although his uncle Slippery has been to our offices, met with me and Mickie, told us what's what. Back to that in a minute.

When I see the kid, the sheriffs are bringing him into the courtroom with the other two mopes are his crew, unshackling him and them before the judge takes the bench so he can take the not-guilty plea, set a trial date, deny my application for bail. The kid's face is all swollen, and there's this big bandage covering all of his left eye, the kid squinting out of his right puffy eye at me. That puffy eye's saying, You the lawyer, so lawyer, you fuck, and get me out of here, like my uncle's paying you to do.

When Mickie and me met with Slippery he sort of alluded to what his nephew told him—through an intermediary—since no way Slippery's going to the jail, even as a visitor. There was some trouble at the time of the arrest, something about a charge of resisting. Slippery raised his eyebrows. All three of us sitting there around Mickie's desk knew. Pull a gun on an undercover, your arrest's going to go down hard. Real hard.

Anyway, Slippery explained his dilemma. The kid was trouble. Too stupid to function in Slippery's business. Yet, what could he do? The kid was his sister's oldest. I think Slippery, smart as he is, had also figured out that, at some point down the road, the kid was going to try and take him out. Family ties not having the same import to his nephew as they did to Slippery. But here was Slippery's problem. He couldn't just let the kid go down. Slippery was the CEO, chairman of the board. His people needed to see that, one of them went in, needed legal counsel, it was there. Also, Slippery, I think, had thought through having the kid snuffed by his own people while he was inside, either now, while he was awaiting trial, or later, if he was convicted and sentenced to a long term. Couldn't do that either. It was one thing for Slippery to order an assassination on the inside of an informant or a rival gang member. But that was not really a viable option for one of his own crew. And especially not for blood kin.

No, what Slippery needed to do was hire us, let us know he wanted best efforts here. If the kid goes down, well, Slippery would think that through next round, how to deal with his nephew while he does his ten to twenty. If we spring him, then Slippery—who, mind you, never actually said this to us—would see to it that the kid would no longer place such unreasonable demands on his time. What does that mean? Not exactly sure. But probably, at some point or another, the kid, along with some of Slippery's other, more senior guys, is on an assignment. Something goes wrong. There's a shoot-out. Maybe a "rival gang" somehow gets tipped off to the meet. Shots are fired. The kid's hit. Maybe from behind, back of the head. But who knows how, all those bullets flying? Could have been anyone did it. Or the kid's driving and the cops stop him. His car's loaded with product. There's trouble. One of the cops on Slippery's tab, been on it for years, shoots the kid dead. In self-defense, resisting arrest, the other cops testify when the time comes.

Slippery only alludes to this with us. He knows we are honest lawyers. No bribing jurors for us. No knowingly perjured testimony proffered at trial. He gets who we are. He knows we will do our best in court, for which he will pay us handsomely. But he also knows we understand the long-term plan he's got for his troublesome nephew. And he knows we don't care about that one way or the other.

You're thinking maybe Mickie and me are as bad as them? Well, let's see. This kid's a menace to society. Does it really matter how he's erased, long as he is? As lawyers we do our job. The rest, well, the rest's the rest.

Like I said, that trial's going to take one, maybe two days. Depends on how long it takes to pick a jury in the morning. And the judges in this court—we're in the local courthouse with this one—rarely sit longer than four-thirty P.M. So after, I will see Professor Mumbles. Mickie won't go, thinks the guy is an unbelievable douche bag. He's wrong. And anyway, Mickie and me need to come up with something to spring Rodrigo. I would call that our highest priority at the moment.

I called Professor Mumbles in the hope that he can come up with some way to convince the court to grant bail to Rodrigo. A legal theory we can't figure out. Some other approach. Something.

His real name is Shannon Luchsman. Irish mother, Jewish father, I guess. Shannon was one of them. By that I mean he used to be a lawyer in a big downtown Philadelphia white-shoe law firm. Associate, not a partner.

Shannon wasn't one of the "Havvad" ones. Nope, he graduated law school from Rutgers same as me and Mickie did, though he's about five or six years older than us. Unlike us clinging for life to Cs and Ds, like drowning shipmates, Shannon was first in his class, editor in chief of the law review. Perfect grades, never less than an A in any course for Shannon. So the biggies downtown accepted him into their associate ranks. I mean, Shannon was so smart, just not from an Ivy is all. How big a deal could that be for a guy like that, right? So they took him.

After working like a dog for three years, he's told, Shannon, you are great. You, my boy, are on partnership track. Keep it up. Stay at those eighty-hour weeks, keep giving us all your weekends. The brass ring of partnership's going to be yours the time comes. At seven years, at his evaluation, he's told the same thing. Keep it up. One more year, Shannon, that's all. Because year eight is when we will consider you for the inner golden circle for partnership and the really big bucks, not to mention the stature, the prestige. Keep slaving. A personal life's just around the corner. Tell your wife you married in law school, the two small kids, all of whom you never see, hardly know. Tell them salvation's at hand.

Then comes year eight. Shannon, he's told, we're going to need another year here. Your class has too many superstars eligible for partnership. Some of them are women, a few blacks. Now, you know they get priority consideration. Need to, you understand. Otherwise it looks bad for the firm. And then there's the guys who work for more powerful partners than the ones you work for. These partners get what they want, and what they want is partnership for their own guys now. We know you understand. Just one more year, go back into the salt mine. Next year. Trust us. By now, of course, Shannon's divorced, the wife is with some other guy has time for her, and for his kids. The divorce is ugly, the custody battle wrenching. Shannon sticks it out, working himself past exhaustion.

Comes year nine, Shannon's told, Sorry, things aren't going to work out. You've been great, just great. You need to leave in six months. Not a day longer. Bye-bye.

That's when the breakdown, been simmering for some time, happens. Shannon goes off the deep end. He's institutionalized for a while. Then when he's back he opens a one-man law office. He's got no one: parents dead, wife remarried, kids he never sees, behavior at times still bizarre. He's in downtown Philly, but no longer in white-shoe land. Shannon's shop is above a storefront in a marginal neighborhood. No more big-firm work. Now his practice is off the street. Divorces, car crashes, petty crimes. But he's a good guy. Under all that still-lingering craziness (I think he knows we all call him Professor Mumbles and I think he thinks that's okay under the circumstances) he still has a legal mind better than the rest of us guys out here on the lower rungs of the legal ladder.

Mickie's wrong on this one when he says the guy's a jerk, waste-of-time crazy bastard can't tie his own shoes. Nope, Professor Mumbles still has what it takes somewhere under all those twitches and other weirdnesses. Okay, maybe his mind's no longer the steel trap it was when he was slaving away with the white-shoers. Now I guess it's more like tinfoil. But he's a good guy. A sweet guy. He'll help us if he can. Depending, I guess, on his medication levels. Listen. And you know goddamn well Mickie knows this too. We need something here for Rodrigo, else it's going to get ugly for me and Mickie. Ugly like I don't want to think about.

CHAPTER THREE

I'm sitting in the waiting room of Professor Mumbles's office. Such as it is. He doesn't have a secretary, does his own typing, printing, whatever, from his PC. There are a couple of shabby chairs, the usual out-of-date magazines no one reads. There's a Mr. Coffee on the side table looks like it's last been cleaned when Juan Valdez commercials were still showing on late-night TV. I mean, the black-brown muck on the bottom of the pot could tar the road outside.

I know Shannon's in there, behind closed doors, in his inner sanctum one-man office. I can hear his snoring. But I wait. I'm early. The trial ended abruptly. Never know what will happen in court. Always a crapshoot, I say. So after court I grabbed a hot dog and Coke and then came up here. Mumbles has a couch in there, on which he's now probably sprawled, sawing wood. I'm not sure, but could be he lives in there, showering and the like I don't know where. But, hell, let him sleep. Like I said, I'm early.

I called Slippery Williams. To tell him what happened. The call was short, to the point in an elliptical way. You know, Slippery's careful with phones. I rang his cell. He said, "Yeah." "Me," I said. Slippery waited. Then I said, "Your boy's good to go." That was it. The details of what happened would be of no interest to Slippery. The judge, the proceedings in court. All Slippery wanted to know was did I spring his punk-ass nephew or not. So good to go was all I said. Slippery got it. "My man," was all he said, then hung up. I'll give Mickie the blow-by-blow later. He'll love it.

Earlier this morning when I show up at the courthouse, check the docket to see which judge's been assigned to my case, I stand there at the bulletin board in the clerk's office and I'm grinning. Well, what do you know? I drew Thurgood (yup, that's right—Thurgood, like you know who) Rufus Brown. Judge Thurgood Rufus Brown. (Yeah, his parents—mother, as we heard it—the father missing after action—named him for the first African-American justice on the United States Supreme Court. As an infant, Mama's cooing into his crib, Baby, you gonna be somebody.)

In an earlier life Thurgood was a fairly awful civil rights lawyer, letting his ever-present boiling temper get in the way of lawyering for his down-and-out minority clients. I mean, this was a man groomed to carry the black man's burden on his back. Mama saw to that. Thurgood has always been hot under the collar.

Then came Councilman Thurgood Rufus Brown, elected for three consecutive terms to the poorest, most downtrodden ward in Camden. Here he actually did good. Thurgood didn't let anybody mess with his making things at least marginally better for the folks trapped like rats in his ward. And now there's Judge Thurgood Rufus Brown.

New Jersey judges are not elected officials. The state governor appoints them to the bench. For the governor, turning Councilman Brown into Judge Brown was a no-brainer. Think about it. Gone is elected-official Brown, telling his constituents, Don't you be voting for none of them white devils up there in the state capital. Hell, they don't know you livin' down here when the money flows for municipal projects. None a that money's comin' down here to you; you know that. And by putting a brother on the bench from one of the worst areas of Camden, the governor may have placated some of the inner-city downtrodden; they might even vote for him the time comes he needs to seek reelection. Hope springs eternal. So, bottom line? Judge Brown's here to stay. He's no longer got anyone he needs to please. The man's on the bench.

This, I tell myself, still grinning at the bulletin board, is what we advocates, using the skills and language sets taught to us in law school, call one big fucking break. Judge Thurgood Rufus Brown. Well, what do you know? So, Judge Brown hates whitey. That'd be me. Although I don't count since my client here isn't. But he hates the cops and prosecution more. White or black. This is a man probably keeps a picture of Rodney King in his wallet. The DA's office would put out a contract on Judge Brown they thought they could get away with it.

Second bit of good luck is the assistant DA assigned to the case calls in sick with the flu. The DA sends another assistant—a black woman, no less, the first guy's white, I'm thinking maybe he's not sick—to Judge Brown's courtroom, has her explain the situation. Me and the kid are already there, seated at counsel table, the kid's shackles removed by the sheriffs sitting directly behind him hoping and praying he'll try something so they can take him back into lockup and beat him some more.

Your Honor, the female assistant DA says, and I swear I can hear a blackness street thing in her voice I'm certain she doesn't use at home with her doctor husband or her colleagues in the office. (See, I know her. She's a first-class lawyer and a really nice person. But today, in here, that doesn't mean shit. We are in court on opposite sides. This is war. Why do you think she's talking like she is to the judge?)

Judge Brown listens to her. Then he looks at me, seeing what is the defendant's position on this request for an adjournment of the case the prosecution has just made. You know, hold the trial next week, or next month, when the prosecutor assigned to it can make it. Well, let's see. The DA assigned to the case, who knows what it's about, prepared for trial, isn't here. The DA himself, afraid of Judge Brown, sends in an unprepared black woman, letting Judge Brown, who is far from stupid, see what the DA's doing is pandering to the court. And that street dialect fits this woman like someone else's too-big shoes.

"Your Honor," I say as I rise from counsel table.

"This man," I say, pointing down to the punk is my client, who's busy cleaning his nails, way too stupid to see what's going on here. "Well, Your Honor," I say, "he's being held without bail. The witnesses are here, ready to testify, the jury panel's only a call away to the clerk's office. We're ready. The DA's sent a replacement for the one's called in sick." (Notice I said "called in sick." I didn't say "sick.") "This assistant is as well qualified as any in the DA's office."

With that I look over at her and smile, so the judge can see me doing this. The woman looks back at me with an absolute forlorn look on her face, 'cause she sees where this is going. Christ almighty, I know she's thinking.

"The defense," I say in summation, "objects to an adjournment. We're here. We're ready. Let's go."

Judge Brown is a big dark man. Big face. Big hands. Big hair. He looks down at me, Cut the theatrics, his gaze warning me, don't push it, son. Message received.

You know, for lawyers there's rule number one and there's rule number two. Rule one: Get your fee in advance. Rule two: you're winning in court, shut up and sit down. I shut up and sit down.

"Motion for adjournment denied," the judge says, telling the bailiff, "Bring in the jury panel so we can get this show on the road."

I think Mumbles is starting to wake up. His snores are becoming more erratic. I hear him clearing his throat in there.

So, I'm in court, it's midmorning, the jury's been selected and sworn, opening statements made. The assistant DA has her first witness on. It's the undercover who posed as the New York buyer. He's a good witness on direct. The guy looks the part, even in his go-to-court suit. You could believe he pulled off his being a street guy and not a cop. He's dark as the judge, but unlike the judge, he's slender, seated relaxed in the witness chair looking ghetto-wily, handsome. Of course, on account of what happened this guy's not going to be an undercover anymore. The street now knows him. Bye-bye to that. If he was a federal agent, the government would move him and his family somewhere else. Let him do his thing in Atlanta, or Vegas. But the guy's local law enforcement. Camden's where he's staying. His next assignment's as a detective, where he'll get more wear out of that suit he's got on today. Else he gets a desk. And I know he doesn't want that. So he isn't happy. Just my damn luck, I can see he's thinking, as the assistant DA takes him through his direct testimony about what happened brings us all here. Of course, she's only had a few moments to prepare with him, Judge Brown giving her ten to fifteen, telling her it was an easy case, that was all she needed. She touches on the arrest, but leaves the details out. She finishes.

"Your witness," she tells me, looking up at the judge, worrying maybe she should of let him tell me that. Judge Brown nods down at me. Go on, he's saying.

So I get up and walk over to the podium the judge makes the lawyers stand at when they question witnesses. I take some time looking at the witness. I don't say a word, just wait as long as I can, hoping Judge Brown doesn't say, Let's go Counsel, you got something to ask this man, ask it. I'm doing this silence thing for the jury. See, in a courtroom silence is often more dramatic than oratory. A period of silence tells the jury, Wait until you hear this.

When I think I better get going else the judge's going to chime in, I say to the witness, "Detective, let's talk about my client's arrest."

See, I'm not going to ask him about what happened before. All that's going to do is hurt me. The facts there are bad, what the kid did, how he tried to sell drugs, then ripped the undercover off when he couldn't. And both of the geniuses in the kid's crew have copped to lesser charges and are scheduled to testify against him later today. No, a good cross-examiner never just goes over the direct when it's his turn. You don't like ask, Now, the prosecutor asked you this and you said that. And it's a fact, isn't it, that didn't really happen? It did too, you say? Well, you're not sure, are you? You are, you say.

That's bullshit and it's not the way to cross-examine. What you do is come at it from your own angle. Don't replow the direct. Do that, you're working for the opposition. And you get paid to oppose the opposition, not appease it. (Nice ring there, wouldn't you say: oppose appease? Anyway.) So I come at it from the one point of strength we got in this case. The circumstances of the arrest.

The witness is looking at me. I see him shift in his chair. He doesn't want to talk about this, what he did, just about took the kid's eye out when they took him down.

I wait just a beat or two more. I know I don't have any silence reserve left in my account with the judge.

"Now, Detective," I say. "The arrest. Tell us what happened."

"Objection."

This comes from the assistant DA, who's on her feet. Yes, I'm thinking. Just like I planned. "Overly broad," she says up to the judge.

"Sustained," the judge says, then turning to me he says, "Break it down, Mr. Salerno."

"Yes, Your Honor," I say.

Now, like I said, this is just how I planned it. See, I asked that too-broad question on purpose, hoping the assistant DA would knee-jerk object, like they tell you to do in the trial practice seminars lawyers go to, except guys like me and Mickie who don't because we learn this on our feet in here and other courtrooms. Question's too broad, you object. That's the rule. But to be good at this, you've got to look around corners, think, Where's my opponent going? Where's he heading?

Where I'm heading is I want to go into what happened when the detective and the other cops on surveillance watching what went down from their nearby parked cars arrested my client and the other two punks now turned state's evidence. How this detective I've got on the stand did what he did to the kid sitting next to me dozing, his head nodding every now and then—right in front of the jury, what an idiot—every last gory detail.

See, if I start my cross-examination by going into all that detail, about a third of the way through the prosecutor's going to object, on her feet saying to the judge—but really for the jury to hear—how I'm milking this, making too much of it, trying to take the jury's eye off the ball. The case is about some nasty young men, she'll say with dripping indignation, first trying to sell drugs and then robbing this undercover police officer. Pointing the jury's attention back to the detective who had to endure a sawed-off shotgun pressed against his face thinking he's about to lose his life, leave his wife a widow, three small kids fatherless, all in the line of duty. All because he's making the streets safe for the city's honest hardworking citizens like those twelve in the jury box.

Or else the judge, not yet seeing where I'm going with this, is going to tell me on his own, without the prosecutor on her feet objecting, and again in front of the jury, Move it along, Mr. Salerno. You've covered this. New subject, or sit down, 'cause your cross is over. Now, that happens, I've got two choices. One: Argue with the judge. The jury hears me say, Aw, Your Honor, this is important, I have more to ask this witness along these lines. Believe me, with most judges, especially Thurgood Rufus Brown, that choice's a loser. No, worse than a loser, because the judge's going to admonish me. Mr. Salerno, I said move on or sit down. You got that? Forcing me to cower and say, Yes, Your Honor. Choice two: When he tells me to move on to a new subject else finish my examination and sit down, is where choice number one ended. Yes, Your Honor, I say, and sit down. Either way, the jury hears enough to think less of me and their attention will have been drawn away from the one thing I've got here that gives this dope dozing next to me a fighting chance. So I ask my first question way too broad, hoping the assistant DA objects, the judge sustains, telling me break it down, Mr. Salerno, because now I have carte blanche to do my cross slow and—I do it right—searing.

"Detective," I say. "After the incident" (see, I'm going to call the sawed-off shotgun near-killing an incident, sanitize it) "you and the other law enforcement officers followed the defendant and his colleagues" (colleagues; yeah, right) "to a house located about half a mile from the incident. Correct?"

The detective shifts again. "Uh-huh," he says.

"You have to say yes or no, for the jury," I tell him, giving him my you-know-better-than-that look I'm hoping the jury's catching. I would like the jury to understand that the detective had no trouble answering questions clearly when the assistant DA had him on direct, but the minute I start he's being, what do you call it? Truculent.

"Yeah," the detective says.

"And you were the first police into the house, correct?"

"Uh-huh," he says, then adds, "Yes."

"You broke the door in?"

"It was locked and the suspects were in there," he says.

Good, he's getting pissed at me. Be sure and let the jury see that, Detective, I'm thinking.

"So you broke the door in?" I repeat.

"Yeah, I guess so," he says.

"You guess so. Okay," I say. "And right behind you were the other police doing surveillance earlier, correct?"

"I wouldn't say they were right behind me," the detective says, wanting to quibble.

"Okay," I say. "They weren't right behind you. Took them, what, about thirty seconds to barge into the house after you?"

"I guess," he says.

Now I stop again and just look at him, a bemused smile on my face. But I don't linger too long with this on account of I sense the jury and the judge are getting it.

"So, Detective, you're the first one into the house, my client's in there along with his two colleagues." (This time the detective smirks at "colleagues." Don't overplay your hand, I silently admonish myself. Ditch the "colleagues" thing.)

"Detective?" I say, indicating to him, You need to answer me.

"Yeah, Counselor, I was the first one in."

When cops call defense lawyers "Counselor," they say it with this wonderful sneer, making it sound like "low-life dirt-bag shit hole," all in one. Okay, I'm thinking, we're getting somewhere here.

"And when you broke into the house you saw the defendant here and his two friends right in plain view, correct?"

"Yeah, I saw them."

"And Detective, the defendant came right up to you, didn't he?"

"Yeah, he came up to me."

"And he spoke to you, didn't he?"

"Didn't notice," the detective says, his eyes cautious now because we are about to get into the good stuff. He knows it and I know it. Thing is, I am in control here. This isn't going to be a conversation about what happened. This is what you call cross-examination.

"Didn't notice," I repeat. "Okay," I say. "When you saw the defendant he was standing there before you in his underwear, correct?"

Now, why this kid sitting next to me was in his underwear when the cops broke the door down is a mystery. I asked him when I saw him briefly in lockup earlier today before we went into court and, to be honest with you, I really couldn't make out what he was telling me. Something about hanging and chilling. Doin' this, that. Best I could make out, the kid and the other two mopes never considered that the guy they ripped off, cop or no, would come looking for them. But he was indeed in his underwear when the detective broke the door to the house down and—as they say—entered the premises. What the kid actually said to the detective is also a mystery to me. When I asked the kid, he just shrugged, didn't say.

"Yeah, Counselor, he was in his underwear."

"So he wasn't armed? There was no weapon under his clothing? Correct?"

The detective straightens in his chair. A good cross-examiner uses his examination to put the witness in a corner without the witness seeing where he's being taken. Then, when the witness is cornered, the cross-examiner pulls the witness's wings off slowly, like he's a little bird, one feather at a time, and then, when the wings are off, he drops the little bird on the floor and crushes it beneath his feet. The detective is now in that corner. If I do this right, he's not getting out.

"So he wasn't armed?" I repeat. "Detective?" I add, meaning, You might as well answer the question because this game's about over.

"No sir," the detective says.

"No sir he was armed, or no sir he wasn't armed?" I ask.

"Wasn't," the detective says.

"Wasn't what?" I say. This is fun, I'm telling myself. Thank you, Detective, I'm thinking.

"Wasn't armed," the detective says.

"And you went right up to him standing there in his underwear and you struck him?"

"I subdued him and placed him under arrest."

"You subdued him. Okay. You subdued him by striking him, isn't that correct?

"I may have."

"May have or did?"

"Did, I guess."

"You did, you guess," I say. Another feather pulled off, almost down to the skin and small bones.

"Detective, are you right-handed or left-handed?"

"What?" he says.

"It's a simple question. Are you right-handed or left-handed?"

"Right," he says.

"Okay. Now, when you struck the defendant, did you strike him with your right hand or your left hand?"

"I didn't strike him," the detective says. "I slapped him."

Bad move on his part, making a nonsensical distinction: strike versus slap. He's trying to wiggle out of the corner, but he can't, it's too late. The judge, who has been watching this intently, chimes in.

"Stop playing games," the judge warns the detective. "Answer the question and cut the cute stuff," he almost booms down at him. Brother or no brother, the judge isn't liking where this is going. Police brutality doesn't wash with him.

"Detective, when you slapped the defendant," (I'll use his word, I don't care) "did you slap him with your right hand or your left?"

"Right," the detective says, quickly eyeing up to the bench, letting the judge know, How can you be doing this to me, we're in this together? Well, not the kind of together the detective has in mind, I guess.

"And Detective, when you entered the premises you were armed, weren't you?"

"Of course," he says, his tone saying, Like you think I wouldn't be, with that piece-of-shit your client sitting next to you almost blew my head off earlier?

"You had your gun drawn?"

"Yeah, I had my gun drawn."

"You carry what, a .45?"

"Yeah."

"And when you struck . . . slapped the defendant with your right hand, your gun was drawn?"

"I said it was, Counselor."

"And your gun was in your right hand?"

"I guess so."

"You guess so. Okay, so when you slapped the defendant with your right hand, your .45 was in it, so you slapped the defendant with your gun. Do you guess so to that too?"

"Must have," he says, like, wow, the thought just occurred to him.

"Fact is, Detective, what you did when the defendant came up to you saying you don't remember what, in his underwear, unarmed, is you pistol-whipped him repeatedly in the face, just about removing his left eye from its socket. That's correct, isn't it?"

"Objection," shouts the assistant DA, who's finally come to life here, I'm wondering what in the hell took her so long. I thought she was better than this. But it's too late. Judge Brown's fever is up.

"Overruled," he all but screams down at her. She slinks back into her chair. I can see that forlorn look on her face way over here behind the podium I'm standing at.

So now, slowly, step by step, I take the detective through the rest of it. How when he finishes banging the shit out of the kid's head, one of the other cops now in the house holding the kid down, he cuffs the kid's hands behind his back. The other two young criminals are on their knees, hands behind heads, other cops pointing their own .45s point-blank at them while they're begging, Please, man, don't be doin' that to me. Watching the kid being knocked half unconscious. Then how the detective asks the kid, his one eye leaking, the other three-quarters swollen shut, Where's the money, you little fucker, tell me now else I'll shoot your goddamn prick out a your pants, you fuck, you.

Downstairs, he tells the detective, woozy, almost passing out, the detective reviving him with face slaps. No gun this time. So the detective and the cop's been holding the kid down, now up, leave the other two perps upstairs, cuffed and ready to go, and take the kid down into the basement. Way the detective tries to tell it, while he and the other arresting are down there, the kid with them, hands still behind his back cuffed, shows them where the bag of money's at. Stuffed behind some old rotting BarcaLounger. Then the detective says the kid tries to escape, so they have to "subdue" him some more with their fists and shoes. He's trying to say how the kid tries to escape from the cellar by running—get this—up the stairs, cuffed, near comatose, underwear, no shoes. Of course, what the jury hears me pull from the detective—word by excruciating word—is that once the cops retrieve the money, they lead the kid halfway back up the steps to the living room, then drag him back face down so he can bang his head against each step and then, for good measure, beat him some more, telling him, This is what you get for trying to off a cop, motherfucker.

Now I'm finished my cross. But I leave it there. I don't say to the assistant DA your witness, or tell the judge I have no more questions. No, instead I leave the detective on the stand, dirty-eyeing me so the jury can observe him doing this, and say up to the court, "Your Honor, may counsel approach the bench?"

Judge Brown's steaming. If you were a blind man sitting with your white collapsible cane in the third row of the gallery you could see this. All he does is crook his finger at me and the ADA, letting us know, Come on up here. Judge Brown then nods at the stenographer sitting on a swivel stool below the bench taking down every spoken word, Bring your machine up here, take down what's about to happen, he's telling her.

Okay, now we're up at the bench. See, I left the witness in place, didn't end my cross on purpose. I finish, say your witness or whatever, the ADA gets another turn at questioning. It's called redirect. She gets a chance to rehabilitate the detective. She can establish that maybe the kid tried somehow to resist the cops, show that maybe what he said when the detective barged into the place was taunting, insulting to the police, something like that. She can redirect the detective back to the rip-off and his near-murder, help the jury see that the detective had good reason for his rage when he subdued the kid. Point is, I've got things poised good like they are, for what I'm about to do.

And what I am about to do would be a loser in most other courts. But, I'm thinking, with Thurgood Rufus Brown, maybe not.

See, sure the cops overreacted. You should of seen how the kid looked at arraignment days after the arrest. They beat him good, no doubt about that. But that doesn't excuse the kid from his crime. Either he tried to sell drugs and then came close to murdering the undercover or he didn't. What the cops did after doesn't affect that. What it does do maybe is give the kid a civil right of action against the city and the cops individually for big-time damages for how they treated him. The boys at Bernstein, Smulkin, Abramowitz & Wolf would make a ton of contingent-fee money on a case like this. But I have a different plan, seeing how Judge Brown's now face to face with me, I'm up at the bench with the ADA and the stenographer waiting for more words here. And I don't want more questioning of the detective. I like things right where they are. So the detective's sitting there pretending he's not trying to listen to what we're half whispering up here when I tell Judge Brown I want to make a motion.

"Let's hear it," he tells me.

"Your Honor," I say in my half whisper, directing my words toward the stenographer now clicking away on her machine. "The defense respectfully moves for dismissal of all charges on the ground of law enforcement misconduct." (I'm kind of making this up as I go.

There's something called prosecutorial misconduct, but that didn't happen here. The DA's office did nothing wrong. But I'm in the right church here if not the exact right pew.)

Judge Brown turns his attention to the ADA. Now, he's aware that, technically, the testimony from the detective isn't over. I know he knows what I'm doing here. The ADA goes through the motions defending her case, but know what? Her heart's not in it. Good for her, part of me's thinking. But the other part's saying, For Christ sake, be a goddamn lawyer, do your job. You're an advocate. Advocate. When she's finished the judge says to her, before he rules on my motion, does she have any more questions for the witness, his look telling her, You better not if you ever plan on appearing before me again. No, Your Honor, she says. The judge then tells the detective, You may step down. Now he's got the record clean before he rules. No more questions for the detective. The record is frozen for all time.

"Motion granted," the judge says. "Case dismissed. With prejudice," he adds. Meaning these charges cannot be refiled at some later time, like when a different judge's around to get the case. He turns to the jury. "Ladies and gentlemen," he tells them. "You are excused. Report back to the clerk's office before you go home." Then he bangs his gavel, and as he rises he says court is adjourned until further notice.

No speeches from Judge Brown, no diatribe directed at the prosecution and the cops about what happened. Judge Brown's way too smart for that. He does that from the bench, it gets in the papers. Black radical judge cuts scumbag loose who almost offs cop. Nope. What Judge Brown's going to do—I know it—is he's going to call the district attorney himself into his chambers for a private session. In there he's going to eat the DA's ass out. Boom down on him, tell him you better get your weak-ass self into a room with the chief of police, tell him, Something like this happens again, I'm going to start throwing every case you bring me out like it was yesterday's garbage. Then I'm going to see to it your police get themselves indicted, sending them away long. And hard. Got that?

Judge Brown leaves the courtroom. Me and the ADA stay at semi-attention right where we are before his bench, as lawyers do when a judge is in motion on his way in or out of his courtroom. The judge ignores me. There's no nod of recognition, no good job, son. Nope. I'm nothing to him. Just another pale-shaded courthouse lawyer. Another hack he hears from day in and day out.

Once the judge is gone, I shake the ADA's hand. Another lawyer custom. Win or lose, you do that. Then I return to counsel table, where the kid's still sitting, now wondering what the hell happened here. The sheriffs have ordered him to get up so they can reshackle him. I can see this little dimwit is thoroughly confused. Jury's gone, but he's still being shackled. What? he's thinking. I'm putting my papers back in my briefcase, I say to him, "They're going to take you back to lockup, do the paperwork, then release you. Then you can go home."

The kid's trying to process what I just said. Slowly, very slowly, he gets it. Somehow this is over. He's won and can go. So now he starts to smile, looking around at no one. Then he starts beaming, because he's thinking he's out of here, back on the street. Good, I know he's thinking. First thing I'm going to do, his pea brain is telling him, is find them two punks was my crew copped against me, and put a bullet, do it this time, pull the trigger, up close in their motherfucking bitch-ass heads. Do it facing them, my Glock held sideways pressed right against their foreheads, splatter their brains all over. Saying as I do, Cop against me, bitch, this what you get.

Well, whatever, I'm thinking. This kid is completely oblivious that his uncle Slippery, soon as he gets the right opportunity, is going to take him out. The kid won't see his next birthday, which is probably somewhere around twenty-two, -three, maybe.

I've got my papers stuffed in my bag and I'm about to leave, but standing before me is the detective. And he is not happy. We're face to face. He's way into my space, too close. Nose to nose. He's evil-eyeing me the way fighters do before the first round, the referee telling them how he expects a good clean fight.

"I'm gonna be watching you," he tells me.

I want to step back, get away from him. I am very uncomfortable with this man so close to me. But that would be a big mistake, I know that. So instead, I hold my ground. I force a smile to my face.

"Meaning what?" I tell him. "You see me somewhere you're going to slap not strike me, maybe give me a little of your pistol-whipping you seem so good at? 'Cause if that's what you have in mind, Detective, you will be sitting here." I point to where my client was seated in the criminal defendant's chair, the kid no longer in the courtroom to see this, the sheriffs now in the lockup with him doing the paperwork. "And," I tell him, "when you go away, Detective, there won't be a jail in this state doesn't have some inmate waiting for you. 'Cause you will be a marked man, all the perps you've taken down throughout your illustrious career."

The detective doesn't say a thing. He just stays planted where he is. I may have outworded him, but I haven't done a thing to diminish his rage. He may be speechless, but he's steaming. We remain locked like that for what seems to me like an eternity, but probably is less than a minute, when the ADA's arm slides between me and the detective.

"Enough," she says, more to the detective than to me.

He isn't moving. I'm not even certain he's hearing her. I mean, to him, my client, who I have managed to put back out on the street, did almost kill him. I did that and this guy is enraged. Yup, really fucking enraged, is how I'd put it.

"I said enough," the ADA repeats, this time adding, "Detective, step back. Step back now."

And after another ten-second eternity, he does. But as he turns, I think I hear him say, under his breath, "Faggot."

He said it. Yeah, I'm pretty sure. That shakes me. What does he know? Or can he just smell something in me? Christ, now I've got this hothead cop after me. On my tail. (Okay, maybe "on my tail" isn't the best way to put it under the circumstances.) I pretend that I suddenly need to rearrange the papers in my briefcase, that I am unfazed by what just happened. The detective leaves the courtroom without another look at me, or the ADA. The ADA shrugs my way, What can you do? she's signaling. You understand, she's telling me with her body language. I return the shrug. Yeah, sure. Forget about it. But, "faggot"?

Oh boy.

CHAPTER FOUR

The door to Professor Mumbles's inner sanctum opens and there he is in all his glory. He's blinking repeatedly through those still-from-the-1980s, too-big eyeglasses, the Coke-bottle lenses magnifying his eyes way out of proportion. Mumbles is a heavy man, big gut hanging over his pants line, his suit jacket (still on, since he slept in it) is wrinkled, his white button-down shirt frayed at the cuffs, yellowed at the edges. His tie's soiled and askew. He's still half asleep, staring at me; his brain hasn't yet touched down to planet earth. I can see he hasn't a clue who I am or why I'm sitting here. He doesn't even really know where he is at the moment. I watch Mumbles run the back of his hand across his mouth, taking away some vestige of saliva. His fingernails are bitten to the core. Then he tries straightening his hair, putting his jagged part back in place. Flakes of dandruff float to his shoulders. Not a pretty sight. I wait a minute or so, letting him come together.

"Hey, Shannon," I say, thinking he's about there.

Mumbles blinks some more at me. Then he gets it, sees me. Recognizes me.

"Junne." He beams, a big smile on his face, because Mumbles likes me. I treat him right. Always have. "Come in. Come in," he says, beckoning me into his office.

Once inside, Mumbles is wondering where to seat me. Where to seat himself. The sofa, he now sees, still has the ratty pillow and blanket from his nap. He grabs them and stuffs them unceremoniously behind it, runs his hand over the sofa to smooth it, then motions for me to sit.

"Sorry to keep you waiting, Junne," he says. "Conference call," he adds, like, What can you do? Duty calls. As I sit on the sofa I can see that Mumbles has disconnected the phone at his desk by taking out the cord from the wall jack, it's lying loose on the floor. So the ring wouldn't disturb his nap, I guess.

I nod like, Hey, sure, no problemo. The sofa still smells like Mumbles's sleep. Mumbles folds himself into the swivel chair behind his desk, which groans from his weight. I can barely see him now, hidden behind the papers piled Leaning Tower of Pisa–style all over his desk. I notice similar stacks scattered all around the floor.

"Uhm?" I say, motioning, meaning, Could you please move some of those stacks so I can see you? This Mumbles gets.

"Oh yeah," he says, pushing some of the stacks aside, which, of course, causes a landslide, Mumbles back on his feet trying in vain to right the stacks falling domino-style onto the floor. I rise to help, but Mumbles waves me away, Don't worry about it, he's telling me.

He leaves the papers where they have fallen, scattered all over the place. What the hell, he's thinking, those cases probably been over several years now. Or was some of that the current stuff I've got in court now? Oh well. Mumbles settles back in his chair.

"Coffee?" he asks me. "I've got a fresh pot brewing out there," referring, I guess, to the molten asphalt lurking at the bottom of the cloudy glass pot on the side table in the waiting room.

"Ah, no, thanks, Shannon. I'm good," I tell him.

Mumbles gives me that you-sure? look. Coffee's right out there, brewing away. Then, as I'm about to get into it, tell him why I'm here, try and get some help, some advice, Shannon Luchsman morphs into full Professor Mumbles. He sits back in his creaky chair. "So, Junne," he says. "Now, what brings you . . . Knee hurts," he mutters, "gotta fix it." Then, back with us again, he tries to finish his original thought, but instead tells himself under his breath, "Pen and paper, need pen and paper," searching his cyclone-hit desk for something to take notes on. I wait.

Mumbles blinks away at me. Where were we? he's signaling, not sure anymore, I guess, of what's up here. Wait it out, I tell myself. I watch Mumbles come back around again. Yup, he's here at the moment. He's found a ballpoint and the cardboard back of a full-with-notes yellow legal pad, which he's holding over his lap backward so he can write on the cardboard, the scribbled-full yellow sheets fanning his legs. Okay, shoot, Mumbles seems to be saying.

This is why Mickie wouldn't come. He can't stand the guy. Well, to be fair, what Mickie can't stand is this. Mickie says he can't sit here and listen to it's-time-for-Wapner bullshit. Sure, Mumbles's rice isn't fully cooked. But locked away in that brain, with all those random thoughts flying around like bats in a big belfry, some of them from time to time escaping as muttered asides to himself, is—I'm hoping—the answer to springing Rodrigo Gonzáles. Let us not forget that Rodrigo is at this very moment sitting in his maximum-security cell, not at all happy, probably trying to decide how slowly to have me and Mickie tortured to death, we don't spring him like he paid us to do.

So I start to tell Mumbles the story. I'm maybe midway through it, at the part where "Mr. Smith" is in Mickie's office telling me and Mick how we have like three seconds left to file something with the court releases Rodrigo from custody, when the phone starts ringing. Now, it's not ringing in here, since Mumbles disconnected the line from the wall before his nap, but the phone on the empty desk out in the waiting room where a secretary would sit if Mumbles had one is ringing. We both can hear it in here, but Mumbles gets confused hearing it. He reaches for the phone on his desk, which is under some of the papers slid from the piles but didn't make it all the way to the floor.

"Hello, hello," Mumbles is asking into the phone, his magnified eyes blinking up a storm, he's wondering what the hell's the matter with the person on the other end doesn't answer back.

I get up off the couch and go over to the wall jack, get on my knees, and reconnect the wire. Now Mumbles has some juice, a voice on the line.

"Yes, yes," I hear him say as I return to the smelly couch.

"Yes, yes, yes," he's saying. "Oh," Mumbles adds, now forcefully pushing more papers aside on his desk as he desperately searches for his appointment book, which is so buried beneath all that stuff he isn't likely to see it until spring thaw.

But I get what's probably happening here. That is no doubt the bailiff from one of the local courts on the line. The judge is up on the bench. Opposing counsel is there, as is Mumbles's own client. And they're all there ready to go, waiting for him. Now, most of the local judges know Mumbles. And his story. They know what he once was. What he now is. And they cut him some slack. So probably the judge has told his clerk, everyone there in court waiting, Call Mr. Luchsman, find out how long it will take him to get over here.

I hear Mumbles tell the phone, "Ten minutes," meaning that's how long it will take him to get over there. Then he remembers me sitting over on the couch. "Twenty," he says, "twenty minutes."

Now he's on hold, the clerk probably asking the judge up on the bench, Mr. Luchsman says twenty minutes, that okay with the court? Mumbles places his hand over the receiver so he can tell me he's on with the clerk, but then changes his mind just as the clerk comes back on the line.

"Yes, yes, yes," Mumbles says, blinking away. "Twenty, yes, twenty. Right, right, right. Goodbye."

He hangs up the phone, sits back in his creaking chair, and retrieves the full yellow legal pad where he's started making notes on the upside-down back cardboard. Has he already forgotten the call? I'm wondering. No, Mumbles knows he's got to go, but first he wants to help me. Like he said he would when I called him and arranged to come over here after court today. He's heard enough from me, I guess, to get it.

I sit and watch as Mumbles starts scribbling madly on the cardboard, tilting it this way and that as he runs out of space.

"Okay," he, well . . . mumbles to me, and a stream of words spray themselves into the room. I am trying to make sense of what he's telling me as he speaks, scribbles, and all the while holds a conversation with his inner thoughts.

"Big problem," Mumbles says. "Maximum security, dangerous scumbag client, unresponsive judge, got to get laundry, need clever motion, got it, asylum, yes, that's it, petition for asylum, divorce alimony payments, shit, I forgot, yes, asylum, best bet."

Then I watch as Mumbles gets himself out of his seat, ripping the pages from the underside of the legal pad he's holding upside down, the pages fluttering down all around him. He hands me the cardboard, now ink-filled in every space, some of it written in circles around the corners, and he tells me he's got to go could I please lock up for him, but a petition for political asylum for Mickie's and my client is our best bet. Make up a case, he's telling me as he walks out of his office on his way to court, then realizes he doesn't have his own case file, returns to the desk, pushing more papers to the floor, and selects what may or may not be the file and leaves.

"That's it, Junne," Mumbles is saying as the door closes. "That's your best bet. Put together a case why your guy needs asylum from death squads or something like that and how he can help the narcs topple his country's junta generals for drug trafficking blah blah blah."

The outer door shuts and calmness settles. Asylum, I'm thinking. Well, okay, if Mumbles thinks it's worth a shot. Sure, Mumbles is damaged goods. Still, fluttering away up there between his ears is more than Mickie or I've got. If Mumbles thinks a petition to the court for political asylum is the answer, fine with me. I'll talk it over with Mickie, but we'll get Mumbles to write the brief for us. Pay him out of our own pockets. Put our names on the papers, not his. He won't care.

Of course, what I should be thinking is first me or Mickie, or us both, need to hit the books, go to the law library. Check this out. See what the law says. Can it work? Or are there problems here? Now, I know Mickie won't. He's never seen a written word he likes. And me? No, I won't either. To tell the truth, it's maybe a combination of being just too lazy and afraid that I won't fully get what I'm reading, so what's the point? Mickie and me will let Mumbles do it. Pay him. No problem.

This, of course, is a mistake. Mumbles's idea will turn out to have as many holes in it as Rodrigo plans to put through us, but as I walk out of Mumbles's inner sanctum, unplug the Mr. Coffee in the waiting room, turn out the lights, and leave, I'm thinking, Now we're getting somewhere.

What I should be thinking—as my old man would have put it— is *Marone*.

Meaning.

Shit shit shit shit shit shit shit shit.

CHAPTER FIVE

It's Monday night. I saw Mumbles last Thursday. Friday I had coffee with Mickie at the courthouse café, Tamara still giving us that look. Not her want-some-of-this-don't-ya? look, standing at our table she's as tightly wrapped in her pink uniform as ever. No, Tamara telling us wordlessly, Poor guys, whatever it is, you both probably ain't smart enough to fix it.

I told Mickie about what Mumbles suggested. You know, putting together (that's spelled "dreaming up") a case of amnesty for Rodrigo. Telling the judge has Rodrigo's case our guy can help topple his whole drug-infested, bribery-riddled government. Only first give him a little supervised freedom so when he does he won't be snuffed in prison before he can help. The judge says, Sure, okay, let's put him in a low- to medium-security facility. He'll stay there, on his honor, won't he? the judge will ask us. Yes, Your Honor, we'll say. Absolutely. So ruled, the judge says. The marshals move him from the shit hole he's in. Then bye-bye Rodrigo, he's escaped back to the jungles of El Salvador and the fuck away from us. Whoops, sorry, we'll say later. The judge is more than pissed. He's blind-rage furious. Okay, so maybe we have some trouble with the court. Maybe the bar association starts proceedings against us. But guess what? Me and Mickie are alive.

Mickie listens, sipping his coffee. Yeah, sure, he says, giving it next to no thought. Part of me's thinking Mickie knows this will not fly, but seeing as he doesn't have any bright ideas of his own, What the hell, let's try, he's saying. Who knows? Anyway, Mickie says, Yeah, sure, get your friend the Nutty Professor to write it up. We can file it with the court with our names on it.

That was it. End of discussion.

We both had cases of our own that day, so we couldn't linger. Mickie left first, then, after a while, I got up too. I didn't go right to court. Couldn't. No. I sat in my car parked on the street. Just sat there. That's when I decided to do Atlantic City over the weekend. I mean, I was really jittery, needed to get away. Well, if you're thinking, Junne, not a good move, yeah, it didn't help. And I don't want to talk about it. Okay?

But now I'm back from the weekend and it's Monday night and I am standing at Mickie's front door, having just rung the house bell. Twice. Wondering what the hell's taking him so long, *Monday Night Football*'s about to start. I ring again and then knock. "Yeah," I hear Mickie shout. "Hold on. Hold on." I wait some more and then, finally, he opens the door.

Mickie's not dressed. He's wearing a bathrobe as he steps aside so I can come in. Minute I walk in the house I smell fucking. He and Cynthia have been having sex, no doubt about it as I follow Mickie into the den where the flat-screen's at. She's not there, but her scent lingers in the room like she did one of those Road Runner vanishing-in-a-flash acts. The flat-screen's been turned off, but the DVD's been playing is still in the machine. Mickie gives me that mano-a-mano smile like, Whoa, baby, was that good, should have seen her move her motor on the couch there. Then he picks the remote off the coffee table and snaps on the porn flick the two of them were watching while they're doing it. Now, Mickie's doing this to me on purpose. *For* a purpose, is more like it. He's showing me, see, this is normal. This could be you, Junne, look at that, really see it. Could be you.

What I see is two girls and a man sprawled over each other, grabbing and humping and groaning. The bedsheet's a purple satin. (Yeah, that I noticed. Big deal, doesn't mean what you think it means. Straight guys'll notice that too. Right?) The girls have those silicone tits pasted to their bony chests wouldn't move in hurricane-force winds, and the guy pumping away at them's sporting a humongous cock with his pubes shaved down to crew-cut length. But I watch. I mean, what am I supposed to do? Say, Mickie, ew-ickie, please turn that off? No. Mick's heart's in the right place here. I know it. So I watch while Mickie's watching me watch them. Then he snaps off the picture, flips from video/DVD to channel select, and finds *Monday Night Football* just beginning, the players horse-trotting onto the field, the announcer all excited like this is a Roman Colosseum fight to the death. Beer? Mickie's asking me when Cynthia comes in, dressed in fresh jeans and blouse, but still residual-smelling of you know what.

"Hi, Junne," she says. "Hi," I say, but I can't hold her gaze. She knows I know what just went on in here. To her it's no big deal. She and Mickie live together. Nothing wrong with a little late-afternoon delight, she's thinking. Well, I mean, they knew I was on my way over to watch the game. Couldn't they have waited until later after I left?

Look, this girl may be a cocktail waitress, but like I said earlier, she's got a Ph.D. You know, it's in something like medieval history, so she can't actually find work with it. She just stayed in school longer than anybody else. But still, she's got to be smart enough to know I'm coming over for some *Monday Night Football,* so she and Mickie can do their own balling later after I'm out of here. That's not—you should pardon the expression—so fucking hard, is it?

I take my usual place on the sofa. Cynthia, who won't stay more than a few minutes and then she'll tell us have fun, guys, and retreat to the bedroom, settles into the matching side chair. She curls her feet under her, gripping her ankles until she's snuggled in. She's not the best-looking woman around, but she does have appeal. I give her that. Her features are just slightly larger than her face deserves, but there is a definite womanly attraction there. Lips just south of swollen, green eyes holding bedroom light, brows curved into the beginnings of displaying some kind of naughty interest. Her skin is pale, hair lightly streaked. Seated as she is, I see tight thighs, nice breasts pressing against her blouse, the outlines of her nipples larger than I would have somehow expected.

I can see how Mickie can be satisfied with this woman, she seemingly not too fussed about her living here in a semitransient state, Mickie not being what you'd call a committer. It will last as long as it lasts. Mickie will treat her well, cheat on her when he thinks he can without too much risk, ball her every other night, never share too much of himself when they're together. For Cynthia, all that is just fine. She's got her own agenda. Whatever that is. Mickie's a journey for her, not a destination. But as transient as it may be, they each have the other. Which I guess is why they were fucking one another's brains out just before I got here.

And yeah, I'm envious. Hurt, kind of, I guess, you know, that my best friend in the whole world had me so completely out of his mind. And, what's the word? I'm coveting their each having somebody. I mean, that's why I drove up to Atlantic City this past weekend. Wasn't it?

It was a bad move. Dumb. Not helpful. But shit. Aren't I entitled to something? I know. Grow up, Junne, you're probably thinking. Get a grip. Yeah, well, you got full control of your own demons? So I drove in from Camden, got there Saturday late morning. I stay at Harrah's. They comp me and Mickie. From time to time we do stuff for them. Small stuff. Defend an employee who violates his or her parole. Maybe a small assault charge for a pit boss slaps around his waitress girlfriend when he catches her flirting with one of the good-looking Spanish kids works in the kitchen. Stuff like that. And we bill them, but it never amounts to much. So they comp us. I don't get a suite or anything, just a normal room. But whatever I sign for, you know, meals, drinks, are comped. When I check out, the front desk person says, Everything okay, Mr. Salerno? Yeah, I say, fine. Then that'll be it, he or she says, gently ripping the bill from the printer and placing it in the wastebin under the desk. Have a nice day, sir.

And you know, you can get—let's call it companionship, if you want it. Whatever you want, if you know what I mean. Whatever. What you do is have a word with the head bellman, guy named Chip, or one of the pit bosses in the casino. Fifty to a hundred bucks slipped into their hand, a whispered conversation what you're looking for, how much you're willing to pay for it. Then about an hour later you're in your room and there's a knock 'cause what you ordered is standing out there in the hall waiting to come in. I don't do that. No, not for me. Mickie has, I think. But what I would be asking for, well . . . I don't do that.

So I get there Saturday, have lunch at the buffet, walk the

Boardwalk outside remembering the Atlantic City of when I was a kid, before the gambling, here with my family for summer vacations. The Hotel Traymore too ritzy for us, walking the lobby, my mom carefully looking around making mental notes how those people lived, my dad telling her for Christ sake, Lydia, let's go to the beach, the kids want to get in the damn water already. The Taylor pork roll sandwiches eaten at the counter farther down the Boardwalk, the smell of the meat, the slopped-on mustard mixing with the sea-salt air, the moving human traffic up and down, up and down the widest boardwalk in the entire universe. As I walk I feel this uncomfortable mix of warm nostalgia and sadness for things bygone. After a while I guess it's too much for me, so I go back to the hotel and take a nap.

Saturday evening I eat dinner in the hotel's five-star. Now, I'm no gourmet, but with the waiters in tuxes, their north Jersey accents slipping through their "monsieur"s and "madame"s like fishy water through a trawler's net, the roaming violins playing show tunes, the food at your table lukewarm on account of there's so much on the plate it requires assembly time before delivery, well, it's pretty awful. Cheesy, you'd call it. My waiter was a nice guy, gay as can be. Didn't seem to notice anything about me, unlike that prick detective busted Slippery's nephew. Still upset about that. Then, after dinner, I'm off to the casino.

They'll serve you drinks at the tables, comped, all you do is place a few bucks' tip on the girl's tray, held up shoulder-high so you can tip and simultaneously check her pressed-up boobs. I'm drinking scotch and I have probably already had too much. I'm at a blackjack table. Gambling's not comped, so I'm telling myself, Be careful, Junne, you're more than half in the bag, the evening's only half done. Watch yourself. As I double down on a bet I see this guy at the other end of the table. He's watching me, a woman I'm seeing is his wife is standing behind him, her hand resting on his shoulder, but she's bored, looking around for something else to do. Wedding rings on them both, but I'm getting a look from the guy. Yeah, *the* look. I'm getting it from him. I see it. He sees I see it.

The dealer wins the bet, what else is new? I shrug now, seeing the guy down the table's shrugging too. What can you do? his smile's signaling. But his eyes are sending me a different message. I smile back, but leave it there. Then the wifey leans in to him and whispers something. Sure, okay, he nods, and she goes off toward one of the roulette tables, opens her evening bag, and buys chips. I leave the blackjack table, pass the guy without so much as a glance, and walk to the bar where there's only a few people sitting. Another scotch ordered and the guy from the blackjack table's taking the stool next to mine. Hey, he says. I don't say anything, just smile hi.

"How's your luck running?" he asks with this he-man bravado in his voice, like he should have ended his question with "pal."

"Crappy," I say, taking another pull of scotch.

The bartender is there and the guy orders vodka tonic, lemon not lime, he tells the guy. Sure, says the bartender, and makes the drink right there from the house vodka, house tonic, both pumped in from a hose and nozzle. He tells the guy, Want a tab or pay now? Tab, the guy says, not looking at me but wanting to, I can tell.

"Me too," the guy says, referring to his luck or lack thereof at the tables.

"Yeah, well," is all I say.

The guy's about my age. A little heavier, like he's fighting a weight problem, has it just under control, for now. He's dark, Italian- or maybe Turkish-looking. I notice the backs of his hands, his knuckles are hairy, his nails clean but cut like a guy makes his living with his hands. I'm thinking this guy with his shirt off, say at the gym in front of his locker, he's going to have a hairy chest, but what about his back? That going to be hairy or clean?

"Where you from?" the guy asks.

"Jersey," is all I say. Then add, "You?"

"Wilmington," he says, then offers his hand so we can shake and be introduced.

I shake his hand, real hard grip, tell him my name's Bill. Frank, he says. Is he really Frank, I'm thinking, or has he made up his name too? Really Frank, I conclude. He holds my hand just a fraction too long before releasing it.

Okay, well, here's how this goes. We talk a while longer. Maybe some more about our luck, maybe we go from gambling to sports, maybe we see one of the waitresses at the other end of the bar, waiting for her tray's refill, and we comment on how hot she is, all the while each reading the level of the other's insincerity. Somewhere during all this, maybe his leg touches mine, reading all the while, or he makes a point and touches my shoulder for emphasis, still reading. Then he says something half funny, half disparaging about the wife, nodding over where she's still at one of the roulette tables, letting me know he's not really that interested in her these days. We do this dance, then I say, Well, okay, guess I'll turn in for the night, shake his hand again, my leg on the stool brushing his. I call to the bartender for my check, the guy says, Hey, don't worry about it, I got it. I go, but I take my time. A few minutes and I'm at the elevator waiting, and without a word, he's there too. We ride up in silence, he follows me to my room, doesn't say a word as I slip the card into the lock. He follows me into the dark room.

Yeah, well. We did all that. All except that last part. Somewhere during my time with the guy at the bar I told myself no. No. No. So I called over to the bartender for my tab, declined the guy's offer to pay. Didn't shake his hand. Just said see ya. I went back to another blackjack table, never giving the guy at the bar another glance. Played a few hands, went up to my room alone. Plugged in the laptop to the high-speed, no charge, that's comped too. I toggled to maledate.com and jerked off to one of those two-guys-per-picture porn slide shows. Then I powered down the computer, got into bed, snapped on the TV, and channel-surfed my way to sleep, switching off the set sometime hours later when I woke up to take a pee. Yeah, that's what I did. And so now you know.

I could have cried, I felt so bad, so . . . I don't know. So lonely, I guess.

Next morning I checked out of Harrah's early and was back at my place in Camden breakfast time. That was Sunday, the rest of the day I spent alone. Called my mother, spoke to her. I almost told her about my Saturday stroll on the Boardwalk and the childhood memories it released, but then the other stuff crowded in on me and I didn't mention it. All I did after that was go for a run, watch football, order in Chinese. Well, no, I made a cake. Yeah, I made a cake. So the fuck what? And now it's Monday night and Mickie and me are in the living room, eating nachos, drinking beer, and watching the game.

It's still second quarter, about seven minutes left on the clock. The doorbell rings, followed by immediate knocking. Mickie looks over to the front door, then to me. What the hell? he's thinking. This time of night, no one's expected. Knocking? I'll go, I tell him, and walk over into the foyer, you can see from the living room where the TV's at. I open the door and there's these two twentysomething Hispanic guys looking out of place in this neighborhood, they're gangbangers, no doubt about it. One standing there in front of the other. The first one's got stringy black hair, ponytailed but strands slipping out, wearing that loose-fitting rap-artist dress they wear, the other guy behind him's heavier, scowling, with the shaved head like Rodrigo has. Like Rodrigo, I'm instantly thinking. Holy shit. The first guy's asking me, "Hey, you Mickie or what?"

I'm not even nodding, just staring at these two guys, when I hear a commotion behind me in the house. I hear movement, a cabinet opening, then slamming shut, then footsteps, Mickie's for sure, rushing to where I'm standing. He's a freight train, gaining speed as he gets closer. Before I know it Mickie has pushed me aside; he's almost bellowing as he reaches past me and grabs hold of the guy's hair in front of me. Mickie has somehow managed to reach around behind the guy because now he's got full hold of his ponytail. I see Mickie whip the guy around and pull him right into the house, Mickie's free hand holding a silver-plated snub-nosed .38 pointed right at the side of the guy's head. The guy's screaming, "Hey, hey, hey." Mickie kicks the front door shut, leaving guy number two just standing out there, this perplexed expression on his face, What do I do now? he's wondering, as the door slams in his face. All the while Mickie's drag-pulling the ponytailed gangbanger right into the living room, shoving him down under the flat-screen, shrieking at him, "My house? You come to my house? You don't come to my house. Not my house. Never. Never." The kid's struggling to get free, but his face is all fear, he's thinking, This loco maniac screaming in my face, his pistol pressed in my head, is gonna shoot me soon, oh, please, mister, don't.

Mickie's towering over the guy, still shouting, his one hand tight as can be on the ponytail, jerking it every time he makes a point, the other hand has the snub-nosed pressed hard into the side of the kid's head. Then I see Cynthia standing at the back of the room. She's rushed from her bed to check on the noise. Her hands are up to her mouth, What is this, she's trying to figure out. Seeing Mickie in this rage, and the gun, she's frightened, unaware how she looks, with her thin-as-paper-to-her-bare-midriff nightie and a thong I can see is the exact same purple color of the bedsheets in the porn flick Mickie made me watch. I see her belly button's pierced with a small gold ring. She looks like she's about to let out a shrill scream, but her sound button's off. She's frozen in place.

Mickie's still crouched over the guy, screaming into his face, telling him—"Tell Rodrigo I know he sent you, you greaseball motherfucker slime-ass cunt. Tell Rodrigo never, never take it to my house. You got that? You got that?" he repeats, the pistol pressed even harder into the kid. Mickie's glaring, waiting for the kid to say something, say anything, not just stare up at him. Mickie's robe is wide open, some of it actually tenting the kid huddled under there, hardly moving now, awaiting his inevitable fate. Under the robe Mickie's got on this wife-beater T-shirt. His guinea tee. He's also wearing these balloony boxers, like some old man would. With the way Cynthia's nightie-dressed, I would have expected some kind of black bikini underwear on Mickie, his pale belly hanging over the top.

Anyway, Mickie knows these two guys were sent here by Rodrigo, just knows it. I'm trying to think that away as I watch all this, wanting there to be some other explanation, some innocent mistake here. It was one thing for Mr. Well-Dressed Smith to be sent by Rodrigo to our offices. I mean, that was upsetting as hell, but in our world that was within code. You know, the do's and don'ts of what we and the scumbags we represent do. But sending emissaries to your house . . . that is outside the rules of the game. Way outside. Even if it's only to deliver a message, as I begin to realize was the case here with these two punks, one maybe still standing out there with the closed door in his face wondering, What now? Else when I opened that door, I would be dead by now. Stone-cold dead, shot there and then, Mickie and Cynthia right after that the second the punks stepped over my body and stormed in shooting. No, this was to have been a message. A warning from Rodrigo, reaching out from maximum security with his crew, telling Mickie, Fuck you, man, I know where you live, you better do what I paid you for.

Yeah, Mickie's got this right.

The doorbell rings, all of us momentarily turning toward it before we in unison silently conclude it's just the other guy out of ideas what he should do next so he's ringing the bell seeing, Can I come in please? Then we all go back to business like the director has yelled cut and then action.

"Mickie." Cynthia has found her voice. Well, sort of, since she says this half whispering, half beseeching. She wants to say, Mickie, please stop, please don't do what I fear you are about to do. She's not there yet, standing statue-motionless, half dressed, still in shock.

We see Mickie take the .38 from the guy's head and level it square in front of his face. "Please," the kid manages. "Please," he repeats, imploring Mickie. It comes out, *Pees, pees.*

Mickie flicks his wrist, the gun flips at the bridge of the kid's nose, cartilage cracking as the kid's bone snaps and blood, bright red and gushing, starts streaming down his face, onto his floppy rap-artist clothes, and then drips onto the eggshell white wall-to-wall Mickie put down himself when he redid the living room last year after he got the flat-screen and the surround sound like in the theaters.

Mickie's still holding the kid, but now he jerks him up, telling him, "You tell that motherfucker Rodrigo he comes anywhere near my house, sends you or any other greaseball punk-ass bitch, next time better bring an army because you'll need it." He's shoving the kid, blood trailing as they go, toward the front door, saying to him,

"You hear me? You hear me?" But the kid's in pain, not answering, wanting to hold his shattered nose in place but can't because Mickie's propelling him toward the front door like a car pulling into the fast lane. Now Mickie's got the door, opens it to throw the kid out, and, sure enough, there's Shaved Head, still standing there, wondering, Uhm, what should I be doing? His eyes momentarily light up like he's thinking, Oh wow, thanks, man, for opening up, I didn't know what . . . then seeing his buddy, nose smashed like hamburger meat, blood everywhere, including on the sleeve and front of Mickie's robe, his mind is now crawling toward, This isn't good. Uh-oh, he's slow-motioning into focus. Mickie shoves the kid right at Shaved Head, who instinctively grabs him like his junior high school coach has asked for a good catch for once, Pedro, please, as the door slams shut in his face yet again.

I stand there. Mickie moves past me, not a word. He goes to the sofa, swoops the remote off the coffee table, and plops down like he's had a hard day at the office. He stares at the flat-screen, the second half now on, gone are the usual intermission beefy four ex-players, sitting at the halftime desk squeezed into silly-styled, tailor-made suits. They have finished yukking it up as they take good-natured but lame swipes at one another and make instantly forgotten season predictions. The game's back on.

Cynthia's on her hands and knees below the screen. While Mickie was dragging the guy to the front door, she must have somehow gone into the kitchen, because she's spraying something onto the rug and trying to wipe up the kid's bloodstains. All she's doing is spreading the mess; that wall-to-wall is gone. But she doesn't see it because she's still in shock. Mickie's wrapped in his bloody robe staring blankly up at the screen, while Cynthia's down there, on hands and knees, her ass facing Mickie, the purple thong covering just about nothing, her tiny nightie hiked up her waist as her tits jiggle with each swipe of rag over the carpet. Under other circumstances Mickie'd be smirking, nodding first at me, then over at her down there mooning us, signaling, How you like that, nice, huh? But Mickie's a zombie, eyes glued to the TV. Cynthia's down there rubbing her little heart out, spreading the stain into a larger, pinker mass. I sit on the other end of the sofa. What else should I do?

After a while, smack in the middle of a play, Mickie toggles the remote and the porn DVD's back on.

That's it for me. I get up.

What I am not about to do is go out there to my car. For all I know, those two hoodlums are still standing there, bewildered. Thinking Rodrigo said scare them but don't hurt them, but now maybe it's okay to kill at least one of them under the circumstances. No. I am not leaving this house. That's not a problem. I have spent the night at Mickie's before. I don't say a word to either him or Cynthia, not Good night, not I'm sleeping here, all right? I leave them where they are, go down the hall to the guest bedroom, throw my clothes over a chair. I don't wash my face, pee, nothing. I am so tired. I crawl under the covers and am near-instantly asleep. I can hear the game's back on. Then I am gone.

Out of the deepest sleep I hear what sounds like a banging, then moaning. As I slowly climb back to consciousness I'm cloudy-thinking that somehow those guys are back in the house and something's going on. Then I realize it's not that at all. I check the bedside clock: 3:35 A.M. The noise is coming from down the hall. Mickie and Cynthia's bedroom. They're balling. The headboard's beating against the wall; she and he both are moaning. "Uggh, uggh, uggh." The beating gets faster, the moaning more urgent. Jesus fucking Christ, I'm thinking. What the hell is wrong with them? Can't they remember even for a second that I am still here? Don't they care one fucking little bit? They're like a couple of animals in heat. Then I guess I kind of realize that Mickie and her are probably coping as much as screwing, you know, over what happened earlier? Either way I cannot lie here and listen to this.

I throw on my clothes and head for the front door. I am going out there and home. I seriously doubt those two guys are still there this time of night. Either way, I'm going. Tell you the truth how I feel right now? I would rather deal with them than deal with this.

CHAPTER SIX

The next day, late morning, Mickie and me go to the prison to see our client Rodrigo. First, we meet for coffee at the courthouse café. He has a huge breakfast, scrambled eggs, bacon, hash browns, toast, the works. Tamara's not there. Day off, I guess. Just as well. Because all I can do is get a cup of coffee down while Mickie sits across from me devouring his breakfast like a guy who spent the entire night in the sack, humping and bumping between the sheets. Which he pretty much did, first with Cynthia on the sofa before I got to his place, then after all that shit went down, headboard knocking into the early morning hours. We don't talk about last night, none of it. Not the punks, what happened, me staying over, why I left in the middle of the night, Mickie not noticing until morning he's asking Cynthia, Where's Junne, he still here or what? We meet at the café, Hey, Mickie says, then we sit down and order. My coffee. His mountain of food. This is the Italian way. Guys grunt, Hey, how you doin', have their breakfast, and then get to it. None of this, That was really scary last night, didn't ya think? Definitely un-macho. (Okay, what happened the other day when Mr. Well-Dressed Smith spooked us in the office was different. Nothing's a hundred percent. Right?) I watch Mickie eat, then we go to the jail.

But, know what? Mickie was prepared for this. Prepared for Rodrigo. I gotta hand it to him. The guy's got the right instincts. The right moves.

So we're at the jail. Because we're lawyers we get to sit in a little windowed room with Rodrigo. None of this he's behind glass, picking up the phone so we can speak, his open hand on the window. The guards, who Mickie and me know for years, bring Rodrigo into the room, hands under his armpits, Rodrigo's shuffling, shackled at the wrists and ankles, his orange jumpsuit smelling ripe. His head's still shaved, but he's sporting about three days' stubble and it looks like he's been in a fight.

"Gentlemen," says one of the guards, Joey Ballastara, from the old neighborhood. "Here's Johnny!" he announces in his bad Ed McMahon voice, like he's done forever, since he's never seen Leno, Conan O'Brien, any of the late-night new ones. He and the other guard unshackle Rodrigo's wrists, but attach his ankle cuffs to a steel bolt on the cement floor where there's a chair for him to sit and a small table for us all, also bolted to the floor. "Will that be all, gentlemen?" the other guard asks in a fake Irish brogue. These two guys are Abbott and Costello. Same act each time, been doing it years and years, both about due to be pensioned out. But they're good eggs. They don't mistreat the inmates without reason; they don't bust lawyers' balls.

"Thanks, guys," I say. They salute, Our pleasure, and leave. Mickie goes into action.

Now, what I expect to hear from Mickie is more of what happened last night when he confronted the kid Rodrigo sent he dragged into the house. But no, Mickie's going at this another way.

First thing he does is he pumps Rodrigo's hand. He leans over the bolted table and vigorously shakes it, Rodrigo dark-staring at him, his squinty eyes saying, What the fuck's with you? Mickie leans back in his chair, big grin on his face like there's no other place he'd rather be than here with this scumbag. He's dressed as usual in one of his badly tailored suits, mismatched tie. He leans back, crosses his legs wide. Rodrigo notices Mickie's Ferragamos. The light in here is overhead and harsh, Mickie's highly polished loafers almost gleaming.

"So, how they treating you, Pedro?" he asks, saying Pedro on purpose, knowing it's not Rodrigo's name.

Rodrigo just stares at Mickie. If I had any doubt that it was Rodrigo's boys last night, seeing this look of his? Doubt's gone. I sigh, but Mickie's just getting started.

"Feeding you all right?" he asks, Mick's insincerity dripping off each word like oil oozing down a dipstick. "Getting any of that good old corn-holing this place's famous for?" he adds, pumping his right forefinger through the circle made by the cupped fingers of his left hand. All the while grinning at Rodrigo, showing him, one of the things we are *not* going to talk about is what happened last night.

Rodrigo's truly baffled. This is clearly not what he expected from us. He's speechless, not that his English is that good in the first place.

"What's the matter, Jesús?" Mickie says, pronouncing it *Haysuuus,* really drawing it out, letting Rodrigo know in no uncertain terms how this is going to go in here. "Cat got your tongue? You know, *el gato*? *Comprende?*"

Rodrigo's fixed on Mickie, then I see he gets it. He reaches into the pocket of his jumpsuit and retrieves a single cigarette, no pack in there. He sticks it in his mouth and waits for Mickie to offer a light. Me, he's ignoring. Mickie shrugs, Sorry, he's signaling, no matches. Rodrigo, still ignoring me because this is not about smoking, removes the cigarette and replaces it in his pocket, then he gives Mickie this crooked Robert De Niro grin. Okay, I got you, he's thinking. Hombre's an iceberg motherfucker, huh? He nods at Mickie, like in appreciation. You know, professional appreciation. Balls, Rodrigo's thinking. You got cojones. He likes that. I'm going to kill you anyway, you don't deliver, Rodrigo's grin's saying, but now I will respect you when you die. Finally, Rodrigo clocks me, quickly, then he's back to Mickie. He may have contacted me first, but Mickie's now the man. I'm wallpaper.

"So, Pablo," Mickie says to Rodrigo, "wanna hear the plan we come up with?"

Rodrigo shrugs. Yeah, sure, he's saying, why not?

Mickie nods at me and I take Rodrigo through it, you know, the stuff I got from Mumbles. We're going to file with the court, say Rodrigo has important information can implicate and then topple his corrupt government, but he needs some protection so he isn't snuffed while in prison helping the Feds, so put him someplace less than full maximum security he promises to be good and stay around while he's helping.

I'm done. I see Rodrigo looking over his shoulder, like, Where are those two bozo guards, I'm bored with this guy's bullshit and want back to my cell block so I can hang with my boys, maybe finish off the motherfucker started with me earlier, doesn't know who I am. Mickie takes over.

"Okay, Jesús (*Haysuuus*)," he says. "We'll be in touch. I'd keep that asshole puckered I was you."

Mickie stands and raps on the window, letting Abbott and Costello know we are done in here. He ignores Rodrigo and walks out, leaving him there ankle-attached to the cement floor. I follow. Rodrigo watches me. His eyes are blank, can't tell what he's thinking.

Not three hours later, Mickie and me are in our offices, there's no court for either of us today, and who shows up unannounced again but Mr. WD Smith himself. Like the last time, Janice pronounced Janiese shows him to Mickie's office. He tells us that Rodrigo would very much appreciate if we would run him through what we told Rodrigo earlier in the jail about our plan. Either Rodrigo didn't get a word of what I said, or we've got this wrong and WD doesn't work for Rodrigo, it's the other way around. Or both. So we take WD through it. When we finish, he says thank you and leaves. Just like that. I'm thinking, Does he buy it? Does he get it? What? But he leaves and that's it. I go to my office and call Mumbles to see how he's coming with the brief, but the phone rings and rings, no answer, no voice mail, no nothing. I tell myself, go over there later in case he forgot already what we need from him.

Mickie and I have dinner that night. I'm there first, get a table for three thinking Cynthia's coming. Mickie shows up late. Just him. No Cynthia.

We're at a place in Philly, been there forever, but it's changed, redid the whole inside, it's no longer the homey family-run Italian place it was. No more booths, tile floor. The place has been decorated, looks nice with muted colors, soft lighting. Same family owns it, the grandchildren now adults running it. Still the same name, Gallo Nero, from the Chianti wine region of Tuscany, where they have this special area for the reservo wines, each with the serial numbers printed around the bottleneck and the emblem of the "Gallo Nero." Means Black Rooster. More about that in a moment.

Like I said, now the décor is different. Chic. You know, soft, modern. And the menu's changed, sort of. The classic dishes are still there, but there's also new stuff. Inventive dishes, mixing the old with the new. I like the place. Thing of it is, though, ever since it got nicer? The place attracts a kind of different crowd. What I'm trying to say is, you know, like guys. You know, guys. Not all guys, plenty of couples, mixed couples, there too, but Gallo Nero attracts more "just guys" than it used to. Personally, what do I care? I just like the food. Mickie, well, the last time I suggested dinner here he like begged off, said, Let's not do Italian tonight, how about steak?

And then there's the thing about the place's name. I mean, I just heard this, maybe it's not true. But the "just guys" who go there joke about the name Gallo Nero, the Black Rooster they're calling the Black Cock. This is definitely not something I'm going to share with Mickie, no way. But tonight, seeing how Cynthia's joining us and we're three at the table not just two guys, Mickie says Yeah, sure, when I suggest the place for dinner. Only, like I said, Mickie shows up without her. As the waiter's clearing the third place setting, telling us no need to move to a table for two, stay right where you are, I'm asking, Where's Cynthia?

Mickie's looking around the place, frowning. Jesus Christ, he's probably thinking, Now I'm sitting here with a guy, just the two of us, like them. When his attention's back to the table he shrugs, tells me Cynthia's gone back home, to spend a little time with her family. Huh? I ask. Meaning? Meaning she's with her family, Mickie says. When's she coming back? I ask. Another shrug. So, I say, it's what happened last night? Now Mickie's angry. What the fuck do you think? he says. You saw her.

The waiter takes drink orders and disappears. We sit there in silence, Mickie still watching some of the others there, which of course causes them to watch him and us, misinterpreting what he's doing. Whoops, I'm thinking. Our drinks arrive and I see one of the other tables, a couple of well-dressed guys, smile pleasantly at our table. Nothing really inappropriate, yet of course inappropriate. So I say to Mickie, She coming back, do you think? Another shrug. Who the fuck knows, he says, let's order.

When our drinks come, Mickie has his scotch down almost before the glass hits the table. But he doesn't order another. We're midway through dinner, at the main courses. There hasn't been a lot of talking here, we're pretty much eating in silence, not the way I want it, but I'm picking up pretty easily on Mick's mood. He did what needed doing at the jail with Rodrigo, but now Mickie's showing the strain of all this. No need for an act here. Not with him and me. I'm wondering how much of his mood is Cynthia. To be honest with you? On account of I know Mickie? That, he will get over. Soon as he's got another babe, meaning if Cynthia either doesn't come back or, worse for her, waits too long to come back. I've got to tell you, a part of me's feeling, she doesn't come back, well, then there's more time for me and Mick to hang out. But honestly? Mickie needs a babe. A come-and-go babe's okay, but he needs a babe. I only wish I felt the same way. Be a whole lot easier. Know what I'm saying?

So we're eating. Mick's ordered the veal scaloppini. With the side order of linguini with clam sauce. White, of course, with the veal. Me, I'm enjoying the pan-roasted calamari with the infusion of a pesto frutti di mare sauce. Very light, yet superb on the palate. Okay, that's what the waiter said when he described it. Tastes great. Superb on the palate? Fuck. Beats me. When it came to ordering the wine, Mick's studying the menu. He looks over at me, says, Dago red? He's joking, I'm relieved he's maybe snapping out of his funk. Then he orders a really expensive Brunello di Montalcino. Yeah, it's still dago red, but really good dago red.

So we're eating. Mick's still not what I'd call talkative. Now and then he's eyeing the "just guys" at the other table, who have lost interest in us and are chatting through their own dinner. I see someone I know from the health club, one of the ones walks to the shower with his towel tightly wrapped 'round his waist, come into the restaurant. He's searching for the friends he's meeting, sees them at a table behind me and Mickie, starts walking our way, sees me, and takes a second, then places me from the gym. He clocks me sitting with another man. I see him thinking, Well, what do you know? Then he's like ready to stop at our table maybe to schmooze. This I cannot let happen, it'll plunge Mickie back into his funk.

"Hi," the guy says, sort of slowing down like he's a glider coming in for a landing.

I look up. "How you doin'?" I say in my best Camden old-neighborhood, harsh-street way, you know, to discourage him?

So, this tone is, let's call it, way out of character for me. Enough so that the guy actually stops, not because he's like interested in my gruffness, but because what I just said sounds so, well, put on, I guess. Even Mickie looks over at me, like, What? Then sees I'm looking over his shoulder at something, turns, sees the guy, looks back at me, shakes his head, and lowers his fork to his plate. All this happens in a second; I'm like slow-motioning it for you on account of that's how it played out for me. The guy turns his attention to the fellas waiting for him at the table past us, smiles coldly at me, and walks by. Mickie's still staring at me.

"What?" I say to him.

He just shrugs, puts the napkin to his lips, then calls, "Check," to the waiter.

I guess dessert and coffee's out of the question tonight.

Now, while all this is happening? Across the river in Camden, some other shit is going down.

Slippery Williams's dumb-ass nephew's been told by Slippery, I want you to go with my best west side crew, down by them warehouses they got past the projects. Dion and Lamont be with you. Nodding at these two thugs in the room looking like linebackers in street clothes. We takin' delivery tonight, but it be tight, I want Dion and Lamont to hang back, on account of we don't know these niggers we buying from like we should. But they young cats, like you, so I want you up front let them see you good when this shit go down. My boys—they your boys tonight, you in charge—they gonna hang back. Protect your own nigger ass.

Slippery's nephew looks back at Dion and Lamont, his uncle Slippery saying they his boys tonight, they cold-eye staring him, but now he's grinning, can't help it, because Slippery say he be in charge tonight.

All right (*aight*), he says to his uncle. But, of course, tonight's the night Slippery's decided this boy's going down. Dion and Lamont told by Slippery earlier, Not a word to any of the other boys, this strictly between you and me, you do it right, I treat you right after. You promoted.

So while Mickie's calling for the check, across the river in Camden Slippery's nephew is standing out front in the parking lot of a shut-down-for-the-night warehouse, Dion and Lamont behind him, they saying, We here, motherfucker, got your back. The kid's waiting, but nothing's happening. Where the motherfuckers at? he's thinking. Should be here by now they want to sell their shit. What they waitin' for? He hears a click. He knows that sound, it's a pistol cocking. He turns and sees Dion and Lamont got their pieces out.

Damn, he's thinking, seeing they're both looking at him, ain't no one else here.

Just then, all three of them hear the chain-link behind them rattling, shouting starts, Freeze, motherfuckers, some white voice yells at them, Police, drop to your knees, do it now!

The kid reaches for his Glock as Dion and Lamont turn and start firing behind them in the direction of the cops, then they start running toward the kid, all three of them now firing off rounds and running as a pack for the warehouse corner, so they can get out of sight, maybe jump the fence on the other side, make it to the street. Their parked SUV's now out of the question. Just as they near the building's corner, Dion takes one in the back of his leg, he slides just as he turns the corner, he's down, but the building's now giving him momentary refuge. Lamont runs past. He sees Dion's down, but he keeps going, scales the fence, keeps going. But the kid stops, kneels down by Dion.

The kid's in a rage. "Help me, man," Dion says, grimacing, trying to hold his leg. "Help me."

"My uncle?" the kid asks, making it clear he's not doing shit until Dion tells him.

"Please. Help me," Dion says.

"Was my uncle told you shoot me?" the kid repeats.

Both of them can hear the rustle of the police making their way to them. They've got a possible thirty-second margin left, if that. This will be Dion's third conviction, so he knows he looking at twenty to life. The kid's Glock is now three inches from Dion's face, the kid waiting for his answer, more an acknowledgment of what he already knows because even he's able to figure this one out.

"Yeah," Dion says, the pain in his leg now white-hot, he's grimacing, starting to sweat through his clothes.

When the police turn the corner, they see the kid, using his pistol like a hammer, beating in Dion's head. The gun butt's coming down on Dion again and again, pieces of skull and brain flying, blood everywhere, the kid oblivious to the cops as they tackle him, wrestle the pistol away, slam him face down on the asphalt, cuff him. All the while the kid's still in a rage wanting to kill Dion some more, he's not finished yet.

This was a bad night for Slippery all around. It seems that, for once, the cops had been running a successful wiretap on Slippery's operations. Just about everyone in his crew's going down tonight. The cops on Slippery's tab keeping it to themselves, seeing that this time internal affairs was part of the surveillance team, watching the rest of them. No point in going down along with Slippery, they easily conclude. So long, Slippery. And of course, to add insult to injury, Slippery's nephew is now in police custody, a murder one charge facing him, the police saying, Kid, help us with your uncle Slippery, we'll help you. The kid nodding, Motherfucking right I'm going to help you, asshole tries to off me. What you want to know?

When Mickie and I leave the restaurant, fall's now really here. The wind's picked up, temperature's dropping so you need coats you're going to stand out here. We're both just in our lawyer suits.

Mickie and me stand there. I think he wants to say something. If I didn't know better I'd say I see tenderness in his eyes. Well, yeah, we're best friends. But this is something else, like Mickie's saying, Junne, all I want is the best for you.

But of course what he says is, Okay, Junne, tomorrow. See you.

Yeah, tomorrow, I say.

He turns and walks to his car.

CHAPTER SEVEN

So the next morning after coffee at the courthouse café—Tamara back at work now but way too busy to more than serve us and smile, How you doin', lovers?—Mickie and me are back at the jail. This time to see Slippery.

How we learned was the call I got from Slippery on my cell after I got back to my apartment from my dinner with Mick at Gallo Nero. The Black Cock. Jesus H. Christ, what the hell was I thinking, taking Mickie there? Anyway, just as I'm at my dresser about to switch off the cell, I've got the thing literally in my hand, thumb on the red button you turn it on and off with, it rings. I about jumped out of my underwear was all I had on, about to crawl into bed, put the covers over my head, and try and figure out how to get through life. It was Slippery with his one phone call he gets after the cops took him down.

After my cautious hello, since I didn't recognize the number on the little backlit display panel—it was one of the three pay phones on the cell-block wall they got—I hear Slippery's voice. Well, first what I hear is that cavernous noise in the background tells me someone's calling from lockup. You know, the clanging, the sound of heavy metal doors slamming shut, calling voices motherfucker this, motherfucker that. It's like 11:10 P.M., a call with sounds like that means only one thing when I get it. Someone's gone down, the cops saying to him, One call, asshole, make it fast.

"Hey," he says.

"Slip, how you doin'?" I say, recognizing his voice, but I already know how he's doing. "I'm down, Junne," is all Slippery says. What else is there to say? I'm thinking, telling him, First thing in the morning me and Mickie will be there, Slip. "All right," he says. I can still hear the racket in the background, some white-cop voice telling some mope standing somewhere too near Slippery move his fat ass off the fucking wall else he'll knock his fucking goddamn head in, you hear me? I'm about to click off, tell Slippery one more time we'll see him first thing in the A.M. when he says, "Junne. Man's coming 'round, see you." "Now?" I say, thinking he needs me to know something he can't tell Mickie and me tomorrow because you never know, the cops sometimes electronically eavesdrop on attorney-client-protected conversations in lockup, we all know they do it. Mickie and me got stuff from the jail guards when we were cops. You tell the DA what you know, but you don't tell the DA where and how you got it. You dress it up, move it from the jail to a made-up source from the street. The DA's hungry for evidence to use in court, so he or she takes it without too many questions. Doesn't say, Detective, where exactly did you say you learned this?

"Now," Slippery says, meaning, I know it's late, but I want you and Mickie to know some stuff before you see me in here tomorrow, so yeah, now.

"Sure, Slip," I say. I mean, yeah it's late, but the man's down. This is what me and Mickie do.

"All right," he says again, and clicks off.

Twenty minutes later my buzzer rings, I go to the front hall to look at the little closed-circuit camera each apartment's got by the buzzer since the neighborhood's not yet at the stage where you're going to be happy you buzz in someone sight unseen. I recognize the guy standing there nervous as a whore in church, he's looking from side to side worrying is anybody clocking him standing there at a de-fense lawyer's apartment after 11 P.M. on a weeknight. It's one of the plainclothes works the Fifth is on Slippery's tab didn't warn him in advance of the takedown on account of internal affairs was on this one watching all of them, uniform and plainclothes alike. I let him stand there awhile longer leg-shifting, then I buzz him in.

I know the guy but only like to say hi to. He's your typical bulging sloppy plainclothes detective, bad everything: dandruffed hair, bitten nails, cigarette cheap booze smell, and, of course, those awful brown pants and dull plaid sport coat, who actually sells that stuff? He doesn't want coffee, a drink. All he wants is to tell me what Slippery wants me and Mickie to know, then he wants out of here as fast as his stubby little legs can carry him.

Sitting across from me in my living room, he tells me the whole deal. How they had taps on most if not all of Slippery's hideouts, the cops learning where most of his stashes and safe houses are. He tells me which ones. Two guys inside Slippery's operation were flipped several months ago. Low-level guys. He gives me their names, mean-ing their street names. Two low-level guys, maybe, but ones who knew enough to cut deals: them for Slippery. Then he tells me about the kid, my former client Slippery's nephew, and how Slippery's takedown of the kid got flummoxed when the kid and Slippery's top

two lieutenants, the kid's would-be executioners, got taken down themselves.

What he's telling me is that Slippery got taken down hard. Getting back up for him is looking like a miracle at this point. The cop says there are still some stashes the arrestings don't yet know about and some bank accounts Slippery can't now touch but they're there, still intact. I get this. Slippery wants me and Mickie to know he can't pay us at the moment, but he's good for it. At least for now, but who knows where the continuing investigation, as the cops call it, is going?

I also get why this nervous lump of flab and mismatched cotton is sitting here. Sure, Slippery whispered to him when he saw him— he was one of the arrestings—after the cuffs were on him, his arms stretched behind his back as tight as the cops could make it, this guy's partner smirking, asking, Slippery, you comfortable, you okay? Slippery hissing at him, See Junne or Mickie tonight, motherfucker, hear?

Sure, he's here because Slippery told him, but he's also here because he's good and worried Slippery's going to reach out and touch him from the jail, internal affairs or no internal affairs, the motherfucker didn't warn him. He wants Slippery to know he'll do whatever he can, but jeez, under the circumstances what else could he do but nothing, please, Slippery, understand the position they put me in.

The cop finishes, says it's late, he's gotta go. Fine, I say, but I don't get up. This, after all, is a dirty cop. Mickie and me were no angels when we were cops. But on the take? No, never. What I'll take is his information. And I won't burn him. That is not in my client's interests. But respect from me he isn't going to get. I sit facing him, waiting for him to get up and get the hell out of my place. He sees this. At first he seems embarrassed, then he flashes anger like he's telling me, Who the fuck you think you are, you sleazebag shyster lawyer, looking at me like that? He stays seated looking at me, I can see his rat mind's composing something he's about to say before he leaves.

"Heard you did a good job, Counselor, for Slippery's nephew when he went before Thurgood Rufus." He doesn't say Judge Brown's last name, telling me Brown's just another jungle bunny far as he's concerned, robe or no robe. And of course he's cop-calling me "Counselor."

I don't respond.

"Yeah," he says to me. "That undercover sure was pissed what you did to him on the stand." He's watching me. Now he's smiling like, Ain't this gonna to be fun, give you a little payback the way you're looking at me, asshole.

I still don't respond.

"Course, he's no undercover anymore, thanks to you," the detective says. "Man says he's got your number, not sure what he meant by that, though," he's telling me, letting me know he damn well for sure does, as do the others at the precinct listened to the undercover after our dustup in court. You know, what he called me when he left the courtroom.

Now I respond.

"Get the fuck out of here," I say.

He nods like yeah, sure, gets up, and leaves.

Fuck him.

I go to sleep, now somehow oddly feeling better, maybe because I'm pissed off and no longer feeling sorry for myself.

So now me and Mickie are at the jail.

This is the same jail our boy Rodrigo's in. Thing is, Slippery Williams is in state—meaning local—custody, while Rodrigo is a federal prisoner. The shit hole they call the Camden County Jail is literally a two-block walk from the courthouse, though you walk it you either need to be watching the locals on the corners eyeing you or be packing, or both. The jail holds both federal and state inmates. Years ago the Feds made a deal with Camden County—Put some of our federal mopes in there in a separate section on account of our federal facilities are so overcrowded, the men are already jammed four to a one-man cell. We'll give you money, so much a head to house and feed these lowlifes we can't cram into our own places at the moment. That "moment" is going on its tenth year.

Same entrance for everyone going in, looks like a red-brick junior high left over from the 1960s. The folks outside on any given day are the same. Women, mostly, black, poor, some heavyset and tired-looking with their kids, waiting to get in and see the man Mama's telling them this your daddy. And the young ones, mostly black but one or two white and Hispanic as well, some no more than fifteen waiting their turns to see their men. Me and Mickie are no strangers to the place, walking up in our suits and ties, obviously a couple of courthouse lawyers. The women eye us, some thinking maybe we're plainclothes so we're the man, Fuck you, motherfucker, account of you I can't hardly get no welfare checks no more and my man in there, where my money at? While some see us, thinking, Shit, my man can't afford no lawyer, you coming and going in there like you please.

But Mickie and me are always friendly to this group waiting out there with their kids jumping and playing around like it's recess and they're having fun. How you doin'? we say, smiling at them, letting them know we are not the enemy. Some nodding, some surprised by our friendliness and returning our smiles, some just watching us, faces blank as paper.

Tell you the truth, this daily gathering of family remnants is heart-breaking. Even if they're not much in the brains or morals depart-ment, and who knows about the brains part, like what fucking chance they ever got, the downward cycle those kids are on, playing out here but really just waiting their turn to grow up so they can be inside orange-jumpsuited. Well, it's just plain and simple sad, sad, sad.

So me and Mickie do our outside greetings and then we go in-side. We don't have to wait in line like the women, the guard holding the door open calling, LaToya Wilson, seeing her, saying, Uh-uh, you can't take no four kids in witch you. Only two, what you gonna do with the other two's your problem, girl, you wanna go in now else lose your turn, come back tomorrow, up to you. We do the metal de-tector, empty our pockets, keys, and watches in the basket lickety-split fast on account of the guards know us. To them we're "Mickie" and "Junne," not "Counselor" or "Mr." We're good for a bottle every Christmas, ten bucks maybe twenty they need it till Friday. We're reg-ulars here. Mickie tells the woman behind the bulletproof at recep-tion we're here for Slippery Williams, state not federal. Take the elevator to three, she says, I'll call up, Mickie, tell them to get him for you and Junne. So we go to the elevator.

We're standing at the elevator, door opens, and who steps out in our faces but Harold "Dumpy" Brown. Mickie and me know imme-diately he's coming from visiting our man Slippery. This is not a good sign.

Dumpy stops smack in front of us, big grin like he's just been thinking about us.

"Well, if it isn't the Gambino brothers," Dumpy says. "How you boys doin'?"

Mr. Harold "Dumpy" Brown, counselor and attorney-at-law. Standing there looking as usual like some twenty-first-century Cab

Calloway. Remember Cab Calloway? The light-skinned 1940s "Negro" performer from those old late-night TV black-and-white movies. The performer with the devilish grin decked out in an all-white suit of bow tie and tails with the all-white grand piano in his all-Negro ensemble orchestra as he prances back and forth across the stage singing "Minnie the Moocher," yelling choruses of hi-di-hi-di-hi and hi-di-hi-di-ho. His pomaded, processed hair falling down his forehead in strands like he's looking black but he's also looking white.

Well, that's Dumpy. Sort of.

"Hey, Dumpy," Mickie says, because we both know he hates being called that to his face.

Dumpy sucks some air through the side of his teeth like he does, as though he's just finished a big picnic dinner. I almost expect him to pat his belly. He's grinning at us because he's Sylvester and he's just ate Tweety.

"Come from your man Slippery," he tells us. "Asked for me to come over visit with him. Know what I'm saying?"

Dumpy's standing there in his usual overdress. He's real milk-coffee light-skinned, hair's pomaded but too kinky to do more than be squiggly wire pasted over the top of his thinning scalp. Pencil mustache he's had forever. But those suits—garish, intense-tone pin-stripes, shirt collar way too high for his neck, iridescent tie, silk pocket hankie. Even, can you believe it, two-tone-tie shoes (say that fast five times) and twin diamond pinky rings.

Mickie and me have known—and hated—Dumpy ever since the days all three of us were cops. Yeah, Dumpy did law school too. Though, after his troubles on the force, he went down to Washington, DC, for a few years, finished college, and did law school at mostly all-black Howard University. His second cousin Judge Thurgood Rufus Brown saw to that, parts of Camden being the small town that it is.

Needless to say, Dumpy's got a good batting average on the cases he's had before Judge Brown. Now, Dumpy is one hell of a good courtroom lawyer. For the right case. Black defendant, street crime, mostly black jury, he knows how to talk to like some Baptist deacon on a hot summer Sunday morning. I give him that. He's smart and he's good on his feet, mostly with that shuck-and-jive street talk he stuffs into his courtroom lawyering like a big foot in an old sock. Still, when he draws Cousin Judge Brown he tends to do real well. Hey, that's the way it is. Nobody in the DA's office dares complain to Judge Brown, saying to him however politely that he can't be fair and square no matter who the lawyer is.

I glance over at Mickie, seeing how he's reacting to Dumpy having just told us in so many words we've been fired from Slippery's case, Dumpy's now the lawyer. Mickie's not going to show anything to Dumpy, no way. Mickie gets that smile of his he has, you know, the boy-am-I-happy-with-life smile.

Grinning, Mickie says, "Now, Dumpy, you up there with our boy stealing our client? Shame on you, being a fellow member of the criminal bar like you are. You behaving like the old days, you doing that." Then Mickie adds, "Dumpy," just at the end like it's part of his sentence, but also an accusation. Same old Dumpy.

Dumpy's sucking in his teeth again. He really does not like being called Dumpy to his face. Reminds him of the old days. His cop days.

See, Dumpy got the moniker on the force. As an arresting he had the habit of "dumping" things on his perps if they came up clean after he took them down. You know, like a knife, maybe a small pistol been stolen and traced to a homicide, or a packet of dope. And on occasion, if he was pissed at who he had down, he'd have the perp held on his knees by a couple of other cops on each side, they holding the perp's head upward, like he's trying to get some sun in his face. Then Dumpy would take that brick he kept in the trunk of his car, along with his collection of knives, guns, bags of dope, then he'd "dump" that brick onto the perp's face. Not from too high up. No, just high enough to break a nose, bruise an eye, maybe. Only once did he step out of character. Way we heard it, he shot off the kneecap of a snitch he was working he figured was holding out on him.

After a while it was too much for the force. The police commissioner told Dumpy take early retirement else proceedings against you going to start. Get out now, Detective Brown, while you still can. Do something else with your life. And Dumpy did. Even though he's an unmitigated backstabbing shit, he's generally considered one of the better criminal lawyers around here. Especially in the black community. Dumpy carries two business cards, one for white folks, the other for African-Americans. The only difference in the two is that printed directly under "Harold Brown, Attorney-At-Law" on the black version is the phrase "Black On Black Get You Back." Meaning, of course, stay away from those white lawyers like me and Mickie.

Dumpy starts to chuckle. "Now, cellophane," he says to Mickie, "you and your boy Tonto here doin' fine. You got you your Italian (he says it *eyetalyon*) goombahs you takin' care of. You don't need to mess with no brothers. You leave them to me. You don't see me going after none a your Vitos, Tommasos, Vincenzos."

"Fuck you, Dumpy," Mickie says, chuckling like he's not fazed by this.

But Dumpy's on a roll here, still angry Mickie's calling him that, and pumped I guess because he's just stolen our client. "Say, Mickie, my man," he says, "you and your boy Junnebug here still needin' to be subletting your space from them Yids got that slip-and-fall practice?" He chuckles, then adds, "You know, them the boys my good friend the Reverend Jesse Jackson say be Hymies."

"The Reverend Jackson 'says be Hymies,' " Mickie purposefully half corrects Dumpy, like, Fuck you, don't pull that anti-Semitic jive-ass nigger shit on me.

Another tooth-sucking.

"Now, don't go and be gettin' all huffy on me, Mickie," Dumpy says, "you know I love everybody, don't make me no never mind who you and snowflake here needin' to office with. Know what I'm saying? But you know how it is. Man gots to be with his own community" (he pronounces it *communitay*).

Mickie's had enough. He reaches over and pushes the elevator button. The door immediately opens because it's got nowhere to go unless we use it.

"Later, Dumpy," Mickie says as he steps around him and into the elevator. He pronounces it *Dumpay*.

I follow Mickie in. I see Dumpy shake his head, suck his teeth, and leave, giving the guards standing there the same kind of banter Mickie and I do.

CHAPTER EIGHT

Once we get up to the third floor we go to the lawyer interview room and wait for Slippery. Not two minutes later, on account of we took so much time downstairs with Dumpy Brown, Abbott and Costello bring our man in. But unlike Rodrigo when we saw him, the two guards step-shuffling him in chained head to toe, Slippery's walking in under his own steam, no cuffs, no nothing. And the guards are treating him with respect. This is Slippery Williams, Camden's biggest drug lord. He's not going anywhere. The man's a professional, he knows the game. He treats the guards with respect.

After Joey Ballastara's tired "Here's Johnny" shtick, Slippery shakes our hands and thanks the guards for seeing him in. Hey, no problemo, Joey says, calling Slippery Mr. Williams, asking, Anything you need, a Coke, some water? Naw, I'm good, he says, but maybe my boys here be wantin' something. Mickie? Junne? he asks. No, we're good, we tell Joey. Okay, then, Joey says as he and his partner leave, telling us, You change your minds, give a holler.

We all sit. "How you doin', Slip?" Mickie says.

Slippery looks tired. He's just an average-looking guy. You wouldn't know he's the king of the hill just from eyeballing him. Maybe five-eight, dark skin, as street African-American-looking as the next guy. Not particularly muscular, not particularly anything. He's got a few jailhouse tattoos blue-inked on his arms, but nothing rap-artist fancy, just some homemade names of past girlfriends, an old teenage gang sign. He's orange-jumpsuited like the rest of them in here—could pass easily for your average mope. But he's not. Slippery is one smart guy. Fact is, he was born uptown in some other place, white instead of black? He'd probably still be in jail, but instead of indicted for drugs he'd of been some Harvard Business School indicted head of Enron or some other Fortune 500 crook with some fancy-assed lawyers instead of us trying to help him.

Except, of course, Mickie and me aren't helping him anymore thanks to Dumpy. At least that's what Mickie and me are thinking as we sit with Slippery.

"You know how it is," Slippery answers Mickie. He chuckles. "Been better, know what I'm sayin'?"

Slippery looks over at me. "Junne, my man, you all right? You lookin' grim, man," he says.

What is he seeing in my face? I'm wondering. I say, "No, Slip, I'm feeling fine, just tired, that's all."

Mickie says, "Well, maybe Junne's looking like he's looking, Slip, on account of we just ran into Dumpy Brown downstairs, man says he was here, you called for him."

Now, Slippery's not only in the game, like I said, he *is* the game. He knows how we feel about Dumpy.

"I didn't call that motherfucker tell him see me, he come see me on his own. You know Dumpy," he says. "He telling me, Now, Slip, why you need them white-milk motherfuckers, you know you need a brother like me take care of you."

Mickie sighs. But Slippery says, "I tell him, Nigger, what you talkin' about? Those two boys been with me since back in the day. They like kin, don't you go givin' me that brother shit about them, know what I'm sayin'?"

Great, I'm thinking, and Mickie is too. Slippery's telling us how grateful he is for what we've done for him. Past tense. He loves us like we're family, but Dumpy's taking over.

Wrong.

Slippery says to me and Mickie, "Yeah, I told Dumpy, You my man, Dumpy. We talk. Come back in a day or two, work it out."

"Meaning what?" Mickie asks.

"You sure you don't want a soda or nothin'?" Slippery asks. We both shake our heads, like, What already?

"Here's the thing," Slippery tells us, leaning forward, arms on the table. "My boys got took down too. Not all, but enough. They be needin' lawyers, right?"

We nod. That's true. And the same lawyer that represents Slippery probably can't represent his crew, might create a conflict of interest on account of what's good for them may not be good for Slippery. The DA is going to press Slippery's lieutenants to flip over on Slippery and testify against him for a deal. Maybe reduced time, maybe witness protection.

"So here's what I'm thinking," Dumpy tells us. "Dumpy be the lawyer for the others indicted with me. Now, I know Dumpy. He one slippery motherfucker." Slippery stops to chuckle at himself for absentmindedly referring to Dumpy as being *slippery*. "You know what

I'm sayin'," he says. "But Dumpy ain't gonna let none a them mother-fuckers flip on me, know what I'm sayin'?"

"Yeah," Mickie says, but there's clearly more here.

"What it is," Slippery says. "Now, you boys know I got a business I need to run." Meaning from in here. He leans in even closer, his eyes shifting up to the room's ceiling like to say, Here's where those may be listening going to be interested, so I need to be careful. "Now, you boys ain't gonna carry no instructions, shit like that, from me to who-ever out there. You don't do that. I know that. Am I right?"

We both nod. Mickie and me don't do that. Slippery knows it, all our clients know it.

"Well, Dumpy, he down with that. It don't make him no never mind. Know what I'm sayin'?"

Yup, he's right. Dumpy would eagerly carry messages back and forth between Slippery and whoever he has left out there on the street taking care of business.

"Thing is," Slippery says, "him and me can talk like we do. You know, say things the boys upstairs they gonna be needin', what you call it, an interpreter understand what we talkin' about."

Mickie and me exchange glances. The man has a point.

"How that work for you?" Slippery asks us.

It works. Sure, Mickie and me are relieved we are still in the case. And Slippery's right, he can put Dumpy to good use.

"Yeah, okay," Mickie says. "But you've got to promise us, Slip, we'd be working with Dumpy, not *for* Dumpy. Can't do that."

"Naw, naw," Slippery says, "you boys good with me. Always been. Always will be."

Now Slippery sits back in his chair. Mickie and I watch him. He's most probably fucked, will spend the rest of his adult life inside prison walls. Slippery's going to give it the good fight, but unless lightning strikes, and that isn't likely to happen, he's done. He knows it. Mickie and me know it.

"Listen," Slippery says after a while. "I can't, you know, take care of you like I do. My assets are temporally tied up." Slippery says this last part in a faux-white accent. We all chuckle.

Mickie glances over at me. Remember the two rules of lawyering we talked about earlier? Number two: You're winning in court, shut up and sit down. Number one: Get your fee in advance. Mickie's asking me, Okay with you for Slippery we violate rule one? I nod yeah. For Slippery, yeah. For all of what he is, drug dealer, occasional killer, the man is honorable. Honorable in our world. Mickie and me have a lot of affection for the man, maybe we are a kind of "kin," as Slippery puts it. You're thinking, What? Junne, give me a break. But that's how it is. It just is.

So I nod yeah, okay, to Mickie.

"That's fine, Slip," Mickie says.

Slippery nods in appreciation. "No matter what," he tells us, looking first to Mickie, then to me. "No matter what. I'm good for it. You down with me. I'm down with you."

"I know," Mickie says.

Then Slippery's shaking his head again. "Motherfucking punk-ass nephew," he tells us. "Should of put that little motherfucker down, waited too goddamn long, on account my sister, his mama." Slippery's thinking, silently going through his regrets, his mistakes, he waited too long with the kid, maybe got sloppy how he ran his business, now the kid's somewhere in protective custody way out of reach of Slippery, the next time he sees him is when the guards lead him to the witness stand at Slippery's trial as a prosecution witness. And there are hours of tapes of who knows what conversations between Slippery and his lieutenants.

Slippery sighs. "Fuck," he says, now kind of half smiling at us. It's a smile of sadness. A smile from a man who knows his fate and knows he needs to come to terms with it.

Mickie and me don't say anything. Both of us are affected by this, by Slippery's miserable fucking dismal situation.

But what can you do? That's how the game goes for guys like him. Up, then down. It's not an unusual story.

After we leave Slippery, tell him we'll call Dumpy, have a meet, get things going for the defense, Mickie and me walk back toward the courthouse. It's near lunchtime and we'll go to the courthouse café have a sandwich.

Mickie says to me as we walk, "Junne, you need to be the one deals with Dumpy. I get any more of that jive-ass bullshit from him, I'm going to deck the motherfucker, swear to God."

"Yeah, okay," I say.

The rest of the way neither of us talks. Slippery's down. What more is there to say?

CHAPTER NINE

"I'll get him," I tell Janice over the intercom phone. "Tell him I'll be right there."

I go right out to the Bernstein, Smulkin waiting room, where Professor Mumbles is at. I don't dally on account of Mumbles wanted me to meet with him at his office, not here. He's afraid these days to be out and about, unless it's the court he has to go to, or maybe wherever it is he eats, sleeps, unless he's bunking in his office on that ratty sofa. When I enter the waiting area I see Mumbles squeezed in among the ragtag auto accident malingerers are the Bernstein client base. It's like a bus station waiting room, the clients, mostly black and Hispanic, lined up shoulder to shoulder against the wall in fading chairs, back-of-head-sized black dots on the walls behind each pasted there like photo negatives from years of sticky African-American hair-care products. Most every client's wrapped in unneeded neck braces, arm slings, and any other show props the

Bernstein boys have told them, saying loud like they're all hard of hearing, Listen to me, this is important, are you listening? You need to have that on anytime you're out of the house. They tell them be careful because the other driver's lawyer will hire an investigator with a video camera, catch them taking out the garbage, their old ladies middle of the day telling them because they're not at work, pretending injury, get off your lazy ass and throw those goddamn empty beer cans in the bin, then get out the kitchen and take that trash out front. The Bernstein boys telling them, You go shooting hoops with the boys down at the corner playground, you gonna get bubkes, understand? Meaning they get nothing. And of course, if these guys get caught on video, not only do they get nothing, but the Bernstein, Smulkin one-third before expenses off-the-top contingent legal fee goes bye-bye too.

I smile at Mumbles, who has all his papers on his lap clutched tightly between his arms; he couldn't find his briefcase in the rubble of his office before coming over here, I guess. It's a huge pile of xeroxed cases, drafted notes, and paragraphs, not even a rubber band around any of it. Mumbles sees me and smiles sheepishly. I can see that the moment he rises, as he's about to, the papers are going to flutter away from him and hit the waiting room fading carpet, losing whatever order Mumbles has managed to keep them in on his way over here.

"Shannon," I say, quickly leaning over and grabbing his unwieldy paper pile as he rises to meet me. "Let me help you with that. How you doin'?"

Mumbles smiles appreciatively at me, but doesn't utter a word. He pushes his 1980s eyeglasses back up the bridge of his nose and nods. He's got his mute button on, I guess. Mumbles, knowing that he's as prone now as ever to be nonstop-uttering a slew of random thoughts if he addresses me simply to say hello, which will cause the assorted malingerers in here to chuckle and titter at him. This man crazy, their glances telling one another. I am glad he came, so I want to get him out of the waiting area and back to my office as quickly as possible. I would have gladly gone to Mumbles's office for this meeting, but no way could I get Mickie there. Come on, Mickie, this is important, I'm telling him. No fucking way, Junne, he's insisting. And I need for Mickie to hear this too. What Mumbles has come up with for Rodrigo. Please, Shannon, I told him over the phone, be better really if you could come over here, meet with me and Mickie at our place. I didn't tell him that Mickie wouldn't go to his place. Didn't have to. Mumbles may be a lot of things. Dumb isn't one of them.

"Come on, we'll go to my office," I tell Mumbles. "Mickie's waiting on us."

He nods sure, okay.

Janice behind her receptionist desk gets off the phone and says to Mumbles, "Would you like some coffee, Mr. Luchsman?"

Janice has never met Professor Mumbles as far as I can remember. I don't think she was working here when Mumbles was less . . . well, less Mumbles than he is now. And yet, she asks him if he wants coffee with a tenderness—not at all like she's speaking to a child or some half-wit—that makes me smile at her instinctive compassion, maybe she doesn't even see it in herself, but it's there with her gentle question.

Mumbles nods yes, please, his sound still on mute. Janiese doesn't say how do you take it, she's just going to bring him the coffee, fixings on the side, telling him, You go on in with Junne, I'll bring it to you. Mumbles smiles, thankful I guess that she hasn't asked him anything further.

Mumbles follows me down the hall to my office, Mickie's already in there waiting.

Mumbles is suited and tied, but as rumpled and smelly as ever. He sees Mickie, rubs his hand through his hair, but doesn't extend a hand to him. Mickie smiles and nods at Mumbles, no hand extended either.

"Hey, Shannon," he says. "How you doin'?"

Mickie will not be impolite to Mumbles, won't display his true feelings about him. Mickie knows we need him, but despite that, Mickie is way too much of a gentleman to behave badly toward this guy. He may find him creepy, bedbug-crazy, but he knows full well Mumbles is not a bad guy. Far from it.

I tell Mumbles why don't you take this seat, pointing to one of the two in front of my desk. I walk around to my chair, then place his big assortment of papers in front of him as Mickie sits in the chair beside Mumbles. I see Mickie push his chair as far from Mumbles as he can without being too obvious about it, Mickie eyeballing the sprinkles of dandruff snow capping Mumbles's suit shoulders.

Mumbles looks from me to Mickie to the pile of papers now in front of him on my desk. I know I need to get this started somehow.

"Okay," I say. "Shannon, I told Mickie about your idea how we go for political asylum for Rodrigo, he cooperates against his country's junta or whatever you call it, then we get him some kind of limited release while he helps the Feds."

I look from him to the pile of papers to Mickie. Okay, let's go, I'm thinking, come on, Mumbles, open up here, teach me and Mickie what we need to know try and pull this off. There's a knock at the door, then Janice comes in, puts a Styrofoam of coffee before Mumbles together with assorted packets of sugar, Sweet'N Low, and powdered creamer. "There you go," she says, doesn't ask me and Mickie can I get you anything, then leaves us, shutting the door behind her.

Mumbles takes a sip of the coffee, black, which somehow turns his sound back on.

"So," he says, like the three of us have been chatting for the last half hour. "What you need is a compelling case for the political climate of your client's country. . . ."

Me and Mickie sit and listen to Mumbles lecture us on the kind of legal brief that needs to be filed, neither one of us so much as taking a single note. If Mumbles notices this, he doesn't let on. We sit and listen as Mumbles rattles off legal precedent from the cases he brought, snatching pieces of paper from the pile in front of him, displaying sentences to us, underlining things, handing them across the desk to me, rattling on. And of course all the while he's saying how he forgot to make his alimony payment again, how if he misses Judge so-and-so's calendar call one more time he will likely be disbarred, how he needs socks he can't find a matched pair anymore, and on and on and on.

Mickie's sitting there more or less next to Mumbles, his right leg jumping up and down like his motor's dangerously stuck in overdrive. Even if he was listening to this he's clearly not anymore. Mickie's dying. Another twenty seconds goes by when Mickie says he'll be right back he forgot he needs to take care of something; he gets up and escapes.

I can see Mumbles knows Mickie's gone for good, but he's here to help us, so he doesn't miss a beat. When he's finished, he pushes his glasses back up the bridge of his nose, waits for me to react.

Did I understand all of what he just said? No. Do I get the melody here if not the lyrics of what Mumbles is proposing? Yeah, I get that. Will this work? I'm thinking, knowing the answer but not letting myself know I do.

Mumbles is waiting, smiling at me, signaling, It's all right, Junne, we both know this is a stretch.

I let out some air, shake my head.

"Jesus, Shannon," I say.

Mumbles shakes his head in agreement, starts reassembling his pile of papers. He smiles at me. He is a friend and will help as best he can. He knows, I guess, that me and Mickie will ask him to write the motion and accompanying legal brief for us, that we will put our names on it when it's filed with the court, not his. He doesn't care. Mumbles is here for me. And for Mickie too, for that matter.

Mumbles shrugs. "Junne," he says, "you never know. We'll give it our best shot."

Shot.

Right.

CHAPTER TEN

Mickie and me had the best time last night. It was like an oasis in the desert. You need to kick back when you can, relieve some tension, right? Seeing Slippery like we did the other day was a downer. Lot worse for Slippery himself, no doubt. Still, for Mickie and me it was a downer. Slippery's toast. A few years from now Mickie's going to be saying, I wonder how Slippery Williams's doing these days on account of he'll be doing his third-offense, life inside no possibility of parole, drug conspiracy and accomplice to attempted murder of his punk nephew up in Rahway.

We still call it Rahway on account of that's where this maximum-security lockdown hellhole is, the name's been sanitized now by the state, they're officially calling the place East Jersey State Prison. You know what they say, a rose by any other name's still a shit hole if it's Rahway.

Anyway, we had a blast last night. A few days after we saw Slippery and then later Mumbles, Mickie comes into my office tells me tonight we're going to the state bar annual dinner down in Atlantic City. The what? I say on account of Mickie and me do not go to bar association things. I mean like never. Continuing education we don't do.

Unlike some other states, New Jersey does not require lawyers to take so many hours of continuing legal education to keep your ticket punched. In the other states you go to these bullshit two-day courses, slipping in and out because what they're saying is needless, useless bullshit. Since in New Jersey it's voluntary, attendance is low, made up mostly of geeks and younger lawyers who'll do anything to spend a day or two out of their oppressive big-firm cubbyhole offices, telling the partner they're slaving for, Gosh, this program looks really interesting and helpful.

No, like I said before, Mickie and me do what we do in shoe leather, in the courthouse, lockup, wherever. But Mickie's telling me we're going to the state bar annual black-tie dinner, the gala that follows the year-end seminars at the grand ballroom of the Trump Taj Mahal in Atlantic City. The seminars may be low attendance, but the annual dinner's a big deal in the state. A real who's who of the lawyer profession. You know, all the judges and their spouses, the senior partners and the young turks and turkettes standing around in their formal attire smiling and joking even though they'd set each other on fire they thought they could get away with it, lessen the odds who'll be around for partnership consideration a few years down the road. Everyone, partner and young ass-wipe included, chuckling at the stupid jokes the judges crack, saying, Now, Judge, that is truly funny.

I'm saying to Mickie, The what? He's saying, You got that right, Junne, my man. We're going, but we're going different, he says, that devilish grin he has plastered on his face. Uh? I say. You'll see, he says. Put on your tux, we'll pick you up your place five-thirty P.M.

sharp, drive to Atlantic City to the dinner. We? I say. What's this we? You'll see, Mickie repeats, and strides out of my office, cat got his tongue.

You'll see? What the fuck that's supposed to mean?

Next time I see Mickie, I'm standing outside of my apartment all tuxed up and Mickie's rolling down the power window of the white stretch limo just pulled up in front of me.

"Junne, my man," he says. "Stay right there." I watch the window roll back up, now I'm seeing myself heavyset-tuxed on account of the window's tinted and beveled. Way up front the driver's-side door opens and I see the driver I recognize get out and walk over to me.

This is a striking woman, her name's Alice, she's been a limo driver and local part-time bartender for a couple of years now. Alice is tall and thin with spiked platinum-blond hair she wears in a man's cut on account of she's a dyke. A gorgeous dyke, but a dyke, make no mistake about that. Alice is wearing a man's suit cut tight on her body, which, though somewhat small-breasted, is nice no matter who's looking, man or woman. She comes over to me, says, "Good evening, Mr. Salerno," not calling me Junne like she normally would, and bows with a flourish toward the white stretch.

Alice keeps a Web site where she advertises for her limo service. All of us have seen it. It's kind of weird. There's beautiful Alice in her man's clothes posing before her limo. And then beside that there's an indoor studio shot of Alice posed backward sitting on a chair, her trousers on but from the waist up bare. She's peering over her shoulder at the camera with a devilish smile; this black-red-green tattoo of a cobra curls from her waist all the way up to the back of her neck. She also has a smaller version of the cobra tattoo wrapped around her right forearm. What that picture's got to do with her being a driver for hire beats me. But like I said, all of us have seen her

Web site, so maybe she's got something there how to get a car hired nobody's thought of before. Despite all that, I like Alice. We all do.

"Why, Alice," I say. "You look beautiful tonight. Butch. But beautiful."

Alice smiles and opens the door so I can see Mickie, who's not alone in there.

"Junne, get in," he says. And I do, Alice shutting the door behind me and walking back around to the driver's side.

"Hi, Junne," the two women seated with Mickie say, both of whom I know too.

Mickie's got on his tux, although the jacket's lying on the seat, his legs are crossed so I see he's got on his fancy patent-leather, for-tux-only slip-ons. He's holding a crystal tumbler of scotch from the fully stocked bar Alice keeps. The two girls are nicely dressed in formal evening wear, both of them showing full-breasted cleavage. They're two of Buffalo Reds's G-noters. What Mickie explains as I say, "Girls, how you doin' tonight?" is that Buffalo has loaned them to us, here's the deal, Mickie is saying right in front of them both, and why not, there's no secrets with them.

They're ours tonight for the night, on the house, so long as we don't fuck 'em, Mickie explains. We take them with us to the bar association annual black-tie, they're our companions, and we introduce them any way we want, they'll go along, but, Buffalo says, no fucking. It's all on the house unless we let them do us. Mickie explains this in front of them, they're smiling like, What the hell, this'll be a different night out for us, what do we care?

"Got it?" Mickie says to me. "Fuck 'em we want to. But then we pay. A thousand a head—so to speak," Mickie says, chuckling at his little joke, the girls indulgently smiling at him. "Thank you, Buffalo, thank you, girls," Mickie adds, tipping his scotch glass to them.

Is this some kind of setup Mickie's doing on me? I'm thinking. You know, this continuing thing Mickie's got to get me to where he thinks I belong, you know, with women? Is his plan that one of these girls will turn my head and, well, turn me back to someplace Mickie's thinking I really belong? No, I conclude. He may want all that for me, but tonight Mickie's just on a kick, wanting me and him to blow off some steam, have some fun Mickie-style.

The one girl seated on Mickie's right is called Wanda. Like all Buffalo's girls, she's got a knockout body, tonight dressed like the Victoria's Secret version of the First Lady. Her auburn hair is nicely styled, elegant, I'd call it, her costume jewelry looking real and understated. While her face makeup has brushed away the pale layer of freckles covers her body, they are still visible on her arms and exposed cleavage. Now, she too is tattooed, but not like Alice. Nobody we know is tattooed like Alice. Wanda's got a small black ace of spades on the fleshy spot between her thumb and first finger on her right hand and a small dagger in its sheath down on her left ankle. Mickie's telling me that Wanda's my "date" for tonight, that okay with you, Junne? he's asking. You too, Wanda? he asks her, like she's going to care.

Yeah, great, I say, smiling at Wanda. She winks at me, but there's no real sincerity there, just playfulness. I watch as Wanda opens her little cocktail dress purse, removes a vial of cocaine, and delicately snorts powder up both nostrils and then as an afterthought offers me some. No, thanks, I shake my head as Mickie hands me a scotch.

The other girl's really the better-looking of the two. She's tall and really beautiful. While her hair's dyed just a bit too jet-black to pass the almost-real test, it's long and silky, she's wearing it wrapped up around her neck. She's got icy blue eyes you can't help but fixate on, they are so alluring. As she crosses her legs and some material from her dress slips away, I get a glimpse of thigh and leg perfectly, I mean perfectly, shaped. For some reason she's called Little Chip. Why? you're thinking. Maybe it's got something to do with what she does, some sexual something or other she's known for. Tell you the truth, neither me nor Mickie knows why either. Maybe there's a Big Chip somewhere. Whatever it is, she's Little Chip. Although she's telling Mickie, as Wanda passes her the vial of coke, Can I be Rona Rosenberg tonight, Mickie? I want to be Rona Rosenberg.

"Yeah, sure, Chip," Mickie says. "You're Rona Rosenberg long as you wanna be."

Little Chip, now aka Rona Rosenberg, takes what I'd have to call two man-sized snorts from off the back of her hand where she's tapped the coke, shudders, then settles herself down next to Mickie, smiling glassily first at him, then at me. I see Alice watching all this in the rearview as we take off for Atlantic City, the head of Alice's tattooed cobra protruding from the back of her man's shirt collar. She's making eye contact with Wanda and Little Chip, since most girls like Buffalo's dig other women more than they do men anyway.

So we ride all the way to Trump's. When we get there Mickie tells Alice go get something to eat, handing her a hundred in twenties. Saying, Hang out at the casino you want, I've got your cell, we'll call when we're ready. You got it, Mickie, Alice says, and drives off to the covered parking.

Once inside Trump, we get our table assignments from the reception desk outside the grand ballroom, walk inside, and go right to the bar. We're standing around just the four of us since nobody's coming over, I mean, what is there to network with guys like us, right? I see Mickie searching the place for his first stop, that devilish gleam back in his eye. He sees what he wants and leads the three of us over to a group standing nearby, drinks in hand, pleasantly chatting.

Two men, two women, the guys looking like ones made big-firm partner in the last couple of years, feeling their oats; the wives at their sides now Junior Leaguers no longer needing jobs, the big BMW now theirs, all private pre-K and beyond tuition for the kiddies, more than covered by their hero hubbies. They watch us approach with what I can see is dread, Mickie, drink in hand, saying too loud, Hey, how you doin'?

Mickie's introducing us, telling them he's Mickie Mezzonatti, and this guy, he's saying, pointing his scotch glass at me, the liquid's sloshing too close to guy number one, he is one hell of a lawyer, I got to tell you, he says. This is none other than Salvatore Salerno, but call him Junne, short for Junior, we all do, am I right, Junne?

I smile but don't speak, taking in Mickie's play here.

"And," Mickie says, "this is Wanda . . ." Mickie realizes he doesn't know Wanda's last name. "Wannamaker," he adds, chuckling. "Wanda Wannamaker," he repeats, pleased with the sound. Wanda smiles pleasantly at them but also stays silent.

"And this lovely creature," Mickie says, gently pushing Little Chip forward toward them, "is the delightful and delicious Rona Rosenberg." Unlike Wanda, Little Chip now Rona extends her hand and demurely shakes with all four of them, smiling sweetly at the women and not so sweetly at the men.

Not a word back, all four of them are staring at us like those movie characters seeing the aliens just stepped from their spaceship on a mission to breed with their species before their own planet disintegrates. That is, all except guy number two, who's lost in the moment staring at Little Chip tonight Rona Rosenberg and, despite himself, he's off somewhere in fantasyland peering at her boobs, letting his eyes wander down her curves to those sumptuous hips and thighs. Junior Leaguer number two sees that hubbie's lost in lust, her eyes darting between him and Little Chip Rona, who's professionally doing what girls like her do when guys like him are doing what he's doing. Mickie sees all this too.

"So, you boys are with one of the big firms, I bet," Mickie says. "Lemme guess," he says, pretending to be searching for some firm name he doesn't give a shit about, his eyes taking in their discomfort with him and us.

Guy number two's still off somewhere, him and Little Chip are naked, side-by-side, ceiling mirrors and a tight-sheeted bed in the picture. He hasn't heard a word said. Guy number one's needing to carry the ball for their group, his eyes darting from side to side searching for an escape route. Mickie's got them boxed in good, still pretending to rummage his memory banks for the name of some silk-stocking white-shoe fancy-assed law firm.

"One of them big New York firms has offices in New Jersey, like Newark or Trenton, am I right?" he's asking guy number one, who is still eye-darting here and there looking for someone else to pawn us off on.

"No, actually," guy number one finally says, understanding that the four of them are trapped and he needs to say something, anything. "We're with—"

Just then Little Chip sees something's got her attention, she's interrupting guy one midsentence, not caring at all because of what she's seeing.

"Mickie, take me over there," she says. I see an older man I immediately recognize who's just come into the grand ballroom with his wife, they're both checking the place for who's arrived by now. It's Judge Herman Sokoloff, Chief Judge of the state supreme court. That's the highest court in New Jersey, takes the appeals from the lower courts, sort of like the United States Supreme Court does for the nation. The appeals judges are even called Justice so-and-so, not just Judge. Like the ones in DC. We still call the New Jersey ones Judge though. Unless you're up there arguing before them. Something me and Mickie don't do much. So Herman Sokoloff's a big deal, is what I'm saying.

Little Chip's kind of happy to see him like she's recognized a friend at a strange gathering. I get it, Mickie does too. Herman Sokoloff, Chief Judge, is a regular client of Little Chip. He's a "G-notee." Now, the state supreme court sits in Trenton, not Camden where Buffalo's girls work out of, but seeing as Herman's a big deal, I'm thinking he's thinking it's worth the drive—safer—to get it on with Little Chip all the way down to Camden—maybe even they meet in Philly across the river be safer still. Whatever and however they do it, they do it, that me and Mickie get.

Chip's pulling Mickie over to Herman standing there with his sourpuss-looking wife searching the room for someone they know. Me and Wanda follow in their wake.

What I see as we approach the judge is a look on Chip's face saying she knows she can't let on what's what between her and him, she's going to be real discreet, not in any way let on. She just wants to pretend that she knows him like from some innocent prior meeting, like she's a fan or something, just wants to say hello, Judge, nice to see you, get introduced to the Mrs. as someone the judge met somewhere but can't really recall and then Chip's moving Mickie and the rest of us somewhere else, now satisfied she's said hi to someone important she knows in this fancy schmancy place filled with lawyers and other society pillars.

But that's not what happens on account of the judge is a dork, doesn't get it that this is simply a girl who's got an innocent intention of pretending she's just a fraction of a somebody knows the Chief

Judge just to say hello to, then move on. I see him stiffen as Chip approaches, holding Mickie's hand like he's her prom date and they're about to say good evening to their high school principal.

I watch as Little Chip says, "Judge," then adds, "good evening," from her Buffalo Reds–paid–for diction class like that is the proper way to speak in here to this important man. She's smiling something like a kid, innocent even. At this moment in time she's not a whore, she's just a . . . I don't know what, but not a whore. What the judge does instead of playing along wouldn't cost him a dime, say, Good evening to you, may I introduce Mrs. Sokoloff, I'm sorry I don't recall your name. No, what he does is he takes hold of his wife's elbow and leads her away, giving Chip nothing more than a cold smile and nod telling her, Someone like me need not condescend to your level to more than give you a two-second half smile, that's it, now if you will excuse us.

I watch Little Chip stand there as the judge and Mrs. Judge escape to another group of people who are all smiles to see them, handshakes and backslaps and kisses all the way around. Chip's watching this, the hurt on her face something she's endured more than once in her sorry life. I watch as the hurt gets pushed down somewhere and the placid face of Little Chip the G-noter replaces it. Whatever, she's defensively thinking. But Mickie's pissed about this.

Look, I get why Mickie's doing what he's doing, like with the first group he had us descend on. To most of the folks in here, me and Mickie are the lowest of the low in our profession. To them we're law trash. Yeah, he's a little drunk from the scotch on the limo ride, but these people he's making fun of in his own way bother him the way they look down their noses at us. So he's rubbing it in their faces. But what just happened to Little Chip is outside of the rules. She's not a player here. This was all Mickie's idea and he took Little

Chip and Wanda here on loan from Reds, but not to hurt either of them.

Mickie grabs Chip gently by her elbow says, "Rona Rosenberg, let's meet some more nice people," and steers her and Wanda and me over to another group of cookie-cutter alike-looking men and women so he can horrify them with his behavior. But after the introductions and the onset of awkwardness Mickie leaves us there. I see him over in the corner with one of the waiters, Mickie's slipping the guy some bills, the guy's nodding, Yeah, sure, that's what you want you got it. As Mickie returns to our group, his game face back on to needle the shit out of our captives, I watch as the waiter switches the nameplates, rearranging two tables, one up front and one way in the back, I'm guessing that's where the table me and Mickie's been assigned to is at.

Not three minutes later someone says over the loudspeaker, "Ladies and gentlemen, dinner is served, please take your assigned seats." People start examining their little name cards got their table assignments. Not Mickie, he knows exactly where we're going. He leads us up front to the table where Chief Judge and Mrs. Chief Judge will be sitting. Mickie slows us up so we arrive just as Herman and his sourpuss wife do, so Mickie can ensure that he can place Little Chip right next to the big man himself. Chip sees what's happening and gets it, her smile this time devilish, letting him know, Thanks, Mickie, I'll take it from here.

So, we are all seated, no introductions made, no handshakes, no "I'm and this is . . ." Uh-uh, the people at this table, this right-up-front table, need no introductions. This may be fucking New Jersey not Buckingham Palace, but believe you me the behavior is photocopy the same. These are the shit-don't-smellers. The rest, like me and Mickie, who they originally put in the back, are the serfs, even the fancy new boys and girls from the big firms Mickie has been terrorizing don't rate a seat up here. I see the other two couples, who were to be seated here, wandering around, lost and confused, then finding their name cards at the back table was for us.

Chip turns to Judge Sokoloff, her boobs just touching his chest, and leans toward Mrs. Judge.

"Didn't we meet at the Associated Jewish Charities women's crafts festival?" she asks as sweet as sugar, now leaning farther into Herman's chest, still pretending to ignore him.

Mrs. Judge is taking Little Chip in. There's something wrong here, but she can't put her finger on it. This woman speaking to her looks only *like* someone who would go to the AJC crafts festival, not exactly like someone who actually did go. She's studying Chip, trying to figure out what's wrong with this picture, Chip's tits pressing absentmindedly into her husband, Herman's, chest, she's innocently blinking her ice blues.

Her eyes alternating to Chip now, Rona's fleshy tits pressing at Herman, his perplexing look as he stares off somewhere into the distance like he's not here. "No, I don't think so," Mrs. Judge almost hisses.

Chip leans farther into Herman and reaches her hand over to Mrs. Judge, forcing her to shake it.

"Rona Rosenberg," Little Chip says. "Are you sure?"

Mrs. Judge shakes her hand and then drops it like it's scaly and wet. She smiles coldly but doesn't offer her own name in return. Doesn't even respond to Chip's "Are you sure?"

"Huhm," Chip says as she lets her hand slip back to the table. "Maybe it was the Hadassah book fair?" she suggests sweetly.

Mrs. Judge coldly smiles maybe, letting Chip know the one thing she isn't going to get from her is an extended conversation about this, or about anything. As Chip continues syrupy-smiling at her, Mrs.

Judge turns to the older man seated to her left, whom she clearly knows, and interjects herself into his conversation with the woman to his left so she can avoid anything further with Chip. While Mrs. Judge is doing this, Chip has let her left hand slip beneath the table. With the dexterity of the pro she is, and without so much as a glance at the judge, she has unzipped his fly and managed with one simple flick of the wrist to release his still-limp wiener.

Chip smiles sweetly at Herman, then pretends fascination with whatever dribble Mrs. Judge is now gaily saying to the older man and woman. The judge shoots a quick glance at Chip, then looks back away into the distance, not sure what to do.

Mickie, me, and even Wanda are watching this, not letting on what we see. The judge is getting aroused, he's sitting up straighter, his face is flushed. None of this Mrs. Judge sees, intent as she is on avoiding any further contact with Chip.

Chip's pretending to ignore the judge. He's pretending to ignore her, although he's losing his game face here as she's wanking him, first with slow deep strokes, then with shorter strokes and faster. She's so good, you wouldn't know what was happening you weren't watching for it. Herman's getting a little purple in the face, his pecker's now at full mast, flagpoling almost to the underside of the tabletop.

Just then the waiter comes over holding those big silver trays they use at functions like these pretending the food's not some mass-cooked rubbery runny glop they individually serve while leaning over your shoulder balancing the tray with their left hand while expertly forking and spooning it onto your plate with their right. The waiter who has been assigned to our table is an older man, Hispanic-looking, chubby, bald, with a crown of salt-and-pepper hair; sweating like a pig in his ill-fitting tuxedo, he starts the table at Mrs. Judge, asking, "Jew like eveting, lady?"

Mrs. Judge can't be bothered, she simply nods to him, Yes, you fool, can't you figure that out for yourself? The waiter's endured much worse in his life, first escaping his country with the shirt on his back and now, despite his degree in mechanical engineering the U.S. won't recognize, best he can do in his early sixties is serve glop at Trump Hotel black-tie functions. He methodically starts spooning from the tray onto her plate. While he's doing this he can't help but hear the man to this lady's right is whimpering.

Now Chip has somehow managed to change hands, her right under the table stroking Herman, she's now looking straight at him like he's just said the wittiest thing, Why, Judge, that is such an astute observation, no wonder the governor made you the Chief Judge of the court. Herman's defenseless. He won't permit himself to look Chip's way, still staring off into space trying futilely to hold things together here.

As the waiter spoons food from his tray onto Mrs. Judge's plate, he notices the judge's chin start to levitate as Herman comes. Trying to hold any sounds as deep in his throat as is humanly possible, chin now way up, Herman starts with a low-growled "Aghaaaah," but he can't keep it in and as the waiter instinctively turns his head to see where the now more audible "Aghaaah" is coming from, he looks down and, from his vantage point, can see Chip's hand firmly wrapped around the judge's spurting cock, pumping it as he shoots his juice upward and back onto her hand.

The waiter is momentarily stunned. "*Jesucristo dios mierda*" (Jesus Christ holy shit), he says as the tray slips downward and its gooey gloppy contents slither onto Mrs. Judge's chest and lap.

She turns from her engrossing conversation, looks down at her expensive sequined dress, screams, and jumps to her feet. Just as she does, the tray the horrified waiter has been holding falls from his hands and lands smack at her feet, splashing whatever remnants of food are left onto her stockinged legs and shoes.

The waiter is in shock, this has never, I mean never ever happened to him before. He stands statue-still, horrified. The other up-front dignitary tables momentarily stop their conversation, but, unaware of the precise cause of this mishap, politely return to one another and resume where they left off. Of course, we all at our table rise in unison to see if we can help this poor lady. All except Judge Sokoloff, that is. You see, he can't exactly get up with his Mr. Happy still enjoying the night air, now dangling limply across his unzippered lap.

Little Chip goes over to Mrs. Judge. "You poor dear," she says, and starts to clean food off her bosom, all the while wiping the judge's jism off the front and back of her hand, Mrs. Judge later wondering how that fabric got so starchy just from the food that stupid clumsy Spanish waiter spilled all over her. But right now what she wants is for her husband to get on his damn feet like everyone else at the table.

"Herman," she all but screams.

The judge does manage to look her way, but he stays seated. He has to. He has the look of a dog his master has just caught pooping on the living room rug.

Mickie, Wanda, and me watch as he hopelessly tries to wiggle his hips under the table to see if maybe he can somehow manage to reflip his annoyingly uncooperative dick back into his pants. No luck. We are all watching him. He knows he needs to keep both hands still pressed palm down on the white tablecloth in plain view—as we former cops call it—because he just came all over Chip's hand.

"Herman," Mrs. Judge orders, meaning, How can you sit there at a time like this? Get on your fucking feet. We watch as storm clouds cover her bafflement and she then, well, storms off to the ladies' room all alone in the world.

The rest of us watch her go and then politely resume our seats, the others at the table smiling what can you do at Judge Sokoloff, but their eyes asking, Why in the world are you still at the table? Someone from the staff leads the waiter back to the kitchen. Little Chip turns to Mickie.

"Wanna stay for dessert, Mickie?" she asks, meaning, all right with me we can leave now, get the fuck out of here.

"Nah," Mickie says, and we all get up and go. Not so much as a have a nice evening you're going so soon from any of the others we have been seated with. As we leave I see Judge Sokoloff readjusting himself as unobtrusively as possible. Chip leans down to him and whispers into his ear, Have a nice evening, see you in Camden, baby, best to the Mrs.

CHAPTER ELEVEN

It's been five weeks since our night in Atlantic City. Camden's autumn has been unusually wet. Rain every week. Damp and gray most every day. It's just plain shitty out there. And winter isn't even here yet. It makes you think about a few days away. Someplace sunny and warm. Yeah, well, for me and Mickie it's Camden. Things at work have been quiet. The quiet before the storm, I'm thinking. It's been the usual. You know, breakfasts with Mickie at the courthouse café, *Monday Night Football* at his place. We go to court, pick up some new stuff, nothing major. That's about it.

Oh yeah, one more thing. Cynthia's back. With a friend. A woman. More about that later.

But today's the day. Meaning today's Rodrigo Day. Mickie and me are in court. So's Rodrigo, sitting to my right, Mickie to my left, I'm the meat in the Rodrigo sandwich. About three minutes ago, just before the judge is due to take the bench, the guards frog-marched him in from the holding pen where he and the other prisoners who have court appearances sit feasting on stale baloney sandwiches and watery fruit juice until their case is called.

We filed Mumbles's motion, asked for a hearing. The prosecution filed their opposition brief, said what we're asking for is bullshit, the judge should deny the requested relief and set a speedy trial date so they can have a jury convict our scumbag drug-lord client and put him in prison for life where he belongs. (They wrote it better, but that's what their brief says in so many words.)

Professor Mumbles is here, but he didn't want to meet Rodrigo, sit up here as one of his lawyers. No, he told me, no need, Junne, I'll just sit in the gallery, watch from there. So maybe Mumbles isn't as crazy as Mickie thinks, seeing as how he knows enough to stay off Rodrigo's radar screen.

We're all in court now, waiting for the judge. Rodrigo's looking around the courtroom like he's expecting someone. He's got that jail-house smell, for sure it's in his orange jumpsuit, but now deep down in his pores as well. It's a mix of male sweat, rancid garbage, sour piss. Once it gets into your nostrils, it's with you the rest of the day. Rodrigo nodded at me and Mickie when the guards unshackled him and pushed him into his chair, but so far he hasn't spoken to us, nor we to him. I'm going to argue this today, since Mickie hasn't so much as glanced at our papers, me asking Mickie, Wanna take a look at this before it goes to the court? Mickie saying, Nah, go ahead and file the son of a bitch, I know you and Mumbles did good, no need.

We see the bailiff enter the courtroom. He puts some law books up there on the judge's bench, fills the water glass, then he returns to chambers to go get the judge, tell him everything's ready.

Rodrigo turns to me and Mickie.

"Who gonna talk to the judge?" he asks us, but he's looking at

Mickie, not me. Rodrigo's kind of leaning across me, his smell is withering. I see that his face bruises have yellowed with healing, his fingernails are bitten to the bone.

"He is," Mickie tells him, nodding at me.

"No," Rodrigo says. The judge is going to take the bench at any minute. This is not the time for a debate with Rodrigo over which one of us will speak on his behalf.

Mickie leans into me so he can whisper better to Rodrigo. Soon as he gets a whiff of him, Mickie jerks back just slightly. "Junne's prepared for this, he will do it."

Rodrigo leans farther into me and closer to Mickie. I could pass out from his smell, it's so bad. Rodrigo motions Mickie closer in so he can whisper direct to him.

Mickie kind of half obliges on account of he just can't get too close under the circumstances.

"You listen, cojones," Rodrigo half whispers to Mickie. "I want you speak to the judge. You, motherfucker, not him" (*no heem*).

Well, Mickie has done a good job of impressing Rodrigo with his actions that he's the alpha male here. In Rodrigo's world you go with the alpha male, always.

I turn away from Rodrigo so I can whisper to Mickie.

"Go ahead, you do it," I say.

Mickie whispers back, "Fuck, no, Junne. I haven't even read the goddamn brief, let alone the cases you and Mumbles cited."

"Come on, Mickie," I say, Rodrigo leaning into my shoulder back, trying to hear what me and Mickie are saying; I swear I'm about to pass out from his smell. If it was some other mope than Rodrigo pressing into me here at counsel table I'd say, Hey, sit back, for Christ sake, will you? Since it's Rodrigo no way.

"Mickie," I say. "Since when has not reading the papers stopped you from speaking in court, come on, man, you can do this, piece of cake."

Mickie's truly worried that he really doesn't get this cockamamie theory Mumbles has cooked up and he's not budging on this.

He's shaking his head at me like a child won't make pee pee, his mother's saying, Please, little Mickie, do it for Mommy. Rodrigo's pressing in to me like a human trash truck. I'm about to plead with Mickie when the bailiff opens the chamber door and shouts, "All rise."

We all stand as the judge swoops into the court and just about leaps to the bench.

"Good morning," he says. "Be seated."

We sit while the judge arranges his papers. "Call the first case," he instructs his bailiff.

The bailiff rises and starts reading from the docket sheet. He's a middle-aged heavyset black man wearing a dark go-to-court suit two sizes too large. There's about a full inch space between his shirt collar and neck. His voice is radio-announcer deep, but his New Jersey accent's as thick as Rodrigo's smell.

"Your Honor [*Ya Hanna*]," he announces. "This morning's first case [*fust case*] is *State versus Rodrigo Gonzáles*. Motion for release to minimum security. Appearing [*Peeren*] for the government is Assistant United States Attorney Melvin Johnson. For the [*fuy da*] defense, Michael Mezzonatti and Salvatore Salerno."

Satisfied he's done his job, the bailiff nods at the judge and takes his seat below the bench so he can go back to reading the newspaper spread like a tablecloth on his little desk.

Mickie and me watch as the judge glances at what we know is our brief asking that he put Rodrigo in a minimum-security facility so he can jump bail and escape back to El Salvador, where he can resume business as usual. The judge looks up over his glasses at us like, Which one of you idiots is going to rise so I can shit all over you for being so pitifully stupid before I deny this motion out of hand?

Mickie's not budging. I kick him under the table, Get up, come on, Mick, do it, please. Mickie stares straight out into space. Rodrigo's leaning in to me, half whispering, half hissing to Mickie, "Get up, motherfucker, I'll kill you." The judge is losing patience. Fuck it, I'm thinking, about to get to my feet, when the prosecutor rises and addresses the court.

"May counsel approach?" (meaning the bench), he asks.

The judge is still looking at me and Mickie, wondering what the hell is going on over here. He turns to the prosecutor, looks at us again, considering.

"Approach," he tells all of us.

So Mickie and me go to the bench, Rodrigo's steaming eyes following us all the way up there. The prosecutor and we wait while the court reporter joins us with his machine, now crouched on his knees beside where the judge is sitting on the other side of the bench, ready to take down whatever it is Melvin Johnson has on his mind.

Mickie and me have known Johnson for years. He's a career guy in the prosecutor's office, been there ever since law school. He's not a bad egg, really, just a meat-and-potatoes prosecutor, does his job; what he misses in imagination he makes up for with thoroughness, preparation. He's black, midforties, neatly but cheaply dressed, always in a white button-down shirt and grayish patterned tie. Melvin's on the thin side, dark-skinned, wedding-ringed, with three or four kids, I'm guessing. Probably not much fun at parties, but a decent guy. He'll probably stay a government-salaried prosecutor till the day he retires, he's the type.

Now, me and Mickie have had our share of cases with Melvin

over the years. I'd say he has a low opinion of us in the gray-matter department. I've already told you that our briefs (you know, the ones Mumbles doesn't write for us) aren't so hot, and our courtroom style is, well, it's not what you see on TV. What bugs Melvin is that we beat him with juries more than he can account for. That's a real puzzler to him. Can't figure it out.

Anyway, the judge is looking Melvin's way, indicating, You're up here, what is it, I'm busy this morning.

Melvin hasn't so much as nodded in our direction. He seems kind of nervous.

"Your Honor," he half whispers to the judge like we do up here. "This motion is nonsense."

The judge is about two seconds away from telling him, For that you needed to come up here and tell me what I already know? I was just about to deny it after humiliating these two morons standing here to your left. But Melvin's not finished.

"However, Your Honor," he says. However? I'm thinking. Uh? I exchange quick glances with Mickie like, What's this all about?

"However, Your Honor," Melvin says, "the government does have a proposal to make concerning this defendant."

Now, ordinarily, when a prosecutor has a plea-bargain proposal, he or she makes it directly to the defense lawyer, sometimes on the phone but usually at a private meeting in the prosecutor's office. Not up here for the first time in front of the judge and on the record. This isn't like Melvin, I'm thinking. What's up with this?

"So," the judge says, ignoring me and Mickie like we're just some bystanders at a party happened to wander in on this ongoing conversation. "Let's hear it."

I can't believe my ears, Mickie's poking me in the back like, Get outta here, our prayers have been answered.

What Melvin's proposing is that we drop this bullshit motion asking for low security for Rodrigo while he gives up the corrupt rulers of his country who've been letting him do his drug business without intervention on account of they're his silent partners. Instead Rodrigo pleads guilty to only two counts of drug smuggling. He rats out others in the Salvadoran drug trade, meaning his competitors, maybe some in his own organization been getting too ambitious, sort of like Slippery's nephew now in protective custody out of reach. In return, the prosecution will agree to a mere seven-year prison term for our man, instead of life no parole. And, get this, he can do his time in an army base stockade, on account of his life would be in danger in the federal prison system. Now, seven years in a stockade's no picnic, but for a guy like Rodrigo it's a cakewalk. Then after, Melvin tells the judge, Rodrigo gets released to the custody of the Salvadoran authorities, where charges are pending against him, so he can serve more time at home. Meaning the U.S. attorney knows damn well once Rodrigo is shipped home he will be a free man on account of no way are those charges on the books, for show only, not for real, going to mean shit to him.

In a nutshell what Mickie and me are hearing is that Melvin Johnson thinks he's got the case of a lifetime, given what his street crime caseload's been like his whole damn career. Rodrigo's a big fish. Melvin's offering Rodrigo a trade. He gets to rat out his competitors and dramatically increase his profit margin, clean his own house by getting rid of those inside his organization maybe too ambitious, be a problem to him in the future. And all he's got to do is seven years' soft time, then he's good to go, since once he is released into the custody of Salvadoran authorities they'll fly him home first-class champagne all the way around. What Melvin gets is one big-fish drug dealer after another to indict and send to jail. Thinking Rodrigo and his government pals will get them extradited here, stand trail. Good for business. Maybe Melvin's thinking Rodrigo's his ticket out of the prosecutor's office; he'll get a judgeship with an impressive string of high-profile convictions, since no way is a private law firm ever going to put this guy on the payroll, what's he got to offer.

And what Mickie and me now get is that Melvin's not telling us this privately like he's supposed to, but up here at the bench in front of the judge and on the record, because he just doesn't trust our ability to get this right without the judge looking over our shoulder making sure we do the needful here, help out the system, help out Melvin.

The judge doesn't ask us shit. Like, How's that sound to you guys? Think it will fly with your client? Nope, what he does is tell us the court will take the pending motion under advisement, go work this out with your client, report back one week's time. Get this done. Now back to your table.

While he's talking I'm looking out over the gallery. I see Dumpy Brown sitting back in the third row, his mope client next to him probably out on bond here for a sentencing for possession of a handgun and distributing some few grams of this or that. The mope's got the look, outfitted in oversized clothes, be a joke like a clown he wasn't some stone-cold killer you look at the wrong way he takes you down not so much as a thought. Dumpy sees me up here looking at him he grins my way, saying, My man, how you doin' today? To his right one row behind I see Mr. WD Smith, like of course he's going to be here, I'm thinking. Of course. That's who Rodrigo was searching for earlier. He's as nattily dressed as ever, looking straight into my eyes. I nod just perceptibly at him. He just stares back at me, no recognition. Nothing.

Oh boy, I'm thinking. The fly in the ointment's going to be WD Smith. Somehow I can't figure, it is. I know it. I just fucking know it.

Mickie and me go back to counsel table. Just as we're seated the judge announces, "The court will take the pending motion under advisement," then gets up and bounces down off the bench and back to his chambers, the bailiff shouting, "All rise. Court stands in recess."

The marshals are reshackling Rodrigo, who's looking over at Mickie and me wondering what the fuck was that all about? One of the marshals says, Mickie, Junne, want some time with this joker in lockup before we take him back to the jail? I see Rodrigo look over his shoulder to the gallery where WD Smith's at. Rodrigo nods, then looks back at us.

Mickie tells the marshal, Nah, we'll see him later at the jail, ignoring Rodrigo as the marshals pull him away like he's a piece of meat in shoes.

I get it. No way can me and Mickie talk to Rodrigo about what just happened up at the bench he's standing in the big holding cell, other mopes standing around waiting for their cases to be called, eavesdropping on what we're telling him. It'll have to wait until later, maybe tomorrow, we go over to the Camden Jail, see Rodrigo in one of the lawyer interview rooms. I look over to the gallery where WD's standing. Only he's gone. His spot empty.

Mickie and me get our coats and take the elevator to the ground floor, past the security guys and metal detector, the lobby busy today with several courts in session. We see agents and undercovers we know coming and going to their cases, a couple of assistant U.S. attorneys saying, Hey, how you doin'. And then we're out on the street. I haven't had a chance to share my thoughts with Mickie about any of this; mostly WD Smith, somehow I can't put my finger on what's bothering me.

We're on the street, Mickie's saying, Well, what the fuck do you know? He's thinking our troubles are over, we can breathe easy 'cause we're out of the red zone now. Just then, we're not ten feet from the street, this car pulls up, some souped-up piece of shit, the windows closed, four homeys inside, Hispanic guys. The oversized stereo's booming salsa music, the bass literally rocking the car on its tires. The back window slides down and who do we see but one of the two punks on Rodrigo's crew paid the visit to Mickie's a few weeks ago. Remember, the guy with the ponytail Mickie roughed up when he pull-dragged him into the living room under the flat-screen. Fatty with the shaved head who was there too is behind the wheel in front.

Ponytail death-glares at Mickie, his nose still bandaged, his voice, I'm thinking, real nasal-pitched, jabbing his finger at him, telling Mickie, You, you mine, motherfucker, just you wait. I can see Mickie getting hot, I'm about to grab his arm, hold him back, say, Whoa, whoa, Mick, not here, it ain't worth it what happened inside just now. But I don't need to because Mickie loses his anger, starts smiling at ponytail, then melodramatically starts looking around at the men and women on the street going in and out of the courthouse.

"Immigration?" Mickie shouts. "We need an immigration officer over here. Immigration?"

Ponytail tells fat boy, Drive the fuck off, get us out of here. He keeps the window down, still death-staring, You mine, motherfucker, wait and see, at Mickie. Mickie, eat-shit grinning, gives ponytail the finger as the car pulls away, the music still pumping through the street.

"Assholes," he says to me as we leave for our office.

Mickie's still thinking our prayers have been answered. Me, I'm not so sure. Can't put my finger on it. But something's not right.

And shit, I forgot all about Mumbles. Didn't even thank him.

CHAPTER TWELVE

Well, we did see Rodrigo. Mickie and me went there this morning, since yesterday after court didn't work. Soon as we got back to the office the phone rings, it's Cynthia telling Mickie, Can you help me here, the son of a bitch's giving me a hard time about getting my old job back. Okay, Mickie says, be right there. To me, he says, We'll deal with your shitbag client tomorrow, gotta go and help Cynthia out.

Big wonder the bar owner across the river in Philly's telling Cynthia, No way am I taking you back, you disappearing on me, not even a call telling me I ain't showing, gotta leave and see my folks back home. Nothing, so no, you ain't coming back, no way. I know Mickie can straighten this out on account of he's known the guy for years—me too, but not from the old neighborhood, just from around. As a favor to Mickie he'll take Cynthia back.

I guess I'm kind of glad she's back. Like I said earlier, Mickie needs a woman around.

Thing of it is, the guys at Bernstein, Smulkin, meaning Arty Bernstein, who's what you'd call the managing partner runs the place where our offices are at, have already complained to me. More than once. Telling me, Junne, have a word with your boy Mickie, tell him leave the secretaries alone. Tell him this is no chicken coop for him to be a fox at. Anything halfway decent out there he's after, hanging at their desks, smiling, asking would they be interested in a drink, maybe dinner when they get off. Those girls are there to work, we're paying them for that, not to flirt with your boy Mickie.

Yeah, sure, Arty, I tell him. I'll talk to him. But the thing of it is, those boys, Arty Bernstein included, doing the same thing. He's seated in my office, suit jacket off but his Saks Fifth Avenue tie high-Windsor-knotted under his spread collar, his braces with the scales of justice strapping his weightlifter's chest tight as bindings around a packing crate. Arty's got what most people would call a Jewish face, you know, nose too big for his tight eyes, hair nicely barbered but on the kinky side, still, he's a good-looking guy. And here's the thing: Arty, some of the others work here, themselves been hustling the better-looking secretaries, taking them for a drink and then later a schtup in some hotel room on account of, unlike Mickie, these boys are all married, their wives telling them, My, you're home late tonight. Wondering why their men smell soapy fresh like they just showered after such a hard day at the office.

Yeah, sure, Arty, I tell him. These guys are our landlords, why start something, know what I'm saying? Anyway, these guys worry me some. Like I already told you, they do well, better than me and Mickie, but the way they run their shop, they're going down one of these days. See, they have plenty of business, but they're paying for it. Cabdrivers, ambulance guys, all of them get a little something from these boys, in cash on the side, they bring people in after accidents, so the Bernstein lawyers can sign them up before any of the other sharks out there can. I also heard that some of the insurance adjusters they deal with, who make real quick settlements so these boys can get their one-third from-the-top fee, also taken care of by them. Arty, some of the others from time to time, have asked me, Want some of this, Junne, wanna work with us on some of this, with your trial skills be a piece of cake. Telling me, Nice money here, you don't mind a waiting room full a schwartzas all the time wearing neck braces and shit.

I've said thanks but no thanks. You know what they say. All that glitters isn't gold. Call it what you want, self-preservation instincts, a sense of what's right, what's wrong. Dunno. Just know that what these boys do's not for me. Not for Mickie. And if Mick's out there prowling the halls on account of Cynthia freaked out after Rodrigo's boys paid their visit, Mickie really horny, needing what he's needing? And the Bernstein boys themselves bad in the apple department? Well, business is business, and I would have a word with Mick, tell him lay off the girls, go elsewhere for that. Only now I don't have to on account Cynthia's back. I told you, this time with a friend, another woman, staying with her at Mickie's, sleeping in the room I sometimes use. I haven't met her yet, the other woman, the friend. We're all supposed to have dinner later in the week, Mickie's already complaining the woman's getting in his way, hanging around the house since she's got no job. Getting in the way how Mickie likes to be alone with his woman at home. His home, know what I'm saying?

I don't tell Arty Bernstein any of this. Tell him only, Yeah, sure, Arty, I'll take care of it. Good as done, you got it.

So, like I said, me and Mickie don't get to the jail to see Rodrigo, tell him what happened up at the bench with the judge, until the day after court.

Rodrigo listens to what we, meaning Mickie, tell him. He doesn't react, just says okay, come back in a couple of days (*cuple dazs*), I'll tell you what you do then (*jew do den*). I got that. The man needs to consult with WD first, get his marching orders, because now I am convinced that WD's running the show, not Rodrigo. After, I tell Mickie all this, say there's something wrong here, but he just shrugs, tells me, Junne, you worry too much, it's all gonna work out, relax, for Christ sake.

Then, while we're at the jail we go to the state side and see Slippery Williams. When we get there Dumpy Brown's already with him, so we join the party. Dumpy's dressed to the hilt—what else is new? He and Slippery are deep in whispered coded conversation, Slippery telling Dumpy what needs doing on the outside, he's needing to run things now from the inside. They both stop when Mickie and me enter the interview room. Dumpy's all false smiles saying it's the Gambino twins; you know, the same shit like always.

"Dumpy [*Dumpay*]," Mickie says, shaking his hand, trying to hold his true feelings behind what I see is a forced smile, then shaking with Slippery.

"Slip, how you doin'?" Mickie says.

"Yeah, well," Slippery says. "You know how it is."

I can see that jailhouse pallor already on Slippery. It's a yellow graying of the skin, darker circles under the eyes, some weight loss, his orange jumpsuit hanging more than it did last time we saw him. It may be harder to tell on a black man, but it's there, I see it.

"Junne." Slippery smiles, glad to see me. "Supp, man?" he says.

"Doin' good, Slip," I say, trying not to let him see what I'm seeing.

But he sees it. Fuck, that doesn't help, I'm thinking. I look away as Dumpy takes control, Mickie I know not going to tolerate this.

"So we talkin'," Dumpy tells us. "You know how to handle the trial, what you snowcaps calling strategy. We strategizing for the case. Here's the thing—" Dumpy begins.

"Whoa, chief," Mickie tells him. "*We* ain't doing shit, Dumpy. Me and Mickie will determine how this case goes, then we'll tell you so you can take care of the underlings." (Mickie stresses this last word, giving Dumpy the look here. Meaning, There's no *we* that includes you, Dumpy, no way, so get that now, save us all trouble later.)

"We clear on this?" he says to Dumpy, eyeing Slippery, letting him know he's got to chime in on this.

"My man," Slippery says to Dumpy. "Now, I told you Mickie and Junne here runnin' the show. You takin' care a my boys also in the case. But Mickie and Junne, they in charge. We cool on that, right?" he says to Dumpy, giving him the look, letting him know how it is.

I see a second's flash of heat in Dumpy's eyes, then he starts into smiling and nodding like this is all a misunderstanding on account of Dumpy's the straightest cat around.

"Hey, Slip," Dumpy says. "Like I told you, you happy with the White Ranger and little Tonto here, I'm good. You the boss, boss."

So we spend the rest of our time with Slippery and Dumpy talking about what we're going to do about this and that in the case. You know, the what-ifs. What if Little Walter, one of Slippery's boys also charged, flips and fingers Slippery as the kingpin of the operation? What if me and Mickie can get the wiretaps knocked out on some legal technicality or other? (We don't spend too much time on that one.) Then, when we finish, Mickie and me leave so Slippery and Dumpy can go back to Slippery running his business from the inside through Dumpy as instructions courier.

Mickie and me know that once we're out of here Dumpy's going to work on Slippery some more to get rid of us for him. Won't happen, not with Slip, no way.

But later, I don't know why, certainly not because I'm worried Dumpy's going to steal our client, I go back to the jail and see Slippery. I don't tell Mickie I'm going. He left earlier anyway, something else with Cynthia, I don't know what, but Mickie's going to be attentive as shit to her. At least for a while, until he's sure she's settled in with him and not taking off again. He gets tired of her, that's different.

I see Slippery alone in the same interview room. To tell you the truth, I got nothing more to say to him. I'm just feeling bad Slippery's probably never going to see outside again. This is like a condolence call, I guess. On account of Slippery's dead to the world, even if he lives a long life. Look, like I already said, me and Slippery go back. Bad an actor as he is, we go back.

So we're sitting, some long uncomfortable silences, some joking he's trying because he knows I'm here to make him feel better. Then, after one of those awkward silences, Slippery says, "Junne, know what bothers me most about my situation?"

"Uh-huh, what?" I say.

Slippery shakes his head. I mean, the man knows how bad his situation is. And he's about to tell me what he's the most upset about.

"Not ever again no pussy," he says, but not funny, not like some dirty goddamn joke. Slippery's a man of the streets. Vocabulary for him is what it is. What he's telling me best he can is that he is grieving over the fact that he will never, ever again be with a woman. Sure, for sex, but for all the other stuff too, what a man gets in addition. Like it is for Mickie. Same thing.

I shake my head like to say, Yeah, Slip, I hear you.

Sort of.

CHAPTER THIRTEEN

I'm coming out of the men's and there stands Mickie, himself now away from the table after I got up to go and take a piss. He's standing near where the cigarette machine used to be when there were cigarette machines in restaurants, now there's a bench between the men's and the ladies'.

"Come on, Junnie," Mickie's telling me. (How many fucking times do I have to hear this?) "You gotta help me out here."

Meaning, he wants me to take Cynthia's friend, seated with her downstairs at the table, waiting for me and Mickie to come back so we can order dessert, coffee. Take, as in take her off his hands and out of his house tonight so he can do Cynthia without her holding her palm over his mouth he's on top of her coming, she's saying, Shhh, Mickie, Debby'll hear.

"What is it about no you're not getting here?" I tell Mickie, starting to go back downstairs to the table. Mickie doesn't let me pass. He's pleading with me.

"Jesus, Junne," Mickie says. "Come on, man, you gotta do this for me. Just one night. I'm going crazy, come on, pal. One fucking night. Won't kill you."

"Mickie," I say. "No. Fuck no. End of discussion."

He lets me pass and we go down the steps together, Mickie's muttering all the way down, Shit, fuck, goddamn it.

I mean, I like Cynthia's friend Debby. She's nice. Not bad-looking, on the short side, her hair's natural dark, cut tomboyish, got a good figure, she keeps up, she says, since she's a massage therapist, telling me she needs to stay in shape, keep her muscle tone up on account of it's hard work.

Mickie chiming in at the table, elbowing me seated next to him across from Debby, "Girl's got strong hands, Junne, fix you up good, huh, Debby?"

This was earlier this evening, when we were at the first-round-of-drinks stage, me and Debby really talking for the first time. We all met here at the restaurant. Mickie telling me earlier, I'll pick the place where we go this time, Junne.

We're in Cherry Hill, near where Mickie's house is at. The Fazanno family has restaurants several places in Camden County. The flagship's here in Cherry Hill called Fazanno's Cuccina. The son, now the owner, the old man probably dead or in Florida— maybe both—opened a new one, a steak place, right next door. That's where we're at tonight. Fazanno's Steaks. Imaginative name, huh? But, I gotta say, the food's good. After drinks, two rounds, we ordered Caesar salads, extra anchovies. Steak Pizzaiola for me and Mickie. Steak in red sauce, you're thinking? What can I say? Sure, it's a steak place, but come on, the Fazanno family knows where they came from. Cynthia and Debby get the grilled swordfish, easy on the butter. Mickie joking with Cynthia he'll take care of giving her some meat later. Cynthia chiding him, "You are so crude, honestly," but I can tell loving it, Mickie being Mickie.

I can see the bar area from here at the table. The Fazanno family likes cops, always have. Even back when me and Mickie were on the force. So at the bar I see cops, off duty, drinking. Not exactly on the house. Not exactly. See, for every three drinks they order, the check comes for one. Same now as it was for me and Mickie. Cop wants to eat, sit at a table, have a meal in one of the Fazanno restaurants in and around Camden County? No problem. Order your dinner, the check comes, you're charged for an appetizer, coffee. But mostly the cops stay at the bar. Why? Because they're cops. And because even for just appetizer and coffee the prices don't work on cop salaries. So why not get a sub someplace else later, drink here?

Sure, the Fazannos like cops, but they're not stupid. They know you treat cops right, they treat you right. And the bad boys? The made guys? At least those who aren't away these days doing ten to twenty for racketeering, eat here too. Yeah, but with the cops here semi-on-the-house, the Fazannos never need to worry about protection money, "trash removal" fees, any of the other stuff the Mob's so famous for. You can pretty much spot the goombahs. They're like the guys you see on TV, the movies. What's that saying? Life imitates art? Something like that.

So Mickie and me are back at the table after returning from the men's. No one wants dessert, coffee only. Debby telling the waiter, Can I have a sambuca on the side, please? So now I know she's Italian too. Her last name's Douglas, but looking at her again across the table, what I see is Italian blood somewhere inside her. Mother, maybe. Mickie says to the waiter, bring us four sambucas, good idea, Deb.

"So, what you got up for tonight, Junne?" Mickie says, still not letting it go, trying to lead the conversation into Debby leaving here with me tonight.

"Early night, Mick," is all I say.

I swear, Mickie's eyes are darting. Me to Debby. Debby to Cynthia. The guy's in a fucking fever. Then he says, big smile, like this is the cleverest thing you could imagine, "What you need, Junne, help you sleep better's a full-body massage. Debby here'll fix you up good. Get rid of all that tension. Am I right, Deb?"

Debby's interested. A blind man could see that. But she's a nice girl; she's not about to go overboard here like Mickie's doing.

"You heard Junne," she says to Mickie. "He needs an early night. Probably has court tomorrow."

Debby nods across the table at me like to say, That's what it is, right? I dutifully nod back, Yeah, something like that, I'm signaling.

The waiter brings the coffee and sambucas, one little coffee bean floating in each glass, you can smell the licorice from here. We're sitting now, no one's talking, Cynthia I think kicking Mickie under the table, telling him leave it for Christ sake.

I look over at the bar. There's about three, maybe four off-duty detectives. One's wearing a jacket and tie. The others are casually dressed, you know, cop clothes, browns, grays, all cheap stuff, I can see it from here. And then in walk three others. Two white and one black. The black guy gets my attention on account of this place is mostly white, you know how it is around here. But this cop's with his buddies, I guess, and when they said, Come on, let's go over to Fazanno's have a couple, end the day, he probably said, Yeah, sure, what the hell? I see them take off their coats, they're staying for a while, have a few rounds with the others already here.

And who is it but none other than the undercover—make that former undercover—beat up that punk kid, Slippery's bad-ass nephew, now salted away in protective custody, who tried to rip him off from the case a few weeks ago. You remember, the undercover I cross-examined on the stand in front of Judge Rufus Brown? The guy I outed, you should pardon the expression. He hasn't seen me, he's shaking hands with the cops been at the bar, maybe meeting some of them for the first time, his buddies he came in with saying, Hey, meet so and so over here from the Ninth. Something like that.

Mickie's saying, "So, Debby, how's the job-hunting going?" trying to change the subject I guess, else he'll so piss off Cynthia he's getting nothing tonight. Debby sleeping down the hall or not.

While Mickie's speaking, Debby's looking across the table at me. Like I said, she's a pretty girl. And she's definitely interested in me. I think she's figuring how to play this; maybe thinking *should* she play this? Debby sighs.

"It's tough, Mickie," she tells him. "I've been to several places, most of the health clubs near here, and no one's got an opening for a massage therapist."

Now, what she said isn't much of an opening, but Mickie, incorrigible as they come, Cynthia kicking him or not, he's going to try and fit through the rabbit hole he maybe sees.

"Maybe Junne can help," he says to her. Then to me, "Junne, who you know's got a health club, a fitness center, maybe where you live in Camden, needs a massage therapist like Debby?"

I shrug, you know, like I'm thinking, now, who could I call for Debby?

"Gosh, Junne," Debby says. "You think you might know someone?"

I'm guessing Mickie's thinking Debby's looking for a job since Cynthia said to her come back to New Jersey with me, you can find work, better here than at home. Stay with me and Mickie until you get settled, no problem, stay as long as you like. Jesus H. Christ, Mickie's figuring, I don't do something she's at the house for who knows how long, no way José.

"What you need, Junne, is some incentive here," he tells me, his eyes letting me know he's going with this, there's no stopping him now. Just then I notice the cop at the bar, the black one whose under-cover career I ruined, notices me. He's like half listening to the other cops at the bar, but he sees me and now he's staring, thinking, I can see, Well, what do you know, look who's sitting over there.

Mickie's saying to Debby, "What Junne needs, Debby, is a little incentive. Give him a taste of what you got, do his shoulders, let Junne see how good you are." Then to me, "Junne, I swear Debby's got the hands of a goddess. I know, she gave me a full-body at the house the other day, it was great, didn't you, Deb?"

The black cop's still watching me, the others at the bar in deep conversation; but not him, he's eyeing me, thinking probably about what I did to him on the stand, maybe more. Debby's telling Mickie, Here? I can't do Junne's shoulders here in a restaurant, Mickie. But she's thinking, Yeah, okay, I could do this, maybe who knows it leads to something.

"No problem," Mickie's telling Debby. "What do these people here care? What are they gonna do, call vice or something?"

Now, Mickie hasn't noticed the cops at the bar; like I said, the man's in a fever, so intent on getting Debby out of the house tonight that's all he's focused on. So his quip about vice cops got nothing to do with what's going on at the bar. I see the black cop's interrupting his buddies' conversation, telling them, See that guy seated over there against the wall at the table for four?

"Go on, Debby," Mickie's telling her. "Give Junne a little taste, do his shoulders, let him see what you got." Debby's giving that jeez-

I-don't-know-should-I look, first to Mickie, then over to Cynthia, who's signaling, Sure, why not, won't hurt anything, all good clean fun.

I take my eye from the black cop at the bar, now telling the others something definitely about me, nodding them in my direction, because Debby's smiling at me, Do you mind, Junne? But she doesn't wait for a response and before I know it she's standing behind my chair kneading my shoulders, the other diners seated nearby smiling over at us, Now, isn't that cute.

Debby's strong hands deep in my shoulders, she's saying, "Wow, Junne, you're tight as a drum. Your shoulders are stiff as an ironing board."

Mickie and Cynthia are watching, smiling, Isn't that great, Junne? Mickie, of course, is thinking more. Debby leans in while she's working my shoulders, says, "Junne, do you really think you can help me?"

I can see the black cop's still talking to the others at the bar about me. The people at the tables near us are back to their meals, having seen enough of Debby doing my shoulders. Mickie's watching, thinking has he done enough to get Debby out of his hair tonight so he doesn't have to worry about her at the house later.

"Yeah, sure, Debby," I tell her, she's working away at the knots in my shoulders, the knot in my stomach's another matter. "Sure. Do what I can," I say. Debby leans in to my back, half whispering into my ear.

"Make you a deal," she tells me. "Help me find a job, take me to dinner, like maybe next week, Tuesday, that works for you. Wednesday, whatever. I'll come to your place after. Give you a full-body massage. On the house. What do you think?"

I can see the black cop's now really into his story about me. He's smirking at what he's telling the others. I'm sitting here, a woman standing behind my chair doing my shoulders, now even part of my upper back. Did I say earlier that I had outed him? The other cops are laughing at what the black cop's saying. Debby's still leaning in, waiting for a response to her proposal.

"Yeah, sure," I say to her. "Sounds like a plan."

CHAPTER FOURTEEN

It's after lunch and me and Mickie are in court. Slippery Williams's sitting in one of the chairs directly behind us, guards armed to the teeth all over the courtroom. Next to Slippery's the two guys are his top lieutenants, now Dumpy Brown's clients. Dumpy's with us at counsel table. Technically we're here on Dumpy's motion he filed on behalf of his two perps. It looks like Dumpy's show today. Only what we're doing, our strategy, Dumpy grumbling, since it wasn't his idea, is for Slippery mainly. So actually it's Dumpy who's here for show.

We're before the judge assigned to the case, Thurgood Rufus Brown, up at the bench telling us be seated after the bailiff announced his entry. How about that? Here we are back with Judge Brown. Big bad brown Judge Brown. Like I already told you, Dumpy's second cousin. Luck of the draw? The clerk's office randomly selecting Judge Brown for his cousin's case? Maybe. Maybe not. (Dumpy knows his way around this courthouse as good as anyone. Lots of homeboys and -girls working in that clerk's office known Dumpy for years, from the parts of Camden are his turf. So draw your own conclusions. Mickie and me don't ask those kinds of questions.)

Judge Brown makes his usual speech, asking the prosecutors do they want him to step down, ask the clerk's office on the floor below to assign another judge on account of the court is "distantly" related by blood to one of the defense counsel in this case. We have all seen this show before.

The two young prosecutors, one white, one Asian, listen to this sitting across the aisle like a couple of stuffed animals. No way are they going to complain. Tell Judge Brown in open court in front of the press, say to his big bad eminence, Hold on, there, Judge, not so fast, so the reporters can do a story for the evening local news: Judge Brown's honesty and impartiality challenged by Prosecutor's Office? These two assistant DAs will appear before this judge in case after case their entire careers: for a few more years as prosecutors and then later, when they are in private practice, no longer on a government salary, they're needing to do well in court to make money. Are they going to complain? I don't think so.

Judge Brown gives it a minute or two, seeing do the prosecutors want to commit career suicide, then he says to us all, Let's proceed. Dumpy rises to address the court.

Mickie's seated next to me, he looks like he's about to doze off. Like I said, it's after lunch and I told Mickie, don't fucking eat the pastrami, no way are you going to stay awake with that greasy shit in your stomach. Does he listen?

"Your Honor," Dumpy announces to his cousin, his voice booming like he's addressing the Roman Forum. Christ, there are only three people in the spectator section of the courtroom, two of them local reporters themselves already after-lunch half asleep.

Dumpy's the same in court, jury or no jury. With a jury his shit works. It's too dramatic for my taste, but it works. With a judge, like today, for motions not trial, to me he's like a kid trying too hard in his high school play.

He says to Judge Brown, "I have a motion which needs resolution before we can prepare for the defense of those accused with these very serious crimes. May I proceed, Your Honor?"

Judge Brown just nods at Cousin Dumpy, letting him know, What the hell you think we're here for? Let me hear what you got.

So, his oratory in overdrive, Dumpy tells Cousin Brown that the defense team has tried without success to contact "one of the key witnesses to our clients' dire need to *project* and *protect* their innocence," as he puts it. Dumpy then levels an accusing finger over at the two young innocent-lamb assistant DAs, who are busily scribbling notes. "But," Dumpy booms, giving it that dramatic momentary pause works so well with juries and is as out of place here in this sleepy half-empty courtroom as a working whore in church. "But," he repeats. "Ah, but." Dumpy's milking this needlessly, I'm thinking. I see Judge Brown roll his eyes. For heaven's sake, he too is thinking, Dumpy, get to the fucking point already.

With one final flourishing "But," Dumpy then adds, "the prosecution has kept this *key* witness under, well . . . lock and *key*," he says, momentarily confusing even himself with his rhetoric. He sucks in his teeth, smooths out his cream-colored suit jacket, giving himself a moment to recover. So, Dumpy says, we need relief from the court. He outlines what we want. This takes another ten minutes, now both Mickie and Judge Brown are heavy-lidded on their way to napland.

But here's the thing.

What Dumpy's doing is a clever strategy. It was Mickie's idea, he laying it out during one of our sessions in Camden County Jail,

Mickie, me, Dumpy, and Slippery all crowded around that small table in the interview room bolted to the floor so it can't become a murder weapon. Not for Slippery, but some other inmate sitting there hearing his court-appointed lawyer who's looking at his watch all the time on account of he's got another appointment, maybe a haircut, telling his man, You want the deal they're offering you, you got to do, I don't know, maybe fifteen, maybe twenty, in Rahway, hey, listen, think it over, I gotta go. That's when the mope takes the table if it's not bolted to the cement floor and smashes the court-appointed's head in before Abbott and Costello can get in there and save him.

Yeah, it was Mickie's idea.

Slippery's nephew (my former client; that's another issue I'll get to in a minute) is in protective custody. Like I already said. I don't remember if I told you his name earlier. It's Alonzo Thomas. Anyway, he will be trotted out at Slippery's trial and will appear as a prosecution witness against Slippery and the rest of his crew been indicted in this case. We won't get to see him or interview him in advance of trial, see how bad his testimony will be, where we can poke holes in his story, try and discredit him as a witness before the jury. Yeah, I know. The kid's going to kill Slippery when he's up there on the witness stand no matter what we do on account of his uncle almost had him killed before the big takedown a few weeks ago. (Am I starting to sound like Dumpy?) But lawyers do what they can. That's our job.

So the kid, Alonzo, is in protective custody. No way is the prosecution going to tell us where they've stashed him, let us go and see if he will talk to us. No fucking way. First, they do, they run the risk we tell Slippery where his nephew's at and he takes care of business with some of his boys still out on the street. No more Alonzo. The DA's office would not take our word that we would keep Alonzo's whereabouts from our clients. No fucking way on that as well. Maybe we were white-shoe big law firm lawyers they'd consider it. Maybe. But those uptown boys aren't taking on the likes of Slippery Williams as a new up-and-coming practice area.

So Mickie's idea is we ask the DA's office, Please can you tell us where Alonzo's at so we can go and try and do a pretrial interview of him. They say, What are you smoking? Fuck no. Then we file a motion with the court asking that the witness Alonzo Thomas be brought to court—still in protective custody—placed on the witness stand under oath, and the judge can ask him will he agree to be interviewed by defense counsel. If Alonzo says, Sure, why the fuck not? we do it right there while he's under oath, find out what he intends to say as a prosecution witness at trial. Get his testimony down so we can use it at trial to cross-examine him with if he makes inconsistent statements. Which almost everyone does, one way or another.

What we get out of this is what they call free discovery. We get a preview of coming attractions. Now, when he heard it, Slippery got to grinning on account of he likes Mickie's idea for a different reason. Mickie's plan would put nephew Alonzo in play.

Meaning? you're thinking.

Well, think about it. The kid's hidden away, out of reach of Slippery's organization—at least what's left of it. No way any of his boys going to get close enough to Alonzo to finish what Slippery's two boys almost accomplished that night out there on the lot before the raid. But if the judge decides to have young Mr. Thomas taken from whatever safe house the cops have him stashed away at and brought to the courthouse to await a ruling on the motion, in case the judge decides to grant it, the interview can take place that day. That means maybe a night in a local jail, maybe even Camden County, then a car trip to the courthouse, the kid shackled, armed guards all around.

Yeah, but he's out there. Exposed. And like I said earlier, Slippery's got assorted law enforcement on his tab. Who knows, maybe even a United States marshal, either guarding the kid or making the arrangements for his courthouse visit. Slippery saw Mickie's plan—you should pardon the expression—as a shot.

Like I said, it puts the kid in play.

Slippery doesn't say any of this to us. Doesn't have to, can read it on his face like a book. So Dumpy's at the table at the jail, like I said, this isn't his idea. He's saying, Waste of time. Stupid fucking idea. (Now, this was before Cousin Brown was chosen to preside over the case.) Then Dumpy catches Slippery's eye. Dumpy sucks air through his teeth, gets real quiet. We agree that Dumpy makes the motion.

That has to do with my prior representation of the kid when he tried to rip off the undercover and almost had his eye taken out. I'm getting to that.

So finally Dumpy finishes outlining what we want here. While we don't know it yet, Judge Brown has in fact already signed an interim order directing the jail officials to bring Alonzo to the courthouse and put him in the lockup cells where defendants in custody wait for their case to be called. He's in there now.

What we heard later from one of the jailers was that the kid was in his own cell, one of three side by side. The other two were packed with inmates who somehow learned that young Alonzo was a rat squealing on Slippery—his own cousin, flesh and blood. (Wonder how that happened?) So the whole time the kid is in there while Dumpy's droning on to the court, the other mopes are letting him know what they would do to him if he were in with them. Things like: Gonna take your baby puny-ass balls and shove them in your punk-ass bitch mouth, I ever see you in the yard back at the joint. The kid's giving it back, telling them he sees them they better step back else he'll kill them. But the way we heard it, the kid was rattled, all those guys nonstop harassing him.

So Dumpy finishes. Judge Brown shakes himself out of his stupor and nods over to the prosecutors, letting them know it's their turn.

One of the two, the white one, a nice-looking kid, I'd say in his late twenties, thin, sandy-haired, overdue for a haircut, cheap-suited like most prosecutors, stands.

"May it please the court," he says. (This kid is young, we don't say that anymore around here.) "The state has a preliminary matter we need to raise with the court. May I proceed?" he asks Judge Brown.

"You here," Judge Brown says. "You on your feet."

This confuses the kid momentarily. Then he gets it. Okay to proceed.

"Your Honor," he says. "The state moves to disqualify Mr. Salerno and his law partner, Mr. Mezzonatti, from their continuing representation of the defendant Williams."

He doesn't look our way, but I am watching him. We anticipated this and think we took care of it with an earlier call Dumpy made to Cousin Brown over the weekend. I'm watching the kid as he tells the court how I represented Slippery's nephew in an earlier criminal case. Therefore, he tells the court, me and Mickie can't represent Slippery here where his nephew, now a prosecution witness against Slippery, was once our client. You see, ethically you can't represent both a prosecution witness and the defendant he is testifying against.

The kid goes on at some length about this, citing cases, giving what I would say was a pretty good law school argument. He really is a nice-looking kid, I'm thinking. I like the way he stands as he addresses the court, like the sandy hair needs cutting.

The kid finishes. Neither Mickie nor me respond. As we planned, Dumpy rises. He tells the court that Mickie and me have agreed that we will not seek to question Alonzo, either now or at trial. He says he has a letter written by us to him that says we will not share with Dumpy anything Alonzo might have confided in us when he was our client. So, Dumpy says, problem solved.

Now, Dumpy would like nothing better than to lose this motion and have us kicked out of the case. Perfect for him, given how he's been trying to convince Slippery nonstop he should hire Dumpy and ditch us. So why does he call Cousin Brown at home, wire this so me and Mickie can stay in? You know why. We are in a jungle here. Slippery wants us. And, like it or not, Slippery Williams is the lion king. Dumpy fucks with Slippery, Dumpy's not Dumpy no more.

Cousin Brown will help on stuff like this, but we have no illusions. When it comes to the real stuff in the case—the evidence at trial, the verdict, the outcome determinative stuff—Judge Brown will be strictly by the book, hands off. He isn't about to risk censure or worse. What we will get from Judge Brown are breaks around the edges. Nothing more. We know this. So does Slippery.

Judge Brown nods back over to the young prosecutor. The kid rises, now he is incensed. That's bullshit, he tells the court in law school language. Either there is an ethical violation or there isn't. You can't slap some paper on it and make it disappear.

The kid waits for something from Judge Brown. A question. A comment. Something. What he gets is nothing, so sheepishly he retakes his seat.

"We are dealing with a man's Sixth Amendment right to counsel," Judge Brown tells all of us. "This court is not going to infringe on such a constitutional right." He then asks Slippery, seated like I said in the row behind us, "Will the defendant Mr. Williams please rise?"

Slippery stands. The surrounding guards rise as well and get in real close to Slippery.

"Mr. Williams," the judge says. "You want to continue in this case with these two gentlemen as your lawyers?"

"Yeah," Slippery says, and promptly sits down, as do the surrounding guards.

Judge Brown gives the kid a there-you-have-it look, then says, "Motion denied. Counsel, proceed with your argument."

A seasoned lawyer would shrug this off and get on with it. This kid's green. He sulks his way through why Judge Brown should not grant our motion and put Alonzo Thomas on the stand. I'm watching, thinking yeah, this kid isn't really ready for this kind of major criminal case yet. That may well help us at trial. But I have no illusions. I can also see that the jury will like him. He's cute, well intentioned. An honest and earnest young prosecutor.

His heart not in it, the kid's argument is brief. He takes his seat. Bring the witness in, Judge Brown instructs the bailiff. Me, Mickie, and Dumpy exchange glances. Well, what do you know? Alonzo was here all along.

Some other guards lead the kid into the well of the court. He stands there while they unshackle him. One of the guards tells him to stand over there next to the witness chair. The bailiff rises and tells the kid raise your right hand. Now the kid's looking around, checking the place out. He sees me, then he scans behind me, sees Slippery. Judge Brown tells the kid in no uncertain terms, gets his attention back, "The bailiff said raise your right hand, do it." The kid raises his hand and the bailiff recites the oath.

When he's finished the kid says, "Yeah, all right" (*yea aight*).

"Answer properly," Judge Brown commands.

Alonzo looks up at the judge, his eyes saying, Who the fuck you think you talkin' to, old-school?"

Judge Brown is not one to be intimidated by punks. He gives the kid a look that says, Two seconds, son, and you're gonna be back in that lockup cell, maybe even the one full with other prisoners love to see you about now.

Mean-spirited and stupid as he is, the kid knows enough not to push this one.

"Yeah," he says.

Good enough, Judge Brown decides. "Let the witness be seated," he tells the bailiff. The kid takes the stand.

The lawyers watch as the kid once again scans the courtroom. I can see he is going to keep his eyes off Slippery. Angry as he is about what nearly happened to him, this is Slippery Williams out there seated behind me and Mickie. Not someone to fuck with. And fucking with him is exactly what the kid's doing. Best not to do an eye-to-eye stare-down with Slippery, his instincts are telling him. Then he sees Dumpy's two clients also seated behind us, next to Slippery. One of them he recognizes. Lamont. Dion, his head bashed by the kid into hamburger meat, is long dead and buried. Lamont was the other lieutenant was out there trying to off him, the one who ran past him and tried to escape over the fence. Seeing him sets the kid off. He death-stares him, then catches himself, decides to be cool, and slouches in the witness chair like he's at his place on the sofa hanging with his own homeboys, BET videos on the HD flat-screen, they're passing a quart bottle of malt liquor and a pipe filled with burning dope.

Judge Brown catches this. We watch the kid being watched by the judge. Since he's in protective custody Alonzo's not orange-jumpsuited. He is in street clothes, the same baggy shit these punks always wear, a sports-team emblem on every single article he's got on.

Only thing missing is the head bandanna and the sports cap on top stuck out at an angle, with the visor pristine untouched off the rack and not beveled and worn straight on the head like the white kids do.

The kid's starting to settle in, his pea brain telling him, Hey, look at this, you the center of attention here, you the man.

"Sit up," Judge Brown commands Alonzo.

The kid looks over and up at the bench, thinking does he want to signal this fool, looking like a big black bull, Fuck you, old man, talk to me like that again you better be holding a Glock nine under that robe you wearin', bitch. Not a good idea, he decides. So the kid sits up.

Now he's staring at me, thinking who knows what. Probably, Hey, ain't that the white motherfucker Slippery got for me to lawyer last time? Man here for me again?

Judge Brown addresses the kid, although he's really speaking for the record. He tells Alonzo he has been brought into this courtroom today on the motion of the defendants who are seeking to determine if he will consent voluntarily to a pretrial interview. The defendants' constitutional right to an adequate opportunity to prepare their defense is paramount under our system of justice, he tells the kid, adding, your interrogation by defense counsel can be accomplished here while you are seated and under oath.

Of course, Alonzo hasn't a clue what the judge just said.

"Say what?" he says to Judge Brown.

Judge Brown looks over at us, then at the prosecutors' table. He sighs, thinking maybe he should have stayed in private practice rather than becoming a judge. At least he'd be making better money, billing by the hour, dealing with mopes like this dim-witted kid on the stand.

"These lawyers want to talk to you. Ask you some questions. That all right with you?" he tells the kid, making it as simple as possible.

Too simple, the nice-looking young prosecutor decides. So before the kid can respond and say something closer to Sure, why not? rather than the no the prosecutor wants to hear from Alonzo, he rises.

"Your Honor," the young prosecutor interjects. "The state respectfully requests that the witness be advised by the court that he is under no obligation to submit to questioning by the defense. That he is well within his rights to decline to be interrogated."

Alonzo watches the prosecutor say all this. Once again he can't make head or tail out of what was just said. He looks up to Judge Brown for translation.

Judge Brown sighs, thinking possibly, Doesn't the Camden public school system teach these morons anything at all, even if they drop out at fifteen?

"You don't have to talk to them," he tells Alonzo. "Up to you."

Alonzo scratches his chin. He yawns. Looks around the courtroom.

Before he can respond, tell Judge Brown, You say I don't gotta talk to these motherfuckers, then I ain't, all right (*aight*)? Know what I'm saying? Dumpy rises to his feet.

"Your Honor," Dumpy tells his cousin. "Would the court grant defense counsel the leeway of some limited questioning, simply to determine if this witness can make a knowing and intelligent determination of his interest—or lack thereof—in submitting to an interview?"

Good move, Dumpy, I'm thinking. Seize the moment before the kid says fuck no and the guards lead him back to the lockup.

Alonzo watches Dumpy, still clueless what these lawyers are saying except when the judge breaks it down for him.

"Objection," the young sandy-haired prosecutor all but shouts, back up on his feet, obviously worried that this situation is about to get out of control. "Your Honor," he pleads, "it's for the court to make this determination, not defense counsel. You allow them to question this witness, the horse will be out of the barn."

I see the kid hear "horse" and "barn," two words he does understand—probably from fourth grade before he left school for the street. Now he is really bewildered, thinking, What the fuck got farm shit to do with this? These motherfuckers crazy, talking about horses and shit.

"Overruled," Judge Brown tells the prosecutor. "The court will allow some limited questioning."

Another break around the edges.

"You may proceed," Judge Brown tells Cousin Dumpy.

Dumpy walks to the podium Judge Brown requires lawyers to stand at when they question witnesses. He looks at Alonzo for a minute or two before addressing him. The kid stares back, his what-you-lookin'-at-fool? stare on his face, but he can't hold it, he's so confused about what happens next here.

"Good afternoon, Mr. Thomas," Dumpy tells the kid.

Alonzo tries a yeah-whatever stare, but he's concentrating on Dumpy, almost cocks his head like a dog does when it can't get the command you just gave him.

"How old are you, Mr. Thomas?" Dumpy asks.

Any lawyer worth his salt knows you need to get the witness lubricated, meaning comfortable answering questions, actually opening his mouth and speaking when up on the stand. You need to do that, get him talking, so you can hear and judge how he speaks and so that the witness himself gets to hear how he sounds speaking from the stand with the mic perched near his face. You ask some easy, unimportant questions first. Then you get to the good stuff.

The young DA is still agitated, worried—with good reason—that an experienced trial lawyer like Dumpy is going to drive his truck through the opening the judge has given him and turn this "limited" interrogation into a full-fledged cross-examination.

On his feet again, "Objection, Your Honor," he says. "The state respectfully asks the court to remind defense counsel of the limited nature of this interrogation. Counsel should get to the point or sit down."

Worried that he may have gone just a little too far with that last comment, since it's the judge and not the prosecution who can tell Dumpy keep going or sit the fuck down, I see the young DA sort of wobble on his feet and then sheepishly sit down. This guy's got a ways to go before he learns how to do this properly.

But he's right, of course. Still, Judge Brown has decided to cut us some slack, so he tells Dumpy, "Can you go right to the meat of this, or do you need some limited leeway?" Judge Brown was a courtroom lawyer, he knows about lubricating the witness well as anyone.

Dumpy decides he can probably skip the preliminaries under the circumstances, and he wants to let his cousin know how much he appreciates the slack he's been given here.

"I can get right to it, Your Honor," he says, then turns his attention back to Alonzo, who has watched all this as bewildered as ever.

"Mr. Thomas," he says, pointing over to the table the two prosecutors are seated at. "You know who those two gentlemen are?"

Alonzo slouches in his chair, then remembers what the judge told him about sitting up. We watch him readjust himself.

"Yeah," he says, the disdain he feels for law enforcement almost dripping off his answer.

"Now, Mr. Thomas," Dumpy asks, "did either of these gentlemen, or any other law enforcement officer, ever tell you that defense counsel had sought the opportunity to engage you in an interview?"

Then, realizing the kid won't get this, adding, "that I wanted to talk to you about Slippery Williams and his crew?"

"Naw, ain't nobody told me nothin' 'bout that."

Dumpy looks up at Cousin Brown, his eyes telling him, See, them two boys over there at counsel table not playing fair, not telling the kid that the defense lawyers had requested an opportunity for a witness interview, it's for the kid to decide by rights, not the DA.

Judge Brown doesn't move a muscle. But the message has been received. Dumpy decides to go for it, thinking the judge's going to protect him when he draws an objection, when he goes beyond simply asking the kid, Are you willing to talk to me now? and instead asks questions about the substance of the case, something he could only do if the kid first says, Yeah, I will agree to talk about that. Everyone in the courtroom knows it, Dumpy says to Alonzo, Want to talk to me about Slippery and my client seated back there about killed you? he's going to say, Fuck, no, just like the prosecutors told us when we asked them.

"Now, Mr. Thomas," Dumpy says. "It's a fact, is it not, that you have never—ever—seen Mr. Williams or either of the two gentlemen seated back there with him, also defendants in this case, in the presence of illicit drugs?"

"Objection," the young prosecutor says, half standing, half seated. His heart's no longer in this.

"Overruled," Judge Brown tells him.

"Say what?" Alonzo says to Dumpy.

Dumpy's back is to me up there at the podium facing the kid, but I can hear him blow out some air, like Judge Brown did earlier. Dumpy downshifts to street slang. I know he doesn't like to do this, but he sees it's the only way.

"You never seen nobody 'round no drugs. Not Slippery Williams, not them other two seated next to him?"

Slippery and his lieutenants are careful. They are never physically in the presence of their product. Never.

I can see the kid now back to death-staring the one of Dumpy's clients seated behind us almost killed him that night. Dumpy sees this too and knows he needs to jolt the kid out of this.

"I said . . ." Dumpy scolds the kid, like his grandma raised him before he took to the street did when he wouldn't listen. "I said, you ain't never seen them boys 'round no drugs. That's a fact, right?"

Alonzo looks back at Dumpy.

"Naw, I ain't never seen them 'round no drugs."

Now, this is good testimony. What Dumpy should do is leave it there. At trial that simple statement can be used to cross-examine the kid after he testifies how Slippery and his crew were dealing drugs. But Dumpy doesn't leave it there. He steps into one-question-too-many land.

You know, there's the old story of the defense lawyer has the eyewitness on the stand. The lawyer's client has been accused of committing grievous bodily harm when he bit the nose clean off the victim in a street fight.

You claim you were an eyewitness to the fight? the lawyer asks the witness up on the stand.

That's right, the witness says.

And you claim you were as close to the fight as you are to me in this courtroom.

That's right.

But it is a fact, is it not, that you did not actually see my client bite the nose off Mr. Jones. Right?

That's right.

Never saw it?

That's right.

That is where the lawyer says thank you to the witness, no further questions, and sits down.

But instead, he commits the courtroom sin of asking one question too many.

Then, sir, the lawyer says, how can you testify with such certainty that my client bit off the nose of Mr. Jones?

Because I saw him spit it out onto the pavement.

Dumpy says to the kid, "So why you be tellin' the prosecution you so sure that Mr. Williams and them others be dealing drugs, you ain't never seen them around no drugs?"

There is no guile in this kid. He's oblivious to tactics or anything else Dumpy is trying.

"What you talkin' 'bout?" he lectures Dumpy.

"I hear Uncle Slippery, them boys he got on his crew on the phone, with they mules and others they got on them all's payroll, talking drugs this, drugs that. Listen," he adds, "that what them boys do, all day, all night, is talk about moving they shit from this place to that, how much they getting, where the supply at. That what they do."

Alonzo sits back in his chair, his expression saying to Dumpy, Fool, what you talkin' 'bout, they not in no drug bidness? That what they do.

Dumpy is crushed. Though I can't see his face, his back still to us; I can see just by Dumpy's shoulders. He is crushed. This was a monumental fuckup. He remains silent, thinking, I guess, is there any way he can dig himself—and us—out of this hole. After a while Dumpy just about half whispers to Judge Brown, "No more questions," and he takes his seat next to me. Dumpy can't look at me or

Mickie, seated on my other side, now fully awake and seething. I can feel his body heat from his chair to mine.

It's now the state's turn to question Alonzo. I look over to see if the young prosecutor is smart enough to leave it alone, or whether he will take a turn at questioning the kid. If he does, there is always the chance that he will fuck up this very good record for the prosecution Dumpy has handed them like a gift.

"Counsel?" Judge Brown asks the DA, meaning, You got any questions?

"Nothing from the state, Your Honor," the young prosecutor says.

Judge Brown glances quickly at Cousin Dumpy. This was a terrible mistake and he feels sorry for him, though he's obviously not going to show it.

"The witness is excused," Judge Brown says, nodding at the guards, letting them know, Go ahead, it's time for you to reshackle this mope, lead him back to lockup. "These proceedings are adjourned until further notice," he says, and rises from the bench.

Now the bailiff stands. "All rise," he instructs, repeating ceremoniously, "Court is adjourned until further notice."

Judge Brown returns to his chambers, followed by the bailiff. The court reporter packs up her steno machine. Alonzo is led from the courtroom, then at a safe distance Slippery and his two lieutenants are cuffed and led away. Dumpy can't look at Slippery, he's fiddling with papers, doesn't look up he's so embarrassed. Mickie nods at Slippery, letting him know me and him will see Slippery later at the jail, assess the damage then. Slippery stays cool. He knows what just happened, though no way is he going to show it in front of the guards or the two prosecutors packing up their briefcases over at their table. And anyway, nephew Alonzo's now in play.

Look, what Dumpy just did was bad. No doubt about it. And he's an experienced courtroom lawyer. He should know better. Yeah, well. Let me tell you. All of us have done this at one time or another. Maybe not as bad as Dumpy just did. But we have. Asked one question too many. Me. Mickie. All of us. You have to understand. You're up there at the podium, you're cross-examining a witness. Adrenaline's running through your veins, your head's filled to the brim with what-ifs as you question. What if I ask this, he says that? What if he says this, do I ask that? Sometimes you get carried away. You fuck up. Show me a lawyer says, nope, never done that? I show you a lawyer's lying about his trial experience, spends his career plea-bargaining his clients because he's afraid of the courtroom.

Now, Mickie knows all this as well as me. As well as anyone. But he's up out of his chair, aiming at Dumpy. Man, is there bad blood here, I'm thinking. The prosecutors still in the courtroom, in earshot, Mickie says to Dumpy, who's still fiddling with his papers, trying I guess to compose himself he feels so bad, "Nice going, champ." Dumpy ignores him.

Mickie's not going to let this go. Dumpy's trying to steal our client and now he's vulnerable. Mickie wants to go in for the kill. He mimics Dumpy's last question.

" 'So why you telling the prosecution that Mr. Williams's dealing drugs, you ain't never seen him around no drugs?' "

I see Dumpy hold it as long as he can. Then he leaves his papers at the table and walks over to Mickie. The two prosecutors keep their distance, but they're watching this. It's only us lawyers in the courtroom at this point, even the few spectators—the two reporters—have left.

Dumpy's facing Mickie. He places his hand on Mickie's shoulder like he's about to console him, say, Listen, I know. It was a mistake. I am so sorry, but together we'll overcome it. That's not Dumpy, I'm thinking, when he says to Mickie, real slow, "Fuck. You."

Then he gives Mickie a shove. Not a big one, doesn't knock Mickie off balance. Just shoves his shoulder back. Then Dumpy adds, "Chump." Right in Mickie's face.

Now, like I said, the two DAs are watching this. Mickie and Dumpy together have just made mistake number two. Never, ever show the other side there may be discord in your ranks. Both of them know better than this. Goddamn it, I'm thinking; Mickie and Dumpy facing each other, neither saying another word.

Then the two prosecutors come over. They shake each of our hands, as is the custom. They don't say a word, just shake.

In Alonzo Thomas's words, that's how we do.

The prosecutors leave the courtroom. I say to Mickie, "Come on, let's go." I see him glaring at Dumpy, his eyes saying, You dumb fuck. Then we leave.

I'm pissed at Mickie. He knows better than this.

CHAPTER FIFTEEN

I hold it in all the way back to our office. Don't say a word to Mickie. Not one word about what he did in the courtroom. Why not? I'll tell you why not. Because I'm was waiting for him to say, Hey, Junnie, sorry, man, big mistake. You know, give him the benefit of the doubt. But no, not one word. So when we get back I follow him into his office. Shut the door.

"Got a minute?" I say.

"What?" is all he says. Like, you know, What is it now?

"What the fuck is wrong with you?" I say. "In front of the DAs. You got to start up with Dumpy in front of the DAs?"

"Fuck you," Mickie says. Then repeats it. "Fuck you."

Now, I know Mickie knows what he did in the courtroom was dumb. And yet, here I am in his office, he's telling me fuck you. I'm telling him, fuck me? Fuck you. And we're off to the races. Screaming at each other, all of Bernstein, Smulkin, Abramowitz & Wolf sitting behind their desks thinking, no doubt, Here they go again, those goddamn guineas, can't they for once behave like lawyers rather than . . . Oh, fuck it. Fuck them too. I'm so fucking mad at Mickie. He won't admit he's messed up and he's taking it out on me. Screaming at me when he should be apologizing. We go on like this, getting nowhere fast, then I open his door, telling him for the last time, Fuck you, man, and I slam it shut.

I don't see him the rest of the day. He's behind his closed door. I'm behind mine. I drive home in a heat. Bad idea. I get home, I'm still furious. I drink my way through dinner, accompanied by some freezer-burned meal my mother off-loaded on me months ago. I eat it too fast like it's a contest. So next thing happens, I'm chewing Tums from the medicine cabinet on account of I can't stop belching. Most of the night I'm tossing and turning, can't sleep, replaying the day— in the courtroom with Dumpy and Mickie, later in Mickie's office the two of us at each other.

The next morning I'm at the office still feeling like shit, Mickie and me aren't speaking. Our adjoining doors opening and shutting, passing each other in the halls, each looking the other way like no one's there. End of the day, I'm still at my desk, now I've got my door open, listening to him, thinking, Is he going to stop in, pretend none of this happened, ask me, Junne, wanna go for a drink? Something like that. Around six P.M. I hear Mickie's door open. He's gone. That's it. Not a word.

Next day I wake up with a sore throat. I stay in bed awhile, seeing will it pass. But I can't swallow. When I do finally get my ass out of bed, I'm bone-sore, sure I have a fever. I take my temperature and sure enough. Great, now I'm sick too on top of all this shit. I stay home. Don't call in. Just stay home. Day two, now I'm sneezing too. Throat's still on fire and I'm working my way through my one Kleenex box at a rate, by nighttime, I'm going to be using the toilet paper as a substitute, my nose already a drip factory, candy-apple red.

I stay in day three. Me, the toilet paper roll by my side, on the sofa, my only companion daytime TV. But see, my mother has my apartment bugged; must be, else how does she know to call just when I'm at my sickest, machine-gun sneezing into the Charmin?

"Hi, Salvatore. What's the matter?" she's asking, hearing me nonstop sneezing before I can even say hello. How in the hell does she know to call me middle of the day at my home, not the office? Unless she tried me there, Janice telling her, Mrs. S, Junne's not here right now.

"Hi, Ma," I manage between two three-second-spaced sneezing fits.

"You're sick, Salvatore," she says, like I've just been hit by enemy fire. I'm lying in a pool of my own blood, clutching at my open wound, screaming, Medic! over the din of gunfire.

I can picture my mother standing at the wall-mounted kitchen phone at her house, stocky like she is, in a dress—she's always in a dress, never seen her in anything else—worried now her baby's going to die. I can see the troubled expression on her face, her lips twisted in agony like she does when she's concentrating on her prayers she's kneeling in the pew at All Saints where the whole family went, my brothers and me were kids, every Sunday. Without fail. No excuses accepted.

"I'm okay, Ma," I tell her between sneezes, then for the umpteenth time blow this ugly green stuff out of my nose that's now on fire like my throat.

"I'm coming right over," my mother announces.

Just what I need: my mother walking into my apartment, her eyes circling, clucking, Salvatore, your place is so untidy. Can't you get another cleaning lady? *Another* cleaning lady? She's balancing two shopping bags of food, enough of her homemade manicotti in one of them to feed the entire building. The rest of the day she's hovering over me, her hand on my forehead every other minute, checking do I still have a fever. Oh boy.

"No, Ma," I tell her, trying as best I can to camouflage the panic in my voice. "I'm fine. I'll be fine. No need to put you out."

"Salvatore," she says. "I'm your mother."

Meaning? I'm thinking. Meaning, I can come over; that's why the good Lord put me on this earth. That and to be a good wife to your father, may his dear soul rest in peace.

Meaning, I'm on my way over and with the absolute best of intentions, and with absolute, unconditional love, I fully intend to make you crazy as well as sick.

"No, Ma," I insist. "I'm okay. I'll be okay. Really. Really."

"Fine," she says. And with that one little word she has let me know how I have hurt her feelings. To the core. With that and a barely audible sigh she has injected me right through the phone with a king-sized dose of guilt. I'm telling you, this woman could teach the Bernstein, Smulkin guys' mothers a thing or two about Jewish mothering.

That afternoon I get other calls. Mickie. Finally. And Mumbles.

Phone rings, I'm thinking it's my mother again, she's reconnoitered, refined her guilt attack, her two shopping bags now full on the kitchen table, ready to go. But no. Mom apparently gave up. It's Mickie.

"You okay?" he asks. He's wondering where the hell have I been, am I still that mad at him I'm not coming in to work?

"Yeah," I say. Then I tell him I've got this terrible cold, is all it is. Probably be back tomorrow, maybe day after.

"All right," he says.

That was it. But know what? Mickie was worried about me.

We're best friends, what do you expect? I'm feeling better after the call. Well, not really. I still feel sick as hell. But you know what I mean. When I get back to the office Mickie won't say anything at first, just Hey or Morning. Me neither. But sometime during the day, either he's going to say, Look, sorry about the other day, or I will. Whichever it is, the other's going to say, Forget about it. And that will be that. Gone and buried. Mickie fucked up with Dumpy when Dumpy fucked up. I fucked up by rubbing Mickie's nose in it. But it will be done. No—what do you call them?—recriminations.

Then Mumbles calls.

He tells me when he called the office that nice girl at the desk—Janice's courtesy of the other day not lost on Mumbles—said I was home sick. "You all right?" he's asking.

"Just a cold," I tell Mumbles.

He tells me he's put together a memo with supplemental cases and authorities on plea bargains, the rights of cooperating witnesses, for the Rodrigo case. Do me and Mickie want it? he's asking. "If you want I could come over, go over it with you, Junne," he says.

I realize Mumbles's call isn't really about a legal memo. He's wanting some time with a friend, home sick or not.

"Sure," I tell him. "You don't mind you might catch something from me. Come over right now, I'll make us some lunch."

"Great," Mumbles says. "Be right there," he says. "Great. Great."

Me and Mumbles spend a couple of hours together. He brings his legal memo for Rodrigo's case. He lays it on the kitchen table where I have laid out lunch. Only tuna sandwiches and canned hearty meal vegetable soup. But we don't discuss the memo. Not once. Nope. We spend the time Mumbles telling me about his kids he never sees anymore, but knows somehow all they're up to, beaming like any proud dad. I tell him about my mother's call and we chuckle over that. Thing of it is? All the while Mumbles is there, the two of us shooting the shit, Mumbles looking bad in his wrinkled worn-day-and-night suit, even a little smelly—for me today that's no problem, my nose stuffed like my mother's manicotti. And not once does he morph into his usual self—no soliloquies, not one he forgot this or that. Mumbles is like almost normal. Relaxed. With a friend and comfortable, I guess.

After Mumbles leaves and I clean up the lunch dishes, I'm eyeing the Rodrigo memo he left behind. I don't pick it up, instead wipe the kitchen table around it like it's radioactive. Fucking goddamn Rodrigo. Just eyeing that memo's enough to put me back into the funk I was in before Mickie's call, Mumbles's visit.

I mean, think about it. Far as Mickie's concerned the Rodrigo problem is about to be solved, seeing what Melvin Johnson, the assistant DA, proposed up at the bench when we tried to argue Mumbles's motion. I'm thinking something's wrong here. WD Smith's somehow the fly in the ointment.

And I know Mickie's probably climbing the walls, Cynthia's friend Debby still living in his house, down the hall in the room I sometimes use. Debby sitting on the couch in the evenings, Mickie needing to stay dressed, Cynthia staying out of his reach. In the kitchen too. (Mickie told me once how he likes to do it in the kitchen. Cynthia, leaning over the sink, he grabbing her from behind, arms around her, pushing his front into her back, saying, How about I pull those jeans down, peel off your string bikini undies? Remember the purple thong she had on that night when those gangbangers of Rodrigo's paid a visit?)

Fuck, I'm thinking again. Slipping into some kind of depression-fueled fatigue. My eyelids like lead, I'm on the couch, sliding into napland.

The phone again.

Now it's Debby calling. Does everybody know I'm home sick? Fucking Janice, I'm thinking.

"Hi," Debby says. "How are you feeling?"

"Better," is all I say, letting her know, Let's make this quick, okay?

"Great," she says, not picking up on anything in my tone. "Listen, I wanted to follow up on what we talked about when we had dinner with Mickie and Cynthia?"

She goes on about how I try and find her a job, we have dinner, she comes over and gives me a full-body massage. "In fact, I could come over now," she says.

"Ah," I say. "Yeah, uhm, jeez. Can I take a rain check, Deb? Still a little under the weather here," I say.

"Fine," she says.

Oh no. That's not fair. Debby doesn't even know my mother. How can she be doing this to me? Is it that one-half Italian blood in her? Or has she been attending those clandestine meetings in the church rectory where the parish mothers secretly meet with the city's Jewish women, show them on the priest's blackboard how to really do guilt, *X*s and *O*s diagrammed like an NFL playbook. Your son says this, you say that.

Debby's off the phone, barely saying goodbye. I get up, go pee, and then flop back onto the sofa. I pick up the remote control, channel-surf my way to *Oprah*. George Clooney's on, telling Oprah about his life, yukking it up, being cute, clever, so the viewers will go watch his latest movie he's promoting. Oprah cooing at him, We (who's this we?) haven't seen it yet, but we hear it's absolutely great. Fabulous.

And I'm watching, thinking, Good-looking guy. What I should be thinking instead is about Rodrigo and WD Smith. What I don't know until later is, I'm home sick, and Mickie's working the case. He's seeing Rodrigo at the jail. Speaking with WD.

CHAPTER SIXTEEN

So, while I'm still slouched on the sofa at home, wallowing in Lady O's interview of Clooney, seeing I'm now almost out of toilet paper too, Mickie's at the jail seeing Rodrigo.

The two of them are in the small lawyer's interview room, Rodrigo shackled hand and foot in one of the chairs. Mickie's in earnest with him now, none of his banter like before. He's telling Rodrigo how it is, trying to let him see, he's got to take the deal's on offer. There's no other way.

Rodrigo's listening, he can't even get his elbows to the table's bolted to the floor, his arms pinned to his waist by the wraparound chain securing his handcuffs. His head's tilted, Mickie has his attention, can see Rodrigo's listening, thinking.

Mickie's thinking, I've got to convince this mope, what's his alternative? He comes after me and Junne, he still stays in jail without bond and then goes down with some other lawyer can't help him when the judge gives him life no parole.

"So listen," Mickie's saying to Rodrigo. "We're not talking about those junta guys, you know, the military leaders, whatever they are, in your country. You got that, right?" Looking into Rodrigo's eyes, seeing does he get this part of it?

Rodrigo remains silent but he nods, Yeah, I got that. Whatever Rodrigo's really thinking, he's keeping locked inside.

"Cigarette?" he tells Mickie.

Neither me nor Mickie smoke, but he's brought a pack with him to the jail. Mickie's prepared for this. He knows how important it is to convince Rodrigo. He reaches into his suit pocket, retrieves the pack, removes the cigarette, leans over, and hands it to Rodrigo's shackled flipperlike hand. Rodrigo manages to reach the cigarette to his mouth, then leans forward as Mickie strikes a match. As Rodrigo inhales a long draw of smoke, Mickie places the pack and the matchbook on the table, letting Rodrigo know, For you to take back to the cell block when we're done.

"This has got some benefits for you," Mickie tells Rodrigo, thinking, What benefits? This fuck's looking at hard time no matter what. But continuing, "You're giving up your competitors. Maybe some of the guys work for you, getting maybe a little too ambitious. Maybe even some of *your* own bosses, getting in the way of your advancement, know what I mean?"

Mickie misses it. I mean, how could he be expected to see it, the way his own mind's going with this, but when Mickie says to Rodrigo he can rat out some of the guys above him are his bosses, Rodrigo's eyes momentarily flash. If he even saw it Mickie would be thinking, Yeah, figured that part of the deal might get your attention. You taking out some of the guys in your organization have their eye someday soon on your position. Maybe even some of those above you, you report to, getting in your way as well.

There's the rub, of course, because Mickie doesn't see that WD's maybe one of those bosses and Rodrigo's head cocked, listening to Mickie, but thinking, Can I do that and live?

"And, shit, seven years," Mickie's telling Rodrigo. "For you—under the circumstances—that's no big deal." Mickie repressing the deal Rodrigo made with me and him. He gives us a lot of money; we get him bail so he can skip and go back home, doing no time, no seven years, no nothing.

Rodrigo doesn't go there, he's still smoking, listening to Mickie, but a conversation this isn't.

"And we'll see maybe we can get you to do your seven in an army stockade," he continues, leaving out the part why, since once he starts ratting, Rodrigo's a marked man in the prison system, a bull's-eye painted on his forehead. "Food's better. Have your own room."

Now Rodrigo aims his crooked grin at Mickie, letting him know, Come on, what you think (*thenck*) you telling me, I'm going to some kind of Holiday Inn?

This Mickie sees, quickly adding, his hands raised, palms out, "Beats what you're looking at otherwise by a mile, don'tcha think?"

Rodrigo lets his cigarette drop to the floor and crushes it under his flip-flop. He stares at Mickie, still doesn't say a word.

Mickie's telling himself, Rodrigo may not like it, but at least he's listening, thinking it over. Sure he is, Mickie convincing himself, I mean, what's Rodrigo's other alternative? But there's someone else thinking here too.

While I'm at home watching Oprah and George, Mickie's not the only one seeing Rodrigo at the jail.

In the general visitors' area, along with the wives, common-law and regular, and other assorted friends and family, WD Smith's seeing Rodrigo. After Mickie's morning visit, WD in his natty suit and tie's sitting across from Rodrigo. Reading him. Carefully watching Rodrigo's eyes as he listens to Rodrigo telling him in Spanish what Mickie's saying, telling WD, No fucking way, man, you know that. No fucking way. But WD's watching those eyes, a better reader than Mickie. Thinking the man's considering this. Rodrigo knows what it may mean to him and his family he does this, takes the deal, but he's inside, has too much time on his hands, starting to get cell-block fever. No matter how hard you are, WD's thinking as he hears Rodrigo repeat, No fucking way, man, sooner or later you start to think, Well, maybe if.

Later, after his jail visit with Rodrigo, WD drops in on Mickie, Janice telling him on the interoffice phone that man's here again to see you. Mickie says be right out, throws on his suit jacket, and meets WD in the waiting area, sees WD clocking the malingerers seated shoulder to shoulder in their neck braces and whatnot.

"Mr. Smith," Mickie says, so WD can see he's standing there. "How you doing?" he says, but doesn't go to shake his hand.

WD looks away from the neck- and shoulder-bracers to Mickie. "Where's your partner?" he says. "He here?"

"Ah, no," Mickie says. "He's been out sick. Wanna come on back to my office?" he asks, thinking, What's he want now?

"No," WD says, staring at Mickie for a while, then adding, "I'll come back when you're both here. Kill two birds with one stone," he adds, with a malevolent wink at Mickie.

Jesus H. Christ, Mickie's thinking. What the hell does he want? He still hasn't gotten it, Mickie seeing WD as Rodrigo's lieutenant, not the other way around. But WD's nevertheless a scary guy. "Listen, no problem," he says, motioning back toward his office. "Come on back and I can fill Junne in when he's better."

"I'll come back," WD repeats, turns, and leaves Mickie standing in the reception area, Janice in her Jamaican accent answering the phones at the desk, "Bernstein, Smulkin, how can I direct your call?"

A shiver runs down Mickie's spine.

So, I'm at home on the couch, Oprah's still on with her next celebrity guest, but I'm tuned out. I blow my nose, wincing at the sandpaper feel of the toilet paper, now down to four squares left on the roll. My nose is so red I could win a Bozo the Clown look-alike contest. I'm going to learn about Mickie's Rodrigo jail visit, WD's Mickie visit. Though neither of us is going to learn of WD's visit with Rodrigo, what WD's concluding about Rodrigo's weakening resolve to hold out on the deal Mickie's dangling before him like a life rope on the high seas. And what am I thinking about now? Debby. Yeah, Debby.

Here's what I'm thinking. I get back to the office, I call her. Take her up on her offer, say, Let's have that dinner, when are you free? She's not bad-looking, like I said earlier, in a kind of tomboy way, her hair's cut like it is. She's got a nice body, firm on account of what she does for a living, small-breasted, sort of muscular. I can do this, I'm telling myself, eyeing the dwindling toilet paper, wondering do I try the paper towels in the kitchen, is all that's left. I can do this with Debby. Done it before.

The little blue pill. My thoughts while I'm doing it my thoughts alone. Right? We go out, have our dinner. She comes over to my place for this bullshit full-body massage we're pretending is something other than she's in my apartment, the both of us alone, seeing where is this going. Debby will be receptive, despite our phone call. Yeah, I can do this. Make Mickie happy, get Debby out of his hair. I owe him that. Who knows, maybe it will lead somewhere. Get myself out of where I am now. Because where I am now is nowhere. I can do this.

CHAPTER SEVENTEEN

Get this.

First day back in, I go to my office, skipped the courthouse café, haven't seen Mickie. I am no sooner in, my overcoat's still on, when Mickie walks in, says, "Seen the paper yet?"

I look up from my desk, I'm peeling the top off a coffee I bought on the way, Mickie lays today's *Courier-Post* on my desk, the print facing me. The story's in the headline: "The Cop & The Hooker," it says. Then underneath, "Arrest Nets Electronic Little Black Book— City Who's Who Implicated." I see a picture of Little Chip (remember her from our trip to AC?), looks like her high school yearbook photo, not some exotic posed shot. I put down my coffee, pull off my coat, and start reading, Mickie asking me, "How you feeling? Better?" I nod, but I'm into the story. Well, what do you know?

Little Chip got busted. It seems that she's been having an affair with a Camden vice cop. I know him. Mickie does too. We used to call him Dudley Do-Right, like the cartoon character, on account of he was one of those self-righteous cops, making sure you knew that each and every perp out there, no exceptions, was scum of the earth. He's real name's Mather Wilson. He's been around for a while. Dumb as a stone, but I always thought, for a cop, despite his perp attitude, he was a straight-up enough guy. A real cop type too, the kind works out in the gym six out of seven. Big arms and chest thick and rippled. He wears a sort of modern buzz cut, what I'd call a five o'clock shadow man. It seems Dudley's married with kids, but according to the article the detective has been . . . "involved" is the word the paper used . . . with Little Chip for over two years. And the paper has her real name: Martha May Grzbowski. Still no explanation for the Little Chip everyone knows her by.

Now, it seems that Chip made the mistake, not only of apparently falling in love with a vice cop, who, by the way, the story says, she first met when he busted her earlier two years ago. She also let him come to her apartment, had their trysts right there in her place. That way he gets to know everything about her. Who she is, where she lives, what she's got—the whole nine yards. Never a good thing for a girl makes her living the way Chip does. I'm reading and I'm not even into the good stuff and I'm already thinking, Man, Buffalo Reds's not going to like this.

So she's head over heels in love with Dudley, he's telling her, Baby, wait just a while longer, I'm going to give up my family, leave my high-school-sweetheart wife, three little kids, forgo my law enforcement career—all I ever wanted out of life since leaving the Navy, all of it just so I can be with you and we can then fuck secure in the knowledge that we mean everything to each other. Yeah, right.

I'm surprised at Little Chip, thought she was smarter than that. But who knows, love has a way of making fools out of anyone, I guess.

Anyway, Dudley's apparently leading her on, month after month, then at the butt end of year two, Little Chip puts it to him, now or never, she says. All right, you want it that way, he says. Never. Chip goes nuts, picks up the phone in her apartment, right in front of him, he's still getting dressed after bed. First I call the little wife, she tells him, then the precinct. He rips the phone from her hand, pulls the cord from out of the wall, wraps it around her neck, squeezes it tight. He's in a rage, doesn't say another word. As Chip's turning blue-purple she's seeing it in his eyes: he's actually going to kill her. But then Dudley suddenly loosens his grip, lets Chip fall to the shag wall-to-wall, coughing and gagging. He leaves, goes to his car. Calls it in. Tells vice he's got a line on a prostitution ring run out of 124536 Elm Court Apartments, city of Camden, apartment 3A. Name's Martha May Grzbowski.

What a fucking dummy, I'm thinking, as I grab a sip of coffee, Mickie still standing there while I finish the article.

So Chip gets busted. The search and seizure of her apartment nets her, what do you call it? Her PDA. Personal digital assistant, or something like that. You know, her electronic Palm handheld thing she keeps all her names and addresses in. And sure enough, there it is: a full list of all of Chip's tricks. Names, phone numbers. Not to mention, next to each name there's a little description of what her clients like in the way of, well, this I don't need to spell out. Right? And it's a fucking who's who—literally—of who's who. In the news article the list is only partial, but guess who's up there at number one? If you guessed Chief Judge Herman Sokoloff, you guessed right. Despite myself, because I'm feeling sorry for Chip, I start to grin. Mickie sees this, says to me, "Got to the list of names, huh?"

Buffalo Reds is in there too. Cell phone numbers, apparently all of them. Apartment address in Philly. This is bad for Chip. Real bad. And, of course, Detective Mather Wilson, old dumb-ass Dudley Do-

Right's in there too. So Dudley's as much of the story as the rest, the paper's describing how he brings the whole house of cards down on Chip's head the same time as his own.

Chip's arrested. Dudley's suspended. All the papers—the *Philadelphia Inquirer*, the big paper around here even though it's across the river, included—are on the story, as are the local TV and radio. Every fucking one of them has teams staking out the houses of those named in the story: Judge Sokoloff's house, the city council-men, all the big shots. Mrs. Sokoloff, going out in her robe to fetch the morning paper, not yet aware of the story since the TV's off, is met by the shouted inquiries she can't quite make out, the klieg lights on her, she's standing there in curlers, no makeup. She's caught off guard, but she's thinking they're here on my lawn because Herman's made some brilliant decision in one of his cases. So she smiles benev-olently at the cameras, waves like she's Queen Elizabeth acknowledg-ing the adoring masses. She closes the door, still smiling, thinking, Oh, that Herman is really something, as she stands, her back to the closed door, reading. From outside, the reporters hear nothing for a while, then a bloodcurdling scream, followed by her bellowing, Her-man, get your fat ass down here now!

I lay the paper down. Mickie sits in one of the chairs in front of my desk.

"Buffalo called," he tells me.

Mickie's looking tired. He's got circles around his eyes. He's put on some weight, he needs a haircut. His hair's shaggy, looks like a kid's, not a lawyer's.

"You feeling all right?" I ask him.

He waves me away, but I can see Mickie's tired.

"Buffalo called," he repeats. Something's troubling Mickie, so I nod, Okay, Buffalo called, what?

"Warrant's out for him," Mickie says, eyeing my coffee, thinking, I guess, he'd like a cup too. I move it toward him, letting him know he can have the rest of it he wants. He waves it away, thinking I guess he'll catch what I got. Tells me, "Buffalo says he wants to turn himself in, but first he tells me to go to the court, get Chip out, she'll make bail easy, what she's charged with."

Okay, I'm thinking. So?

"Tells me," Mickie continues, "Tell the bitch you'll take her back to her place, but first I need her to pick something up for me. Gives me an address on the north side, near where Buffalo used to hang before he moved across the river."

I'm just not getting it, so I'm looking at Mickie. Yeah, so? I'm thinking. Buffalo wants Chip to take care of something before he goes in. What's the big deal about that? Then I get it. Buffalo's not about to let a whore like Chip hang loose enough, long enough, she's being pressured by the DA, letting her know, she implicates the johns, and Buffalo along with them, she gets a deal. You know, maybe not a pass, maybe just a couple of months inside, that's all. And, of course, Chip knows a whole lot on Buffalo. Remember the girl I told you about, made the mistake of complaining to Buffalo in front of his other girls, got her throat slashed? I'll bet you Chip was one of them standing there when he killed her.

Mickie asks me will I go with him, bail Little Chip? Am I feeling up to it? he's asking, still eyeing my coffee but sensibly staying away from it.

"Sure," I tell him, sneezing quickly into the paper towel I brought from home. Now I'm also thinking, we deliver Chip over to that address on the north side Buffalo Reds's telling Mickie needs doing, what happens to Chip?

But we go over to the court, Little Chip's in the lockup. It doesn't take long and we've got her out, $10,000 corporate surety bond, Buffalo arranges it when Mickie calls him, tells him what's needed. We sneak out of the courthouse the back way. The entire city's press corps is outside waiting to jump on Little Chip when she and we her lawyers make our joint exit out the big bronze and glass front doors, so they can shout at her as we lead her down the steps and walk around the block to our car, Who was your favorite, Martha May? How you feeling about Detective Wilson now? Still love him, what he did to you? Shit like that. Court security tells us, Yeah, sure, Mickie, Junne, take the basement entrance, where the judges park, slip out the back, hey, no problem.

So we're at the car. The Merc S-Class Mickie mostly drives, but today I'm driving. We put Chip in the front passenger seat, Mickie in the back. On her last car trip, she's in the back, her hands cuffed behind her, two cops in the front of the cruiser that's taking her downtown, the cops snickering at her, saying things they'd never dare say to their wives. So we put her in front, next to me, let her see things will be better now. But Buffalo's seeing to it they won't.

We're in the car, Chip's looking awful. Remember how pretty she was in the limo on the way to Atlantic City? Well, that's not the girl seated beside me staring out the windshield, no light whatsoever in her eyes. Her dyed-black hair's dirty, unkempt, greasy-looking strands hanging on her neck. One or two of her false nails have broken off, her skin's got that jailhouse pallor, and her clothes the rancid, stale-piss smell I swear it takes no time flat to get you're inside even for one night like she was.

Mickie and me told her when we got to the car, We'll take you home, but first Buffalo wants you to go to the north side, pick something up for him. Yeah, sure, okay, she said, not thinking anything about it.

Once we're in the car, Chip turns to me, asks, "Can you make a stop for me first, baby? I need something, know what I'm saying?" (Gone is the finishing school diction Buffalo paid so dearly for.)

Meaning Chip wants to score some coke, maybe something else she can get to settle her nerves.

I look in the rearview to Mickie. I mean, do we really want to be with her she's trying to score dope from my car? But my eyes are saying to Mickie, Oh, what the hell? He shrugs, What the hell.

"Yeah, Chip," I say. "Where to?"

"Can I use your cell?" she asks. "Make a call first."

This I cannot do. She uses my cell to make a score, who knows? She calls the wrong guy, has a tap on his phone, my cell number gets picked up, now I'm in the shit along with Chip.

"Tell you what," I say. "I'll pull over in a gas station, you can use the pay phone. There's change in the center compartment by your elbow," I tell her. Chip shrugs okay, no problem. Like I said, she's not thinking what I'd call too clearly here.

I clock Mickie in the rearview again as I pull away. He's just staring at me, what we are about to do. And I don't mean the dope run. But fucking with Buffalo? Bad business.

At the gas station, Chip goes for the phone, I tell her Mickie and me will drive around the block, since I'm jittery at the thought of sitting there while she's calling God knows who. Then we take her to a 7-Eleven on Franklin Chip directs me to, saying, Be just a minute. She's reaching for the door handle. Mickie's eyes in the rearview are burning into me. I nod at him, letting him know he's right, we can't do this. I take hold of Chip's arm, I do it low, under the dashboard, in case Buffalo has anyone out there watching us, making sure we're doing what he wants done here. She turns back to me, wondering what the hell am I doing.

"Like I said," I tell her. "After this we go to the north side, take care of something Buffalo wants."

I'm holding her arm too tight. She feels the pressure, begins to see something's not like she thinks it is. She's studying my eyes. I'm not saying anything more, just straight-on looking at her. It takes a few more seconds, then I see she's getting it. Her eyes fill with understanding. She turns pale, ashen.

From the back Mickie says to her, "Think there's a back door in there?"

That's all he says. If you were watching the car, you wouldn't even notice he'd said anything. Like I said, Chip gets it, sees what me and Mickie are telling her. I let go of her arm. She leans over, gives me a peck on the cheek, whispers, "Thanks, baby," half turns to Mickie, says, "You too," and she's out the door.

We wait what we think is the right amount of time, then Mickie gets out of the back seat and walks into the 7-Eleven. It's now empty except for the Haitian girl behind the counter, who tells him some woman, with this other customer was in here before her? Like he was waiting for her or something? The woman asking her can you please open the locked back door for me? My husband and his bad-ass buddy out there in the car been beating me, doing bad things, and I need to get home fast so my boyfriend and me here can get my babies before they get hurt too. Mickie then goes outside, giving me a quick she's-gone look, and goes to the pay phone on the wall. He calls Buffalo, tells him what Chip just did when we took her to make a score she said she needed real bad before me and him could take her over to the north side like he asked us to.

Buffalo's enraged, but he doesn't have time now to think it through, did Mickie tell him the straight up or not? He's got to find that bitch before she disappears on him. All he says into the phone is

"Motherfucker," then hangs up. He'll think on what happened later, see if Mickie and me played him or not. Now Buffalo's got to try and get that girl before she's gone.

Mickie walks back to the car. I get out. We look at each other.

Mickie's shaking his head, telling me, "Buffalo cools down, decides you and me played him? Fucking Rodrigo's going to need to get in line he decides he wants to kill us, wait until Buffalo's finished first."

Mickie grins at me because, know what? What we did was right. Damn straight. I turn and walk toward the 7-Eleven.

"Where you going?" Mickie asks.

An hour later, Mickie and me are in a bar. This is not something we do middle of the day, but we're seated side by side at Donkey's Place up on Hadden. The place is in one of the worst neighborhoods around, but we're okay in here. The wizened old men seated down from us, scraggly whiskers covering their hollow cheeks, staring into their midday draft beers like the answer's somewhere in there, don't pay us any mind. Nor does the hag one barstool away from Mickie, mumbling softly to herself who knows what. We're in suits and ties, sure, but we both have the look from the old days, never left us. So no one pays us any mind in here. Middle of the day and we're drinking scotch. And Mickie orders himself a cheese steak, since Donkey's makes a mean one, probably best around.

Me? I've got one of the three boxes of Kleenex I bought when I went back into the 7-Eleven I walked in after Chip skipped and Mickie called Buffalo. It's right next to my scotch, I'm alternating sips and nose blows. But I'm starting to feel better. Maybe it's just the scotch. Maybe what we just did. Who knows?

Mickie's still chuckling, his mouth half full of cheese steak, he quick-sips some scotch, then says, "I was Buffalo, hell, I'd be asking directory assistance for all Rona Rosenbergs living in the United States."

I smile at that, shake my head yeah, because of course Buffalo's got no idea of the game we played when me, Mickie, Wanda, and Little Chip did Atlantic City a few weeks back. But he ever does find Chip, he'll kill her sure as night follows day.

The rest of the time we're there, Mickie's telling me about his jail visit with Rodrigo. And WD's visit, who's waiting on me so he can tell me and Mickie something important, Mickie's surmising. I try and tell Mickie how I'm thinking WD's going to be a bigger problem for us than Rodrigo. But he's not getting it. Doesn't want to, maybe.

But he will.

CHAPTER EIGHTEEN

Debby and me have a nice dinner at Gallo Nero. Though neither of us is eating all that much. Both of us are kind of nervous about what the night could bring. There's a lot of small talk. About her job search. We joke about Mickie, what it's like for her living there, how he says what he says. That Mickie, I'm telling you? she says. What comes out of his mouth. But yeah, we agree, he's salt of the earth. You and he been friends for like ever? Debby says. I nod. For like ever.

Halfway through the meal I excuse myself, go to the bathroom. I go in a stall because I need the privacy. Bathroom's empty. Still, someone walks in, I don't want them to see me pull my Viagra out of my suit pocket. Without water I manage to get the little blue fucker down, then I step to the urinal and pee and I'm back at the table. I'm hoping I've timed this right. Not too sure, really. Which, of course, only increases my anxiety. Not good, I'm telling myself, as I half listen to what Debby's saying, something about her needing to get out of

Mickie's place, Cynthia's a dear to tell Debby, No, stay as long as you like, honey, don't mind Mickie, he's just being Mickie. He really loves it you're here.

Got to go soon, I'm telling myself. Get her to my place before this Viagra kicks in. Thinking, It's going to kick in? Shit, what if it doesn't? What if I can't . . . you know? I think maybe Debby's in midsentence, the plates have been cleared, the waiter's gone, after telling us, Let you guys rest, be back in a minute see you want anything else. Yeah, she's in midsentence. I don't even wait for her to finish, I'm so nervous. I interrupt, say, Want to go to my place? Yes, she says, real quick, whatever she was talking about out of her mind fast as electricity through a current. Check, I tell the waiter. May have shouted it. Think some of the other diners looked our way.

Anyway, we drive to my place, in Debby's car. (I cabbed it to the restaurant.) If she's driving too fast, me telling her, left here, right here, I don't say anything. And then there we are. I've opened a bottle of wine. Fumbled with the foil, just about tore my finger off peeling it from the bottle, then struggled with the cork. Almost dropped the bottle in the kitchen wedged between my knees, I'm pulling on that cork like there's no fucking tomorrow. But now we're on the sofa, side by side, our wine glasses mimicking us on the cocktail table, both of us downing the first glass like it was ice water.

Debby's sitting close to me. Too close. She's smiling, waiting for am I going to make my move, kiss her? I'm just a little bit frozen at this point. I'm smiling back. But yup, just a little bit frozen. Debby runs her fingers through my hair.

"You have nice hair, Junne," she says, her smile saying, All right, let's go, here.

I smile back, but inside I'm at that place where the bowling ball's rolling down the lane. Is it going to hit the pins or drift into the alley and then fall down the slot, the pins untouched? Okay, I'm thinking, here we go, can I do this? All the while Debby's smiling at me, her hand's still in my hair, but she can't hold it there much longer, both of us realizing that. Think your thoughts, Junnie, I'm telling myself. I know this is awkward, but like I told you earlier, you got to do what you got to do. My thoughts? Come on, you don't need to know that. You know what I'm doing. What my feeble mind's trying to conjure up so I can lean toward this very nice girl who's waiting on me. Okay, I've got something. Never you mind what. I've got something. I can feel arousal down there in Viagraland. Well, actually, more like down there, down there. I lean in to Debby, our lips meet. Gently at first, then her mouth opens and her tongue's pushed its way into my mouth. I've got my eyes shut, but I squint them open and see hers are closed, she's rigid, leaning in to me, her breathing's heavy. I wait just a bit longer, then separate us.

I do it slow, like, Wasn't that nice, not like, Okay, how about we call it a night? I even smile at her, murmur, Uhm, trying to tell Debby, Nice kiss, really nice. She's smiling at me, seeing what am I going to do next. I think I may be frozen a little again because I'm just sitting there, now I'm worried that I'm idiot-grinning at Debby. She's waiting, seeing am I going to lean in to her again. When I don't, her hand's back in my hair.

"How about that massage I owe you?" she says, looking off past the sofa, thinking I guess, Is the bedroom over in that direction? Through that closed door?

"Uhm," is about all I can manage out of my mouth. I think I say it more than once at this point. Debby's not noticing anything. She's switched on, hot, I can hear it in her breathing, and her focus is on taking care of that. She gets up off the sofa. I stay where I am because I can't move at the moment. I'd like to. But I can't. Then Debby reaches her hand out for me. I take it and gently she pulls me up. Now we're facing each other, standing there in the living room. She steps in to me. We are body to body. Crotch to crotch. Like I said, the Viagra's kicked in. Debby feels how hard I am down there. The smile I see on her face now is a bit different, there's a gleam there. It's, you know, kind of devilish. Debby leans farther in to me, I'm rock-hard. She's obviously thinking, Now we're getting somewhere. We're mouth to mouth again, her tongue's . . . you know. I'm telling myself, Junne, back to thinking what you need to be thinking. We stand there, kissing for a while. Then she breaks off, gently, smiles up at me, and says, "Bedroom that way?"

"Yeah," I say. To me my voice sounds kind of high-pitched, but Debby doesn't seem to notice. She takes my hand again and leads me there.

I sit on the side of the bed. Well, at first I just stand there in the bedroom, like a mannequin, I'm not sure what to do. So I sit. Debby pulls me up again. Slowly she unbuttons my shirt, helps me out of my undershirt, which gets stuck over my head. Then she rubs her hands over my chest. I'm just looking at her hoping she doesn't see fear in my eyes. Debby's still devil-grinning, like, This is fun, isn't it, Junnie? I watch as she steps back, unbuttons her blouse, snaps off her bra, strips down to her panties. Her breasts are indeed small, her nipples hard, protruding, her body almost boyish, yet still feminine. It's her ass and legs—her flat tummy—I'm thinking, that's where her real female look's at.

"Junnie," she says, slipping off her undies. "Lay on your stomach, I'll start on your back."

Meaning, Get undressed, and hurry, we're going to pretend start a massage and then we're going to screw, I'm so horny I could burst, so get those pants off quick.

Okay, I'm naked. She's naked. Debby's straddling my rear—I can feel her heat down there, she's rubbing my shoulders, her hands moving slowly south toward my ass.

"Boy, Junnie," she says. Her hands moving from my shoulders to my back, rubbing, kneading. "You're stiff as an ironing board." I'm lying there, face down, my erection's still rock-hard, "Yeah, I know," I say. But my mind's concentrating on what I need to be thinking. I'm really working at this, here. My head's swimming in thoughts I'm needing about now. That bowling ball's slowly making its way down the lane, but those pins are still far off. I guess you could say the ball's wobbling somewhat from side to side, but it's still possible it can correct its trajectory and make it all the way down there and hit those pins. If I can, I'm going to get it there.

Debby touches my shoulder, letting me know, Why don't you roll over now? I do, and Debby sees my erection. I mean, I'm as rigid as an elementary school ruler. That's all she needs to know. This girl is ready. "Condom?" she says hoarsely. I reach over to the night table drawer. See, I have prepared for this. I start into removing it from the package, but I guess I'm not doing it fast enough, because Debby's got it out of my hands. I watch as she bites the corner off the package and she has that sucker on me in two seconds flat. I'm working on my thoughts, over and over. Really concentrating, hard as I can.

Bowling ball's picking up some speed, here.

Okay, it didn't take much longer, Debby's breathing hard, she's under me. I guess she's had enough of the preliminary stuff. I don't need to spell it out. Debby's under me, I'm in her, her legs wrapped real tight around me. We're, you know, doing it. And believe you me, I'm working as hard as I can, here. Concentrating like I've never done before, Debby under me, moaning, holding on to me tight as she can, rocking with me. Inside, my head's exploding with flashing scenes like some museum painting of Adam expelled from Paradise. Thunder and lightning. Gray-yellow sparks are flying. I can almost smell the flint. I've got the torments of hell in my head, I'm running simultaneous loops of scenes I'm needing to see to do what I'm doing here in my bed with Debby. My eyes are squinched shut, I'm grimacing. I'm hard at work. Giving it everything I've got.

Then I feel Debby's hands on my shoulders. I open my eyes. Debby's watching me, and immediately, I mean immediately, I can see she knows.

Gently she guides me off her. I lie on my back, both of us are still breathing hard. I start to say something. I'm not sure what's about to come out of my mouth. I think I'm about to apologize. Say something like, I am so sorry, so sorry, Debby, I . . . Debby's at my side, still panting. She puts her finger to my lips, says, "Shhh." Repeats it when I keep trying to say something, still not sure what, to her. Our eyes meet. I can see the tenderness she's showing me. I look down at me. I'm still so erect. In fact, I'm so erect it's starting to hurt. Debby gets this.

I pull off the condom, start to move off the bed. Debby's hands are on my shoulders, she's pushing me back down.

"First, let's take care of this," she says. "Junnie, close your eyes."

But I don't. I watch as Debby's hand closes around my erection. I swear I'm throbbing, but my head's empty now. I'm just so embarrassed.

"Close your eyes, Junnie," Debby repeats.

I do. Debby moves her hand on me, slowly at first, then faster. My eyes are shut tight. But not like before. Debby's bringing me to orgasm. At this point I don't know what's in my mind. If anything's in my mind. When I come, I almost scream, my back's arched, Debby's still not saying a thing, my eyes staying shut.

When she's finished, I'm still hard, on account of the Viagra, I guess. But I can feel it going down, the tension's off with the release of my orgasm. Debby leaves the bed for the bathroom, comes back with a towel, and cleans me. When she's finished I can't look at her, so I turn to my side my back's now to her. I feel her get off the bed again. Then she's back. She touches my shoulder, wanting me to roll over and face her. I do. Debby's got her bra and panties back on but not the rest of her clothes.

She strokes my cheek.

"I'm so sorry," I say.

"Shhh," is all Debby says.

I lie there. The bowling ball's stopped in front of the pins. It's motionless. It didn't hit the pins, I guess. But it didn't slide off into the side alley either. It's just sitting there, middle of the lane, smack in front of the pins. Immobile.

And you know what? I tell her. I tell Debby everything. Everything I've been holding in my whole goddamn life. It just comes out. Takes me probably an hour before I finish. Debby lies there next to me, on her side, listening. Not saying anything.

I'm still naked. My hard-on's gone. Took a while. I'm pouring my heart out to her and for the first part my dick's sticking up, semistiff. Tell me that isn't awkward, but Debby pays it no miñd; she listens to every word I say. And know what? I don't cry, don't gasp for breath. No, I just tell her. Tell her all of it.

When I finish there's this silence. I look over at her. She smiles at me. Pecks me on the cheek, strokes my hair, though not like before, when we were on the living room sofa, she in heat, me chemicaling my way there. I say, Be right back, then get off the bed and go into the bathroom to pee.

I'm standing at the toilet; I didn't completely shut the door, the stream hitting the water in the bowl's making too much noise. So I try and aim for the rim. My aim's not great, the stream's splashing from bowl side to water center, then back again. I'm wondering, Debby's hearing this, a man she aborted sex with, telling her what I just told her, and she hears him after sex (sort of) peeing, water splashing, then not splashing, then splashing some more. Why the fuck am I worrying about this, I'm thinking, as I finally shake myself finished, then pull down the lever to flush. I turn and see myself in the mirror over the sink. I flip the cold faucet, splash some water on my face, look at myself. What do I see?

I don't know. I just don't know. Don't even know what I'm looking for. I leave the bathroom, pick my underpants off the floor by the bed where I dropped them earlier. Now we're both semidressed. I lie back on the bed, where I was before. Debby hasn't moved.

"Know what?" Debby says.

Here it comes, I'm thinking. The advice. Junne, you need . . . A shrink. Or. To come out of the closet. Or. To develop a thing for men who aren't heterosexual. Or. All three. A sweet and well-intentioned lecture from Debby on what I need.

I look at Debby. I search her face for the superficial advice she's about to give me.

"I'm thinking . . ." Debby continues, propping herself up on her left elbow, "I'm thinking you and I should live here together. For a while, maybe."

Uh? I'm thinking. Debby sees this.

"Look," she says, her hand once more touching my hair, gently stroking, then it's back at her side. "Mickie wants me out of his house. That's no secret. I've stayed too long, he's right. I'm in his way, know what I mean?"

I nod. That part I understand. You know, about Mickie and he's needing her out of there so he can be Mickie—with Cynthia—in his own home. That's a man-and-a-woman thing. That I understand.

Duh? you're thinking. Junne, you can't really be this slow.

"I'd like to live here, with you," Debby says. "If you'll let me, Junne."

She wants to move in? After what just happened? Here I'm expecting some well-meant lecture: Junne, here's what you need to do, you know, with your problem. What she's telling me, she wants to move in with me? Like I said, Uh?

"Think about it," she says. "I'm out of Mickie's hair. You've got a woman here, living with you. Takes some pressure off. What people think how we're living together's their business. I can sleep on the sofa. I don't mind. What do you say, Junne?"

It's simple. Helps her. Helps me. You know, Debby's not some supereducated, what you'd call sophisticated-thinking kind of person. She told me at dinner earlier she did two years at a junior college, then dropped out. Didn't interest her. Took up massage therapy and loves it. Says she went to school for that, but now she reads up on stuff. You know, new techniques, new methods she folds into her massage technique.

Debby probably never had, or didn't fully understand, her psych course, if she had one. She's not a reader, I'll bet. At least not much of one. But she knew. She knew and she stopped us and then she listened as I told her what I have never. Never. Told anyone in my whole goddamn life. All the details. Not even Mickie knows this. And then, what she says is, Can I move in with you, Junne? Be good for both of us.

Look, I'm no genius either. My law degree doesn't mean shit. Like I've told you before, I'm not one of those guys really gets it. Really understands all the subtleties and complexities of the law. Like

Debby, I'm just an average person, same as most everyone else alive, trying to get by. Nothing special. But Debby's figured it out. Even if she can't articulate it. Can't textbook-explain it. She's being a friend. Not judging me. Not telling me what I need—what some college course tells her I need. Debby's giving me an act of friendship. A nonjudgmental act of friendship. How much is instinctive. Meaning from the heart. How much is deliberate thinking. I don't know. And I don't care.

I'll take someone like Debby any day. Over most of those smarter, better-educated, even well-meaning people who might be able to prescribe some solution when it's not really a solution I need. A friend, that's what I need. Like Debby.

"All right," I tell her.

She smiles at me. Okay, then, her smile says.

"You take the bed," I tell her as I lean over and peck her cheek.

CHAPTER NINETEEN

It's the morning after. I'm in the office. I'm passing by Mickie's room from the coffee area down the hall the Bernstein, Smulkin lawyers let us use. I'm feeling better, my cold's now no more than a bad memory. I take a sip of the coffee the Bernstein boys make us write down on a sheet by the cabinet every time we take a cup and then end of the month bill us for. These guys are making big bucks with their slip-and-fall auto-accident practice and they make us pay a dollar twenty for each and every cup we drink.

Mickie sees me, he's standing at his desk like he just got in himself. He's shit-eating grinning. So Debby must have told Cynthia last night after she got home. And Cynthia saying to Mickie they woke up this morning, guess what.

"So," Mickie says to me. "You the man, uh."

Here it comes, I'm thinking. Mickie's going to chase this like a frisky dog does a speeding car. He's liking this. Me and Debby. Me and a woman. Asking me things about last night he should know better not to. But before he gets another word out, the interoffice phone on his desk bleeps. He holds a finger at me, letting me know don't move.

He answers by pushing the speaker button so I can hear Janice's voice out here in the hall.

"Mickie, that man's on the phone again, wants to know are you here," she says.

Mickie's eyes shoot to me. WD again. Shit, we signal each other as I step into Mickie's room, close the door behind me.

Mickie sighs, tells Janice okay, put him through. Another bleep. This time the outside line kind, and Mickie pushes the speaker button again.

"Hello, Mr. Smith," is all Mickie says, frowning at the phone.

WD doesn't speak right away. Then he says, "Mr. Mezzonatti. You got me on the speaker?"

"Yeah," Mickie says, looking my way. "My law partner, Mr. Salerno, is in the room with me. How you doin'?"

I don't say anything to WD. Not Hi, how you doin'? Nothing. Neither does WD for a moment or two. Then he says, "Good. Got you both. Good."

Me and Mickie wait some more.

"Would it be convenient for both you gentlemen to meet with me?" WD asks.

Mickie looks my way while he answers. "Sure," he tells WD. "When would you like to get together?" Then adds, "Perhaps later today. Perhaps tomorrow?"

"Perhaps," Mickie's saying. He's using "perhaps" means Mickie's off balance. Nervous.

As he should be.

"How about right now?" WD asks.

Mickie's looking at me again, signaling, Now?

I nod, Yeah, okay. Now, if he wants now.

"Okay," Mickie says. "How soon would it be convenient for you to arrive here?"

"Arrive here?" Jesus H. Christ. We haven't even seen the guy and Mickie's so spooked he can hardly speak.

"Better idea," WD says. "I'm downstairs in front of your building, in a car. How about you and Mr. Salerno come down now?"

Sounds like a question. But WD's not asking us. He's telling us. No doubt about that. None.

Mickie's looking at me. What am I gonna say to Mickie? No? Tell him to fuck off?

"Yeah, sure," Mickie tells WD. "Be right down."

Mickie presses the off button, says, "Meet you at the elevator." I don't think anything of that and go to my office to get my overcoat because it's cold as a bitch outside.

I'm at the elevator and here comes Mickie. He's got his overcoat on like me. I press the down button. Neither of us is speaking as we wait for the elevator. We ride down in silence too. Each of us wrapped in our own thoughts about this, I guess.

We get to the street and, outside our building, parked tail to nose at the curb are two cars.

Not good, my glance at Mick's telling him, just as the window powers down on the first car's passenger side near the curb. We see WD Smith. He looks at us, at our obvious discomfort, Mickie clocking the second car, trying to see who's in it. How many. WD grins at us.

"Relax," he says. Meaning, We wanted you dead, you'd be dead, not standing here at the curb.

He leans back, unlocks the back door, pushes it open. "Won't you join us?" he says. Another command.

I go in first, slide over so Mickie can get in. We're sitting there, WD turns his head back toward us. I see the driver adjust his rearview so he can get a better beam on Mickie. We both recognize the driver. His nose is still bandaged, but the bandage is now smaller, under his eyes he's still bruised, but more green-yellow now. The ponytailed gangbanger from the night at Mickie's house is death-staring Mickie through the rearview. WD sees this too. He smiles.

"I believe you've met Rodrigo's colleague, Carlos," he tells us, mostly Mickie.

Mickie's watching Carlos through the rearview. He doesn't answer WD.

"Okay we take a little drive, park, and we can then talk? Review things?" WD tells us. Without waiting for a response, WD signals Carlos and he puts the car in gear, pulls from the curb. I don't look back because I know car two's going to be right in behind us. I'm sure Mickie does too. No one speaks. We drive the short distance to near where the jail Rodrigo's in is at. Carlos parks on the street, the jail in view. What's WD doing here? I'm thinking. Parking where Rodrigo can see us through some upper floor's barred window? See us down here, all together?

Something's wrong here. What the hell's going on?

WD turns back toward us again.

"I've met with Rodrigo," WD tells us. He's now turned his body in his seat so he can face us better. Carlos behind the wheel continues watching Mickie through the rearview. What's the saying? If looks could kill . . .

"Rodrigo wants you gentlemen to know," he tells us. "Well, he has decided to reject the deal the prosecutor has offered. He will not cooperate with the government."

Okay, I'm thinking. But why are we hearing this from WD, in a parked car, a backup car parked behind, near the jail where's Rodrigo's at, the chance he can see us down here a thousand to one? What the hell's going on?

WD's not finished. He's still turned toward us, not a hair on his head's out of place, his part's plumb-line straight. Even from the back seat I can see he's as immaculately dressed as ever, one of those dark velvetlike strips stitched onto the collar of his overcoat, like he's some banker just arrived for the executive committee board meeting. And he's sitting next to ponytailed Carlos, dressed like the gangbanger he is. All this *and* at least two more thugs in the car behind. This is a show WD's putting on. I'm beginning to see this as I sit here next to Mickie, who's thinking who knows what right about now.

"Another thing," WD says. "Rodrigo doesn't want to see you anymore, except in court. You will pass anything you need to tell him along to me. I will see that he's informed. Those are his instructions from this point forward."

What? This is bullshit, I'm thinking. Rodrigo's told WD he no longer wants to meet with his lawyers? No longer wants to hear for himself what his lawyers have to tell him affects whether he stays in jail, makes some deal, gets bail, doesn't get bail? Now I'm starting to get it. WD's frightened things are about to get out of control. Out of his control.

He's been seeing Rodrigo some more at the jail. Taking his temperature. Gauging how Rodrigo's telling him he's still not going to take the deal he's been offered. Won't rat out his competitors, some of his own guys maybe getting too ambitious. Maybe even his bosses. Like WD. And WD's thinking Rodrigo's softening up. Rodrigo's thinking maybe this is his only way out. Do his seven years, be done with it. Wait it out, while his house back in El Salvador gets cleaned out courtesy of the U.S. federal government. Wait it out and when he's back . . . well, maybe the field will still be open, seeing how he's the one helped with the housecleaning.

WD sees it coming. Can see Rodrigo telling me and Mickie, mostly Mickie, on our next jail visit with him. Okay, cojones, he's telling Mickie. Make the deal.

What happens then, after we tell Melvin Johnson, sitting in his drab room in the U.S. Attorney's Office, Christmas pictures of his three cute little kids, his loving wife, maybe even the dog by the fireplace in the frames on his desk. Maybe some of those "for Daddy" crayon drawings Scotch-taped to the walls. What happens then, is Johnson calls the marshals service, and just like that, Rodrigo's put in solitary, moved lickety-split out of the regular prison population. Otherwise, as me, Mickie, Melvin all know, word gets out on Rodrigo. What he's decided. It gets out. How? Who? Doesn't matter. It just gets out. Rodrigo's a dead man. Rodrigo's put down like some old infirm dog. Put down fast, money's no object. Plenty of men in the joint with Rodrigo willing to take the chance. For the money. For the thrill of it alone. Makes them numero uno on the entire cell block for some time to come. So Melvin has Rodrigo moved, sitting twenty-four/seven in his own cell, on a separate wing on a different floor of the jail. Maybe even he's put in some other facility, away from the Camden County Jail. Then guys like WD, who've got a whole lot to worry about, can't reach Rodrigo anymore.

Yeah, WD's worried. I can't see any of that in his face, as he's turned toward Mickie and me in the back seat, telling us what's what. What WD's pretending is what's what. But still, all of this. The two cars at the curb, the call to Mickie in his office, saying both of you come down here now. Then all of us parked here by the jail, what WD's telling us Rodrigo "wants." The man's worried. And make no mistake about it. This is far from good for me and Mick. WD's bland delivery of what he's saying doesn't mean shit. What he's telling us— all this bullshit—means the man's good and worried. And that ain't good for us.

"Here's what Rodrigo wants you two gentlemen to do," WD continues telling Mickie and me. "He wants you to tell the prosecutor your client's seriously considering the proposal. Don't tell the prosecutor no. No deal. Instead, you tell him Rodrigo's considering."

WD leans his arm over the back of his seat. He's wearing a very strong cologne. Something thick and musky. I see Mickie try and crack his window to get rid of some of that smell, but the motor's turned off so the window doesn't move. Instead, he unbuttons his overcoat, then his suit jacket.

WD is saying to us, "You tell the DA that before your client provides his final answer. You know, as a precondition. A show of good faith from the government. They first agree to bail your client. The amount of the bail's irrelevant. We'll make it. Whatever it is. You tell the prosecutor, Rodrigo gets bailed, he'll gladly be restricted to home confinement, wear one of those electronic ankle bracelets, so he can be around-the-clock monitored. Everyone can be assured he won't go anywhere, just stay at his place and make his final decision. You tell the DA, he does that, your client's probably going to say yes to the deal, become a cooperator."

All right, so WD's thinking, we manage to get Rodrigo temporarily bailed on false pretenses. Ankle bracelet or no ankle bracelet, WD and his crew can snatch Rodrigo, smuggle him out of the U.S. What they do with him then, keep him on the team or snuff him, they don't need to decide now. But either way, WD's problem's solved. Mickie and me are maybe left holding the bag, when first Melvin Johnson, then later the judge says to us, Where's your goddamn client? Did you help him escape? But that's no big deal. Me and Mickie can handle that. What we can't handle is this. Because there is no fucking way anyone, Melvin, the judge, anyone else on God's earth is going to bail Rodrigo. WD's smoking dope he thinks this is a plan. This is what the uptown boys call your classic nonstarter. Meaning it's fucked from the get-go.

Just then, WD looks down at Mickie's lap. Like I said, Mickie has his overcoat, his suit jacket unbuttoned. I see what WD's looking at. Mickie has his .38, the one from his house that night, he must have taken it to his office, kept it in his desk, in case Carlos was told to pay him another visit, this time at work. It's stuck in his waistband, the gun handle's sticking out. That's what Mickie did when he hung up from WD, told me, I'll meet you by the elevators. He took the gun from his drawer, stuck it in his waistband before coming down here. In case.

Christ, WD's seeing that gun. I see his eyes flash, then he smiles at Mickie. Not a nice smile; his smile's saying something way different from nice.

WD nods down at Mickie's waist. "What are you planning on doing with your pistol, Counselor?" he asks Mickie. "Going to shoot me and Carlos dead?" He raises his hands and pantomimes between his forefingers and thumbs the headline in the local paper. " 'Lawyer Charged with Gangland Killings,' " he recites.

Mickie is embarrassed. His face reddens. WD's smirking at him.

"Listen, Counselor," he tells Mickie. "Lawyers go to jail for stealing their client's money, for cheating on their taxes. Not for gangland killings. Put that away before you accidentally shoot your weenie off," he tells him.

Then WD turns to Carlos, says something to him in Spanish.

They both have a good laugh over what he's said. Two years of high school Spanish and I still can't understand a word he's said. Well, one word. *"Bandido."* WD's saying something, I guess, about Mickie's thinking he's some kind of *bandido.* Carlos and WD are having a good laugh over that. I can't understand the other words, but to me at least, it sounds like WD's speaking Spanish without an accent. Meaning like maybe he too is Salvadoran, or some other kind of Hispanic. Not American, despite his accentless English.

Mickie's hot. He's not liking this, them poking fun at him and his .38 stuck in his pants. Yeah, he's still scared of these guys. But I really don't know where Mickie is on what's really going on here. I'm thinking maybe he's still not getting it yet. But when Mickie's hot, as you saw from a few weeks ago, he sometimes acts before thinking things through. I can't let that happen. That hot Italian blood's one thing in the rack with Cynthia, another with a .38 stuck in his pants, WD and Carlos making fun of him in Spanish. Belittling his manhood.

WD and Carlos are still joking. Mickie's face has gone from red to pale. I can see that in about two seconds here it's going to start. Mayhem is seconds away. I'm watching Mickie. WD and Carlos are too wrapped up in their little joke to see where Mickie's going with this. Mickie's reaching down for the .38. I see it.

All this is happening and I realize something else. I can't tell you how or why. But like in a flash, a split second, Mickie's hand is inching for his pistol, I see it, realize that WD has a plan B. Like I say, all this is about to go, and it's like I can see directly into WD's mind. Can read it. Maybe it's the adrenaline shooting through my veins, realizing we all four of us are seconds away from bloodshed, pain, and death.

The minute Rodrigo goes into solitary, WD's fucked. Rodrigo's safe from reprisal and he's free to tell the government whatever he wants, his deal's in place. He can't be touched. So, if Melvin Johnson doesn't fall for the play WD's telling us "Rodrigo" wants. Some sort of bullshit show of good faith letting Rodrigo be bailed and ankle-braceleted. The minute we report that back to WD, he's got to act fast. Before Rodrigo goes into solitary and then it's too late. Plan B?

Shit, I see it. It's the Shakespeare move. Kill all the lawyers. WD has me and Mickie killed. Makes it look like Rodrigo did it. Had his own lawyers killed. Just like he's been threatening to do. Two local lawyers, maybe not the most highly regarded, but still two former cops, two members of the local bar. Big story in the papers. Melvin Johnson, the United States Attorney's Office, the judge—none of them are going to want to do a deal with a scumbag like Rodrigo has his own lawyers killed. Two local boys. They won't cut a deal with him he's begging them for it. Rodrigo goes down, gets sentenced, and stays in the regular prison population in whatever facility he's sent to. WD wants, he can have Rodrigo dealt with later.

To all of Camden, New Jersey—the law enforcement, the DA, the news-reading public—our deaths will have been by Rodrigo. That's WD's plan B, I know it, can see it as I watch Mickie's hand inching toward that .38 stuck in his waistband, it's just about touching the gun. Mickie glances at me, but I don't think he can actually see me. Then his eyes are back on WD and Carlos in front of us.

"Okay, we'll do it," I tell WD.

He and Carlos stop their joking. WD looks back at me. Then he sees Mickie's face, can tell something's wrong, looks down at Mickie's hand. But Mickie's moved it away. He's just blank-staring at WD. Expressionless. Still, WD can see something residual in Mickie's eyes. WD's considering, thinking, We got a problem here?

"We'll do it," I repeat. I wait while WD's eyes move to me.

"All right," he finally says. One more glance at Mickie, just to make sure. Then WD nods at me, letting me know that's that.

"We'll be in touch," he tells us. "Rodrigo wants you to take care of this as promptly as possible. We clear on that, gentlemen?"

I nod yes. Mickie's still blank-staring at WD. WD waits until Mickie slowly nods his assent.

"Okay, then," WD says. "You gentlemen wouldn't mind walking back to your office, make that call to the DA. I have another appointment and I really must go."

WD waits while Mickie first rebuttons his overcoat, then opens the car door. I slide out his side after him. We both stand there as the two cars pull from the curb and drive away. Then we start to walk back toward our office. It's not all that far, but it's really cold out. Sunny, but bitter cold. We finish buttoning up, hunch our shoulders against the weather, and begin walking.

Along the way I tell Mickie everything I've been thinking. All of it. He listens intently as we walk. Doesn't say a word. Takes it all in. We're about a block from our office. Mickie stops. Shakes his head.

"All this," he says, shaking his head. "All this on account of taking that scumbag's case. Never in a million years would anyone be able to figure out all this would happen. It's Rodrigo. Then it's not Rodrigo. Shit."

"I know it," I say.

Because there is no way out of this. Me and Mickie are fucked. Me and Mickie decide to see Rodrigo, despite what WD said? I mean, after all, he is our client. He says yeah to the deal, goes into solitary? WD has us killed, does it fast, hoping it's not too late before Rodrigo spews his guts to the DA, tells Melvin Johnson all about WD Smith, whatever his goddamn real name is. If we stay away from

Rodrigo, try and get him false-pretense bailed, and it doesn't work? WD has us killed. Either way we're dead men.

Mickie looks at me, shakes his head. I shrug. Then we finish walking back to our office. We don't say anything more. I mean, what more is there to say?

We are fucked.

CHAPTER TWENTY

Shards of early morning sunlight cut across my bedroom. I guess I didn't pull the curtains all the way closed last night when I went to sleep. Debby's in the bed, her back to me, she's curled on her side, legs up. Asleep like that, she looks like some teenager, not a grown woman, asleep with her covers tossed aside.

It's cold in here. I'm fully awake, on my side, the covers up hugging my neck. I'm watching Debby sleep. We're not touching. Her body's half an arm's length away. She's still deep-sleep breathing, that nightshirt she wears, just some V-necked long white cotton job with double leg slits, is hiked up, so I can see her legs, her ass, and her panties she sleeps in. It's cold in here, but sleeping Debby doesn't feel it.

When she moved in from Mickie's I told her, Take the bed, I'll sleep on the sofa in the living room. No way, Junne, she said. This is your place. Sofa's fine. Up to you, I told her. Second night? Middle of the goddamn night, what happens? Without a word, Debby comes into my bedroom, doesn't say a word, gets in on the other side, and goes back to sleep. No touching. Nothing but Debby middle of the night slipping into the other side of my bed.

What's that all about? Tell you the truth, I don't know. It doesn't happen every night; although Debby hasn't been here with me that long yet. Is she waiting on me—despite everything I told her—to, you know? Make a move? I don't think so. I really don't. And what about me? Am I feeling it? Lying here on my side, scrunched under the covers, watching Debby. Seeing her bare legs, her panty-covered ass? Watching her rhythmically breathing? Do I feel it? Do I, despite everything I've said, want to pull my arm from the covers, touch those legs, run my hand down her back, pull her toward me, and make love to her as she wakes, rolling her body into mine? Honestly?

No. Believe me, I wish I did. But, no. I don't.

Soon, when Debby wakes, she won't turn toward me, won't smile good morning. She'll slide out her side of the bed, go to the bathroom, sit and pee on the toilet. I'll hear the toilet flush. She'll stand at the sink checking her face at the mirror. I'll hear water splashing. Then she'll come out and go back to the living room. Not a word to me as she walks by. Not even a glance. I'll lie in bed while I hear her pulling the blankets off the sofa and putting them and the pillow in the hall closet where I told her on the first night they can go in the morning. Next I'll hear her pad into the kitchen to make coffee. After I'm up, shaved, and dressed for work, it's in the kitchen where I'll see her. We'll exchange good-mornings. Nothing will be said about her slipping into my bed. Weird. I mean, what's that all about?

I don't know. I don't say anything to her about this. Like, Deb, can you stay on the sofa, that would be better? No. She doesn't mention it. I don't mention it.

Deb's got a job. Actually, it was Mickie, not me, that wound up helping her. There's this guy he knows, opened one of those upscale gentlemen's salons over in Philly. Place is called something like the Grooming Den, something like that. Mickie says it's the new thing. Get your hair styled, manicure, aromatherapy—whatever the fuck that is. And all kinds of massages. You know: deep-tissue, Swedish, shiatsu. All that stuff Debby knows how to do. I asked Mickie, This place on the up-and-up? You know, because to me it sounded like something was what it wasn't. Know what I mean? Yeah, sure, Junne, Mickie said. It's the latest thing. Up-and-up. Strictly, he said.

So Debby's got a job. She's sound asleep over there, pattern-breathing, her back to me. I'm lying here, under the covers, watching her sleep. And what am I thinking about? You know what. WD Smith, Rodrigo, all of them. The fact that if there's a way out of this shit me and Mickie are in? It's the best-goddamn-kept secret of the century.

It's been four—no, five days since me and Mickie took that ride with WD and his thug crew. Five days, and what have we come up with? Nada. Nienta. Bubkes. We are fucking lost in space. Over and over again me and Mickie have run through this. We do this, WD has us killed, makes it look like Rodrigo did it. We do that, WD has us killed, makes it look like Rodrigo did it. Or we do nothing, then Rodrigo has it done, no need to worry about WD, Rodrigo has us killed because we've done nothing.

Debby's sleeping over there and I am lying here worried sick me and Mickie can't get ourselves out of this fix. Best we've come up with so far?

Believe it or not, it was Mickie's idea. Shows you how desperate he is. Mickie told me, Let's get Dumpy Brown involved. Have him meet with us and the prosecutor Melvin Johnson. See if we can talk

Melvin into bailing Rodrigo like WD wants—big cash bond, home detention with an ankle bracelet while Rodrigo considers Melvin's deal offer. Here's the thinking. It's a little ugly on account of it's racial. But look, much as I feel uncomfortable talking about this, Mickie's idea isn't way out in left field. His idea's in the ballpark of how the world—our world anyway—really works.

Melvin Johnson's black. Ditto Dumpy. Melvin's looking to our client Rodrigo as his possible chance of a lifetime. His ticket out of the United States Attorney's Office. We talked about this. Remember? Melvin's an average guy. Average lawyer. Without something more than he's got, he's a prisoner of his job until he retires. For Melvin it's the same old cases day in and day out. Low salary. No promotions. The job's great for two, maybe three years as a young DA, four to five max, but then it's a treadmill to nowhere. Putting one scumbag low-level perp away after another. Melvin's got a family. He wants to provide best he can for them. Make his kids proud when they get older. That's my dad, the . . .

Melvin's a professional man. Make that a black professional man. Because this is America, who you are, where you come from, still matters. It may matter more negative than positive, but it matters. You're a Jew. You're Italian. Irish. Wasp. Or African-American. It matters. You know it. I know it. We can pretend it doesn't matter if we want, but that's bullshit. It matters.

So, much as Mickie hates Dumpy, he's thinking let's involve him, take him to our meeting with Melvin Johnson when we make our pitch for bail; WD Smith not in the room, but we can feel his presence like crosshairs aimed at our backs. Let Melvin see Dumpy's in on this. Let him think maybe, I do this, what they're asking for their client? Dumpy looks good. And if Dumpy looks good, then maybe, down the line, Dumpy helps me. For openers Dumpy's cousin is

Judge Thurgood Rufus Brown. An opening on the bench comes up? Maybe Dumpy has a private word with his cousin. Whispers in his ear: I've been hearing good things about that brother been in the U.S. Attorney's Office all these years. How about we make him the new judge on the bench? Put another homeboy up there? Or maybe even, Dumpy's looking to add someone to his own small office. Thinking, Melvin might be all right for that. I'll give him a call. Be good for my clientele see a brother used to be on the other side, knows his shit from the get-go helping out on the defense.

So Mickie's telling me, Let's get Dumpy in on this. What do you think? Mickie doesn't spell it out. Not that he wouldn't. He's not shy about saying stuff like this. But why? I get it. Yeah, sure, I tell Mickie. Dumpy? Let's do it. Then Mickie says, You call him. I can't speak to that motherfucker, ask him without losing it. Sure, I'll call him, I tell Mickie. Better than that, I say. I'll go see him. Ask him in person.

And I do. Dumpy's sitting there behind his desk, his too-bold pin-striped jacket on the hook behind his closed door. Dumpy sitting there in his monogrammed two-tone dress shirt with the white collar, Windsor-knotted iridescent tie, his protruding belly straining his shirt buttons. His wavy strands of hair are as usual hard-pasted over his shiny scalp. Dumpy listens to me, sucking his teeth, not saying a single word until I finish.

I don't tell Dumpy the real reason me and Mickie are asking him to join us on Rodrigo. I mean, why? Dumpy gets it too. He's not offended. It's what it is. When I finish, I wait for Dumpy. Wait for him to tell me, Yeah, sure, Junne, I'm there. Or. Junne, man, love to help, but I'm way too committed right now, just can't do it. Meaning, Fuck you and fuck your asshole partner; you can't pay me enough to bail you two motherfuckers out of your troubles. Couldn't care less. You go down, I get my man Slippery Williams all to myself. Become lead counsel in his case. Of course, maybe Dumpy's thinking, while he's watching me wait on him for his answer: Slippery's going down, sure as beans is beans. Better these two Eyetalians there right up front in the courtroom. Be better for business for me. Then I can say, If I had been in the lead chair, wouldn't have happened, no goddamn way.

I'm watching Dumpy, can almost see his mind turning, this way, then that.

"All right," he finally tells me across his desk.

But that's an "all right" with a tail attached to it. There's more, I can hear it in his voice. So I wait.

"Ten thousand," Dumpy says to me. "In cash. Up front. Before the meeting with the DA."

Interesting, I'm thinking. Dumpy's in, but he's in playing hardball with us.

"And I want Mickie to give it to me personally. Without that, no deal," he says.

Dumpy sucks his teeth. That ten grand will come from us, me and Mickie. Out of our pockets. We're not about to ask Rodrigo or WD for money. Five from me. Five from Mickie. Dumpy knows this. It's his punishment for Mickie. What Mickie did in the courtroom that day after Dumpy fucked up with that kid Slippery's nephew when he had him on the stand. It's more than that, though. Me and Mickie are being charged a tariff for what's written on Dumpy's business card. You remember? The other one? The one for his own people saying, "Black On Black Get You Back." Dumpy's charging us a white man's tariff for the use of his blackness. Fair enough, I'm thinking. I'm about to tell Dumpy, let me talk it over with Mickie, but the way I say it? Dumpy and I will both know we've got a deal. But before I can speak, Dumpy adds one more condition.

"Junne," he says. "I'll do the meeting. Okay? But I won't enter my appearance on the court record as co-counsel along with you and Mezzonatti. Don't want your client to even know I'm there. Clear?"

Interesting. I'm wondering, Has Dumpy picked up something on the street? Has he heard anything about what's really facing me and Mickie here? Does that account for Dumpy's requiring us to keep him in deep background? Keep him safe? Could be.

"Clear," I tell Dumpy. Because there's no way can I ask him, Dumpy, what in the hell have you heard? Please tell me so I can tell Mickie. No way. So I tell Dumpy, Yeah, clear.

Debby jerks her leg in the bed, I'm still watching her sleeping. Then she stretches herself awake. I don't move. I'm under the covers watching Debby wake up. She pulls her arms over her head, arches her back, and stretches some more. She gives off a soft moan, then slips out of the bed and slow-walks her way to the bathroom. Not so much as a glance my way.

I stay in the bed, waiting for Debby to finish in the bathroom, go back to the living room. I'm lying there, I can hear her peeing. My thoughts are still on Dumpy. And Rodrigo. And WD. It's a long shot, with Dumpy. But like I said, that's the best me and Mickie have come up with. Under the circumstances.

I hear the toilet flush. Then, after a minute or two, the tap water in the sink running.

It's the best Mickie and me have come up with. And Dumpy's caution? What he may have heard? Don't know. Makes me even more nervous. But what can you do? Mickie and me will try this with Dumpy. I mean, what else can we do? How much worse can this get? Right?

CHAPTER TWENTY-ONE

Another late-night call. My cell rings. I'm half awake, half asleep. The TV's on and I'm still on the sofa long past when I should have turned the damn thing off and gone to bed.

I fumble in my pocket for my phone while it rings the stupid chimes it came with, since I can't figure how to download an electronic song like others I hear.

I clear my throat. "Hello?"

"Junne Salerno?" a woman's voice I don't recognize says. It's not Debby's. She's still out, not sure where at this hour, but she goes out, I don't ask. Her staying here's not working like I thought it would. But it's not her voice.

"Who's calling?" I ask, not wanting to acknowledge it's me on my own cell this woman's dialing, like who else could it be?

"This is Miriam Luchsman," she says. I don't know her, but I know the name. Mumbles's wife. Make that former wife. And her name's no longer Luchsman, I'm thinking, since she's remarried, or would she for some strange reason keep her first husband's name? In the brief silence before I respond, my groggy mind's trying to play catch-up with this. She's using a name I will recognize. There's something she needs to tell me. I know it's bad before I hear it.

"Shannon is dead," she tells me. Hit by a car, she adds. Mumbles was killed as he crossed the street after dark right near his office, out of the crosswalk, against the light. No one saw a thing. The neighborhood full of people and no one saw a thing. In that part of the city, full of down-and-outs, no one ever sees a thing. Not when the police are the ones asking.

Mrs. Luchsman, or whatever her name is now, tells me the cops found my number on a piece of crumpled paper in his pocket, had my home and cell. Must have been what Mumbles wrote down when he called my office when I was out sick and Janice gave him the other numbers before he called me at home.

Mumbles's body needs formal identifying. She can't do it. Just can't, she says. Will I? Please? Yeah, sure, I tell her. I'll take care of it, I add, then snap off the cell. There's no goodbye. No I'll call you tomorrow and let you know. I press the red power button and switch off the cell for the night. I sit on my sofa, sleep now gone. I can still see me and Mumbles at my kitchen table, our lunchtime tuna sandwiches half eaten, and he's telling me all about his kids he never sees. He's beaming. Now he's dead. I turn off the TV and just sit there.

★

I look down at Mumbles on the slab the assistant coroner rolls out of the cold box, one of God knows how many other corpses stacked like reading files in some grotesque giant-sized filing cabinet. I'm hit by the draft of cold air, the smell of decaying flesh just hinting but still penetrating your nostrils, like something too old from the fridge at home.

Mumbles looks gruesome; the car not only ran him down, it ran completely over his body. At least that's how it looks to me. Must have, the young coroner says when I ask. Strange. It hit Mumbles, then plowed right over him. His head was . . . well, never mind. An accident? I'm thinking. Or?

I confirm the body, then ask the guy for the bathroom, where I throw up. Not the first to do that in here, I bet.

It turns out Mumbles did live in that shabby office above the storefront. Slept on the couch, showered and shaved at the downtown Y; that is, when he showered and shaved. Took his meals wherever in that awful neighborhood, the people living there making fun of him, this has-been. A white-guy, broken-down lawyer with rumpled suits and Coke-bottle glasses. Sitting at the counter eating something fried and greasy, all the while out loud reminding himself of all the things his poor wasted mind's telling him he hasn't done and needs to.

Poor Mumbles.

After, I go to work. I see Mickie. I'm in his office, the door's closed again. I tell him about Mumbles, how it happened. What Mumbles looked like at the morgue.

"Jesus," Mickie says, shaking his head. He lets out some air. Clearly feeling this.

Sure, Mickie didn't care for Mumbles. But he didn't see him the way he does Dumpy Brown. Mickie knew Mumbles was broken. And he knows he was my friend.

As a young lawyer Mumbles had it all, at least for a short while. Under all that misfortune—that beyond-repair damaged mind—was a nice guy. A decent guy. To live like he did, then die like that, is just so tragic. An accident? I'm again thinking. So is Mickie, I suppose, as we sit there in silence around his desk. Or was it more?

Mumbles's name wasn't on the legal brief we filed with the court in Rodrigo's case. And though he was there in the courtroom the day of the hearing, he was in the gallery, just another spectator. Like Dumpy. Like WD Smith. I mean, WD doesn't know who Mumbles is. Was. How could he?

Later that day, I'm in my office and I get a collect call from Slippery Williams from the Camden County Jail. Inmates can use the two pay phones on the wall. First they need permission, need to explain why or who they're calling. Lawyers are on the approved list, of course. I take the call, say, Slip, how you doing, man? You know how it is, he tells me. Then he says, Junne, can you come visit me, man? Yeah, sure, I say. What's up? Then I realize whatever's on Slippery's mind he's not about to tell me on the jailhouse phone, cops somewhere in the jail sure as shit listening in on the line. So I don't wait for an answer, tell him I'll be there later in the afternoon. Slip tells me okay, then hangs up the phone. Wonder what he wants.

I spend the rest of the morning at my desk, pretending to work. I start this. I start that. But all I can manage, really, is to sit there thinking about Mumbles. Mostly I'm just feeling so sad for him. But to be honest, I'm thinking, could Mumbles have been killed intentionally, you know, as a warning to me and Mickie? WD letting us know we better come through on this crazy-ass idea of convincing the prosecutor Melvin Johnson to agree to bail Rodrigo. Ankle-bracelet him and bail him. If we don't, then Mickie and me are next. WD's plan B. Kill all the lawyers. Blame it on Rodrigo.

Debby calls from work. Says she's on a break, in between appointments, just wants to say hi. Hi, I say to her over the phone. (By the time she came in last night I was asleep. I left for the morgue early, before she was up.) How you doin', Deb? Job okay? I say. I don't tell her about Mumbles. I mean, she didn't know him. What's the point? Christ, her middle-of-the-night visits, middle-of-the-day calls. One thing I definitely do not need right now is another complication in my life. I try and cut the call short without sounding more than just busy. Then I sit at my desk pushing paper, hardly reading anything. I skip lunch, tell Mickie to go on without me, and then I go to the jail to see Slippery Williams. I don't tell Mickie about Slippery's call, about my going over there. For some reason I just don't.

Slippery's looking the same. No better, no worse. Maybe he's lost a few more pounds, his orange prison suit hanging on bony shoulders. We shake hands in the room, then sit at the bolted table. Slippery thanks Abbott and Costello and they leave us alone.

"Junne," Slippery says. "You ain't looking too good. You sick or something, man?"

"No, Slip," I tell him. "I'm fine. Just a little tired, is all."

Slippery's watching me. He's not buying it, but he lets it go. I mean, what's he gonna say? I'm the lawyer come to visit him from the outside. He's the convict, living in a cell block on the inside. He's going to tell me what I need to make things better for me? Come on. I see Slippery shrug.

"Junne," he tells me instead. "That Spanish motherfucker Rodrigis, in here in the federal section, your boy, right?"

Meaning my client. And remember how I told you that the federal prisoners are segregated in this Camden local jail from the rest of the prisoners?

"Yeah," I tell Slippery. "Rodrigo," I tell him. "It's Rodrigo."

"Yeah, Rodrigo," Slippery says, giving it his best shot at saying it with a Spanish accent. He smiles at this because it comes out somewhere midway between street black and TV-commercial white. Like some kind of *Saturday Night Live* skit.

"Well, the motherfucker crazy," Slippery tells me. "He on the cell block yellin' and screamin' he gonna do this, do that. Sayin' his lawyers no-good motherfuckers working for the wrong man. Some shit like that."

I'm wondering just how Slippery knows this, but it doesn't matter. He's Slippery Williams, he's a king on the inside here, just as he is on the outside. Something happens in here and he needs to know about it, he's going to know about it. Plenty of mopes in the federal section here know it's important to keep Slippery informed on events.

"He sayin' some bad shit, Junne. What he's gonna do his lawyers don't do something, do it soon."

Meaning, of course, what Rodrigo is going to do *to* his lawyers. I don't say anything. I mean, what am I going to tell Slippery? Tell him about the no-way-out, one-way street me and Mickie put ourselves on?

Slippery waits for my reaction, sees me Mount Rushmore him. But he's not offended. He's just providing me with what he thinks is some advance warning of something brewing over in the federal wing could affect my safety. And Mickie's.

"Another thing," he tells me. "Before all that crazy shit your boy's pulling over there in federal? I seen him, you know, where we see people?"

Like I said earlier, when visitors see prisoners here, they don't get to use the two little rooms. Those are reserved for lawyers, maybe when a priest comes to tell an inmate about a family death. Maybe not even then. The rest of the visits take place in a large room, armed guards all around, a long scarred wooden table probably been here since the nineteenth century separates the prisoners and their visitors, inmates seated side by side on one side, visitors on the other. What Slippery tells me is that he's sitting there talking across the table with one of his crew, giving him instructions he doesn't need to bother Dumpy Brown with when they visit in one of the little rooms. Slippery sees Rodrigo several seats away having a discussion with some guy who's been there before. Someone who comes to see Rodrigo regularly, Slippery tells me, the guy he's seeing is always well dressed, suit and tie, real sharp-looking.

So, on this occasion, before Rodrigo's cell-block outburst of the other day, Slippery's talking to his boy, telling him what needs day-to-day doing out on the street, but his attention's diverted over to where Rodrigo and his well-dressed visitor are having what looks like a muffled argument. Slippery's telling me their voices are rising, then Rodrigo jumps to his feet, says something to his visitor in Spanish. The visitor hisses something back in Spanish, then Rodrigo retakes his seat, just as the guards start moving in his direction.

"Spanish, huh?" I say. Not knowing what else to say.

"Yeah," Slippery says. "The dude next to me's some Spanish doper, his old lady's visiting. So I say to him, What that motherfucker just say? He say what he say to the motherfucker in the suit and tie is, I'm not going down alone. No fucking way am I going down alone. Then the dude in the suit tell him sit down, calm down, everything be okay. But I don't think the man buy it, the doper say to me. No, the doper tell me your boy Rodrigis, he just sit and repeat what he just say to the man about not going down alone."

"Rodrig*o*," I remind Slippery. He shrugs whatever, but I get the picture.

Well, any lingering doubt in my mind who's who, what's what between Rodrigo and WD Smith's gone for good. Lingering doubt?

Shit. No lingering anything at this point. What Slippery's telling me is gold-plated confirmation. I need to tell Mickie about this. I'll go back to the office and tell him, I'm thinking, when Slippery tells me more.

"That fat dude, you know, the lawyer lost his marbles, always talking to hisself. He a friend a yours, Junne, ain't he?" Slippery asks me.

"Yeah," is all I say, but whatever Slippery's about to tell me I do not—repeat, do not—want to hear.

"Motherfucker got hisself killed," Slippery says.

"I know," is all I say.

"Wasn't no accident," Slippery says. "People on the street see him crossing middle of the fucking street. There's this car, lights off, double-parked, waiting. Your boy steps off the curb and that car rams in gear, way I heard it, runs smack into the motherfucker. Hits him good. Stops, reverses gears, then runs over the poor sonofabitch. Straight over him."

No witnesses, the cops told Mrs. whatever her name is. Yeah, right.

Slippery's shaking his head at this tale of random violence. Okay, not random. But I'm thinking, the life Slippery lives, steeped in violent death, and here he is somehow disturbed that Professor Mumbles, my friend, is victimized by this seemingly intentional hit-and-run. Everybody's got their gray areas, I guess.

"Now, why would anyone want to do that to that harmless crazy motherfucker?" Slippery asks, shaking his head at the absurdity of it all.

In the background Slippery and me can hear the reverberating noise from the cell blocks, inmate shouts, jokes, curses, guards screaming back, the rattle and clang of steel on cement. Slippery shaking his head, thinking my friend Mumbles's death is so seemingly senseless. Of course, Slippery has no idea that Mickie and me approached Mumbles to assist on Rodrigo's case. Slippery's totally unaware of the connection. How could he know?

I'm steaming. Goddamn it, I'm thinking. They did have Mumbles killed as a warning to me and Mickie. Those lowlife sons of bitches. Goddamn it.

I'm in the elevator, heading down to the ground floor. I didn't make the connection for Slippery. I mean, why? What's the point? All I did was thank Slippery for the heads-up on Rodrigo, told him I'd be back soon and visit with him some more. We didn't talk one lick of business about Slippery's case the whole time I was there.

The elevator doors open on the ground floor. I walk out and head for the metal detector at the front door, the jail guards processing the day's remaining visitors. I'm midway there and who do I see, walking my way, having just entered, bypassing the metal detector, since he's armed and a cop, but the detective, the former undercover I had on the stand. The guy sees me just as I see him. He's been joking, exchanging pleasantries with the guards. He's here at the jail, I guess, to interview some perp. Something like that, given he's no longer an undercover. Now he's a cop functionary. I'm walking toward him and I see he's smirking, Well, look who's here. I am definitely not in the mood for this right now. I look away and try and walk by him.

I try not to think about our confrontation in the courtroom when the assistant DA had to step between us, or about the time he was at the bar in the restaurant when I first met Debby at the dinner with Mickie and Cynthia. The detective elbowing his buddies, joking with them about me sitting there, Debby's behind my chair massaging my shoulders. I try and walk past him, leave it be. Like I said, I am not in the fucking mood right now.

The detective steps in my path. "Well, well," he says, that smirk in full view. "What are you doing here, Counselor?" he says. "This one of your favorite places? All those mens up there?" He says this last bit like some kind of street black drag queen fag.

I stand there, the detective's demeanor telling me I move right, try to pass, he moves right. I move left, he moves left. So I just stand there. Don't say a thing. This, he misreads.

The detective looks me up and down. None of those standing around, not the guards or anyone else, as yet sees what's brewing here. "They don't let you stay overnight, do they, sweetie?" he says to me.

That's it.

I grab his lapels and with all the force I can, I spin him hard toward the cinder-block walls to the side of the inside entranceway and run-push him backward with all the force I can muster. The detective is off balance and so he has to reverse-trot just so he can stay on his feet. In about two seconds flat I slam him hard as I can against that wall. So hard I can hear the back of his head smash full force against the cinder blocks. I see his eyes roll back in his head. He's semiconscious. Dazed, but still awake. I think about slamming my fist into his gut, kneeing him in his groin. But I don't. He's a cop. An armed cop. I do more than I've done and I risk charges. I also sense that the jail guards, now to my back, everyone else in the lobby area, are stunned by what I just did. I have just another second or two before they move into action.

So I lean my body in to the detective, place my lips right up against his right ear.

"Now, you listen to me," I whisper to him. "One more fucking comment like that. Ever. One more look. You know those mens up there?" I say this just like he did, like some black drag queen, mimicking the way he said it to me. "Some of those mens up there are my clients. Some of those mens out there on the street my clients too," I tell him.

I can't tell if the detective can actually process what I'm whispering in his ear. His eyes are trying to focus. He's trying to shake off the impact of the cinder-block wall I slammed him into. But I continue.

"I ask them, Detective, those mens—they owe me. I ask them, they'll slit your goddamn throat. Leave you in the street to die slowly. Make it look like a bust gone bad. No one will know what really went down. How you died."

The detective's coming around. My fists are still on his lapels, but I can feel he's under his own feet now. I release him. The detective remains standing. I turn and walk away and out the door. The guards don't bother me. They let me go. They don't know what just happened, but I guess I have enough goodwill with them, they're giving me the benefit of the doubt here. They'll leave me be. Nothing will come of this. The detective won't make an issue of it either. He'll move from the wall, walk to the elevator, push the up button, won't look at the guards, the visitors coming through the metal detector. He'll leave it be too.

Motherfucker.

CHAPTER TWENTY-TWO

It's Saturday night. Thanksgiving is next week, Christmas around the corner. I can't tell you how much I hate this time of year, those holidays. Think about it. Sure, I've got family. I go to my mother's, or one of my brothers'. We eat. Christmas we do midnight mass together, exchange gifts before, when we all do the traditional Italian seven fishes dinner. You know about that one?

Festa di Natale, we call it, begins with *la vigilia*, the vigil, the feast of the seven fishes. Ends in time for midnight mass. Why seven? Lucky seven? Superstition? Well, in the old country, the northern Italian people don't do this. You've got to come from Naples on down south to Sicily to do this seven-fishes thing. Do the Sicilians, the others admit that this lucky number seven's what it looks like? No way. Ask them, they'll tell you seven fishes at dinner are because of the seven sacraments of the Catholic Church: baptism, penance, Holy Eucharist, confirmation, marriage. I forget the rest, but let's stop for a moment on marriage. Something not in my cards, right? Oh yeah, there's also the seven sins: pride, envy, greed, lust, and some others. Lust would be a good one to spend some time on here too. One sacrament not in the picture for me. One sin coming right up.

I saw this commercial on TV last night. Some old guy's living with his married daughter. He's got Alzheimer's, wandering around his daughter's house in some open-button sweater, the old guy's not sure where he is, who he is. But it's okay because there's this new pill the daughter can get her doctor to prescribe, help her poor dad so he can look at her and half the time think, Hey, I know her, she's my what-you-call-it. I'm watching that in this funk, this shit Rodrigo's got me in, and I'm thinking, if I make it to that age? (Let's put a big *if* here.) If I make it to that age? Won't be any grown married daughter looking after me so she can pop me some pill so then I can think, She looks familiar, don't I know her? Nope, guys like me. We make it to then? We are alone. Full fucking stop. We're the never-married old uncle, the kids in the family whispering about, sitting at *la vigilia*, slurping fish soup, the rest of the seven-fishes dinner stuck to our half-shaved chins, maybe stuck to the threads of our open-button sweaters.

I'm sitting on the sofa, but my feeble mind's elsewhere. Debby's in the bathroom getting ready because, like I said, it's Saturday night. We're invited to Mickie's. Debby's putting on makeup like we're, you know, a couple going out. I'm dressed, ready to go, sitting on the sofa thinking for me, Thanksgiving, Christmas, nothing but grim fucking reminders of what my future's looking like. If I have a future. And the sin of lust. How do I deal with that one, way I think about certain things? How the fuck do I deal with that?

Like I said, I really hate this time of year. But it's Saturday night and Debby's in the car with me driving over to Cherry Hill and she's looking pretty. Saturday-night pretty. She smells nice, perfume's lost on me, but, yeah, sure, she smells nice. She's a good person. Still, I'm kind of uneasy about us. I mean, ever since that night when I opened up, ever since then Debby's been fine. Still, there's something making me uneasy. I push all that out of my head. We get to Mickie's, go to the front door, Mickie and Cynthia greet us like we're a couple. This I let go too. I mean, Mickie thinks me and Debby are, you know. Cynthia too, right?

We order in Chinese. You know the drill. You sit around waiting for the "twenty minutes" the lady tells you on the phone in some thick Mandarin accent. Almost an hour later the food shows. Then you nuke it in the microwave so everything you ordered has the consistency of Elmer's glue. The four of us sit at the kitchen table, all the dishes we ordered now on serving plates, the selections either beige or white-colored. We're drinking beer. Mickie's doing Mickie, joking about how me and Debby are sleeping these days, elbowing Cynthia seated beside him across from us.

Mickie's trying, but I can see his heart's not in it. He's as upset about all that's happening as me. But Mickie's at least trying. Like I said, being Mickie. Me and Debby are fake-giggling, Cynthia happy-smiling, but the beat's missing from all this.

Then me and Mickie are in the living room, in front of the flat-screen. It's Saturday night, but late in the football season, so some NFL game's on, even though it's not Sunday afternoon. Something in the schedule, I don't remember now what, but there's a game on. We're sitting there, watching it, beers and munchies on the cocktail table, even though we've just gorged on bland Chinese. We're watching, but not watching. The game's between teams neither me nor Mickie care about. But it's a game, so we're on the sofa watching.

Sipping our beers. Debby and Cynthia are still in the kitchen, at the table, beers in front of them too. They're smoking cigarettes. I can hear their chatter, but with the game on I can't really make out what they're saying. But they seem to be having a good time, because they're yukking it up. That much I can hear.

Mickie and me watch one of those funny beer commercials they show during football. Best thing on TV, those beer commercials. Mickie turns to me and smiles. "Fucking Herman," he says. I nod. He's not referring to the commercial, but to Judge Herman Sokoloff.

In the middle of all that's happening with Rodrigo, yesterday, a Friday afternoon before the weekend, who comes to see us? Professionally, you know, to retain Mickie and me as defense counsel? You got it. Judge Herman Sokoloff himself.

Remember when me and Mickie went to Atlantic City with Little Chip and Wanda what's her name? How it was kind of a reprieve from what was going on then? Well, yesterday afternoon—I've got to admit—was like a mini-version of that. The meeting with Judge Sokoloff didn't last even an hour, but it's got Mickie smirking next to me on the sofa here, the game on, neither of us really paying attention, Mickie's saying, That fucking Herman.

Yesterday I'm in my office, trying to review some documents I got in discovery from the DA's office for this drug case I took on months ago, pre-Rodrigo. The judge assigned to the case just now getting to it, telling me and the DA in court earlier in the day, been waiting on him for months, Let's move this case, Counsel, the court cannot tolerate further delay in this matter. Yes, Your Honor, we both tell the court, sure thing. Thinking, but not saying, Intolerable, this delay caused by you sitting on your fucking lazy ass, now blaming it for the record on the lawyers. Sure thing, Your Honor. Whatever you say. After, I'm back in the office, Mickie comes in, says, Can you join me and Judge Sokoloff in my office? I look up from my papers to see is Mickie making some kind of joke here.

He's in my doorway, his eyes and head nodding toward his office, letting me know, This is no joke, Junne, Herman's in my office sitting there right now, waiting on me. On us. Apparently he called, said, Can I come right over, Mr. Mezzonatti? My lawyers said I should see you and your partner. I was in court, like I said, during that call, then when I got back Mickie was on the phone. Now Judge Sokoloff, the Chief Judge of the appellate court, is here.

The newspapers, the local TV, are still having a field day with the story of the hooker and her Palm handheld. Little Chip's gone, disappeared after Mickie and me dropped her at that 7-Eleven. Buffalo Reds is still not sure if we tipped Little Chip off or not, but he's giving us the benefit of the doubt. For now, at least. No one's been charged with anything yet. I mean, the hooker's AWOL. Her Palm device listing her clients, their sexual preferences, and of course Buffalo, isn't admissible in court by itself. It's what you call hearsay. Without Little Chip's testimony, telling the jury, Yup, that's my PDA, now let me tell you what all that stuff I put in there means, there's simply not enough for the DA to make a case. He's got a grand jury going, investigating, calling witnesses, but so far no indictments. Once Little Chip took a powder, Buffalo turned himself in, but he wasn't charged, released on his own recognizance, meaning he didn't even have to post bail.

All those listed in Little Chip's electronic little black book been the subject of continuing stories—this one called to the grand jury, that one denies he ever slept with Little Chip or anyone else, ever, except his sixty-five-year-old diabetic wife.

It seems that Judge Sokoloff's been called to the grand jury, not by subpoena, but by letter invitation. Targets of grand juries, the ones the grand jury is looking to indict for crime, can't be subpoenaed to testify. You can't force them to come. (So to speak.) You have to invite them. It's a legal thing. It has to do with protecting their rights, not coercing them into appearing before the grand jury and taking the Fifth on account of they don't want to say what they know will incriminate them under oath. If they're forced to appear and take the Fifth, the grand jury indicts them for sure because they're now thinking, This fucker's got to be guilty, why else won't he testify? So the targets get invited by letter. That way if they do come it's voluntary, no compulsion.

Herman got a letter. He went to his fancy uptown lawyers, sat for about a second and a half in the waiting area with the priceless abstract art collection on three of the four walls, before he was ceremoniously ushered into the senior partner's massive corner office, three Brooks-Brothers-suited junior partners already in respectful attendance. Herman's offered coffee, served with the firm's best china, the firm name logoed on both cup and saucer. He shows them the invitation letter, which was hand-delivered that morning to his chambers, inviting him, "at a time of your convenience to appear before the grand jury and explain the circumstances surrounding the inclusion of your name and certain other identifying features in an electronic device recently uncovered by law enforcement from one Martha May Grzbowski." (That's Little Chip's real name, remember?)

Naturally, Herman tells the senior partner, then the gaggle of juniors now perched attentively on the edges of the various sofas and easy chairs surrounding the glass and steel coffee table in the spacious corner of the senior partner's spacious office. Naturally I came to you immediately. Naturally, the senior partner says, the gaggle nodding, Naturally. But here's the thing, Your Honor, the senior partner says. The way he says it sounds like "Your Grace." This law firm may not be the best forum for the redress of your grievances. Translation: No way is this prestigious law firm, one of the best in all of New Jersey, going to be associated with you while you go down the tubes, vilified in the press, then tried and convicted for having some kind of kinky sex with a hooker who keeps electronic records. No fucking way. You're just a judge—sure, Chief Judge, but so what? Just some judge too full of yourself to be careful how you get your rocks off. When you're gone, this law firm will still be here raking in massive bucks from our corporate clients, who do not want to read in the paper that their lawyers had anything to do with your pitiful sinking ship.

Actually, Your Honor (Your Grace), the senior partner respectfully explains to Herman. Actually, for a matter like this, he tells Herman, I really believe that your interests would be better served by counsel who regularly practice in the courts where these kinds of cases take place, lawyers with more in the nature of a local practice, ones who are on closer terms with the officials involved in matters such as these. (For this you don't need a translation, right?)

Like who? Herman asks, making a mental note, he ever gets his ass out of this, no way will this law firm ever, fucking ever, get a favorable ruling on any case pending before his court so long as he lives.

The senior partner gives Herman Mickie's name, tells him that this "superb" local lawyer and his partner specialize in cases like this. Be perfect for you. The juniors hide their snickers. Mezzonatti and Salerno. Perfect, their eyes silently communicate to one another. Law trash for this trash case. Bye-bye, Herman. You are going down. With lawyers like these, down for sure. Just a matter of time, but you are history.

So I walk into Mickie's office and there's the man himself, seated in one of the two chairs in front of Mickie's desk. He doesn't even turn around, see who's there as me and Mickie walk in.

"Judge," Mickie says. "This is my partner, Salvatore Salerno. Everyone calls him Junne."

Herman turns his head, smiles. What he doesn't do is get out of his chair, shake my hand. Once a judge, always a judge.

"Your Honor," I say in greeting, and take the chair next to his as Mickie sits behind his desk.

Herman's looking a little peaked. Not as full-blooded as when we last saw him in Atlantic City, all tuxedoed up, Little Chip playing Rona Rosenberg under the table jerking his weenie while Mrs. Herman's cold-shouldering her.

Herman's looking at me, then at Mickie. I'm thinking he's going to say something like, Weren't you . . . ? Didn't I . . . ? You know, putting two and two together. But nope. Herman's not making any connection between us and that awards dinner in A.C. when we sat at his table with Little Chip and Wanda. We didn't even register on him, are that insignificant, I guess. Mickie shrugs at me. He's thinking what I'm thinking: Well, how do you like that?

Herman reaches in his pocket, retrieves the invitation letter to appear before the grand jury, and offers it to Mickie. He reads it, then hands it to me. We've seen hundreds of these.

"Mr. Mezzonatti," Herman says.

"Mickie," Mickie tells him.

Herman ignores this. Goes right on, saying, "I intend to accept this invitation and tell that grand jury everything I know."

Me and Mickie wait, because when clients tell lawyers like us they're going to tell everything they know, they are about to lie their asses off. Herman doesn't disappoint.

"I have no earthly idea who this woman is," he says with what sure looks like conviction. It's spelled bullshit but looks like conviction. And of course, if we let Herman go before the grand jury, take the oath, and then lie his ass off, commit perjury, "conviction" is going to be the operative word when he's tried and found guilty of making a knowingly false declaration to the grand jury that invited—not compelled—him to tell his story.

"How my name got in that thing of hers, that Palm whatever it is, is as much a mystery to me as I suppose it will be to you once you gentlemen" (not going to be any Mickies or Junnies passing his lips) "fully learn my case."

Mickie nods knowingly at Herman. Me too, when Herman looks over at me for the assurance to which he believes by divine right he's entitled. All his trysts with Chip in Camden? What happened in Atlantic City at the dinner? So far as Herman's concerned, none of that ever happened. That's his story and he's sticking to it.

"Coffee, Judge?" Mickie says.

He shakes his head no, Herman wants to get this over with as soon as possible. No Bernstein, Smulkin pay-as-you-go Styrofoamed brew for him. I mean, his having to sit here with the likes of us, having to discuss this sordid business, is certainly beneath the likes of him. He's the Chief Judge, for Christ sake. Herman squirms his meaty frame around the chair, absentmindedly tugging at his suit jacket, like it's the robe he wears on the bench. Like he tugs at it when he's exasperated with some lawyer's argument, annoyed that the lawyer has failed to see the point of the insightful question Herman has asked him, a truthful and candid answer to which would tank the lawyer's case, fuck his appeal to a fare-thee-well.

And speaking of robes.

The grand jury's invitation letter mentions "certain other identifying features" appearing next to Herman's name in Little Chip's PDA. The papers already had a story on that one. Next to Herman's name, in the "notes" column, Chip put "robe" and "cop hat." There was some nasty speculation what she meant by that.

"Mr. Mezzonatti," Herman says. He looks over at me, but says nothing because he's already forgotten my name. He looks back over the desk at Mickie. "I fully intend to tell that grand jury I do not know this woman. Never met her. Never had sex with her."

Does that sound familiar? Didn't a recent President of the United States try that one out on all of us? What is it with these smart people? Why are they so fucking stupid? They think maybe because they're powerful, unlike the rest of us schmucks out here, they can simply will the truth away? Make it disappear like some mirage in the desert? There, then not there?

Whatever, me and Mickie are thinking, because the way to handle a grand jury invitation letter is pretty standard stuff. For us, at least. Like I said, we've done it a hundred times. What you don't do, is let your client go into the grand jury and commit perjury. I can't tell you how many times some poor schmuck of a client goes into the grand jury because his lawyer doesn't know any better, or worse, actually believes the bullshit his client's telling him how he didn't do anything, I swear to God, he's imploring his lawyer. What happens is the guy never gets charged with the underlying offense because the DA doesn't have enough evidence. But now the DA has perjury and he makes it stick at trial. Bye-bye, client.

"Judge," Mickie tells Herman. "Junne and me completely agree that you need to get your story out." Whoops, "story" is not the best way to put this, Mickie realizes, so he quickly adds, "What really happened here." That's still not got it, Mickie's looking my way. I see the gleam in his eye, despite himself he's enjoying having Herman in here, just another uncomfortable perp for all intents and purposes. Mickie gets himself in gear.

"Judge," Mickie continues. "What I mean to say is, we agree that someone of your stature simply cannot stand by and let these scurrilous allegations go by without an adequate response from you."

Okay, Mickie's got his bullshit meter on now.

"The thing is, Judge," Mickie says, "a man of your stature should not have to appear like some ordinary witness before this or any grand jury. I mean, with your crowded docket, your official responsibilities, it places unreasonable demands on you, on your position as Chief Judge."

I watch Herman listening to this. He doesn't get it yet. Doesn't yet see that what me and Mickie need to do to protect his portly ass is keep him as far away from the grand jury and perjury as possible.

"So?" Herman asks Mickie. Meaning, Will you please get on with it so I can get out of here and return to my life as a highly respected etc., etc.?

"So," Mickie says. "What me and Junne suggest you do is write a letter to the DA, tell him you would like nothing better than to provide all the information anyone needs to put to rest these false and misleading accusations about you. But, given your extremely crowded docket, you would like to invite the DA to your chambers, where you will happily provide him everything he needs, all of which he will then be more than free to share with his grand jury."

Ding, ding, ding. Herman gets it. His eyeballs click, three cherries come up on the slot machine of his brain. Herman sees the DA in Herman's chambers. First, he's not under oath. Second, no grand jury. Three, me and Mickie will be there in the room ensuring that Herman utters nothing but bullshit, cutting him off whenever he might get too close to actually lying, telling the DA, What Judge

Sokoloff is saying is . . . Four, Herman can tell the press he made a full account of this matter, dispelling completely all these falsehoods. And five, if the DA leaks the grand jury invitation letter to the press, we leak the judge's invitation letter, the one inviting the DA.

Herman may be stupid in matters of kinky sex, but for this he's a fucking genius. He nods at Mickie, nods at me, whatever my name is.

"You will prepare this letter, Mr. Mezzonatti? Have a draft sent to my chambers?"

"Sure thing, Judge," Mickie says.

I'm wondering if Mickie's going to address the possible conflict we have here. Remember, in the past, the wherever-she-is Little Chip has been our client. Buffalo, who's still around, is also our client. My guess is no. First, technically speaking Buffalo sure as shit's not admitting anything. Chip's gone. Herman's saying nothing happened. So we have what we lawyers call a common defense. Well, sort of. Herman says nothing happened, ditto Buffalo for sure. Voilà, no conflict. Anyway, Mickie asks Buffalo to waive any potential conflict between him and Herman, he'll do it. Buffalo thinking, Now I got a judge owes me, can't be but good. Buffalo will be wrong. What possible good can some appellate judge ever do him? But think about it. Who's going to benefit from getting Herman's pompous fat ass out of this?

"I will of course insist on paying you gentlemen for your services," Herman says, meaning, You both aren't actually thinking of charging me for this, are you?

Mickie holds his palms upward, fingers spread. "Wouldn't even consider it, Judge," he says. "Be an honor for us to represent you. Really."

Herman smiles. Okay, he's thinking, the time comes, you two bozos actually get me out of this, I'll owe you. Fair enough. But those sons-of-bitches other lawyers who sent me here, didn't want to soil their hands, help me like they should have. They are fucking toast, bet on it.

There is some action on the flat-screen, one of the defensive players face-masks the running back, the replay from every possible angle fast, then slow-motion, showing the guy grabbing the front bar of the running back's helmet and jerking him back with every ounce of his 325-pound girth. Mickie's ignoring this, smiling at fucking Herman. I'm smiling back. In the kitchen I can still hear Debby and Cynthia gabbing, but now they've lowered their voices.

What's that all about? Is Debby telling Cynthia about me? About us? What's not happening? Why? I can't be sure, but for some reason that's what I'm thinking she's doing. Thinking that Debby needs to, can't keep it in and not tell someone. Someone like her best friend.

Later, Mickie and Cynthia are in bed after me and Debby have left. She's saying to him, Debby told me that Junne's, you know. Mickie, that true? What does Mickie say? I can see Mickie shrugging, telling Cynthia, Nah, not Junne. She's got something wrong here. Maybe Junne's tired of her or something? Got another girl. Who knows, let's go to sleep, Cynthia, I'm beat. But what's Mickie thinking? *Finuk*? Probably. It's Italian. Spelled *finocchio*, pronounced *finuk*. Means fag. No, it's not that little Italian puppet. That's *Pinoc-chio*. But think about it. Sweet little floppy-wristed puppet, and its nose grows like an erect dick. Those old gay Disney movie types pulling an inside joke on all those kids and their parents taking them to the movies, saying, Look at that Pinocchio, isn't he cute?

And what's it matter? First thing Monday morning me and Mickie go to see Melvin Johnson, Rodrigo's prosecutor. Dumpy's coming. Mickie gave him the ten thousand in cash, gave it to him personal, like Dumpy insisted. Will it help, Dumpy joining us? Will Melvin Johnson be more receptive to WD's plan we tell Melvin, Rodrigo's seriously considering your offer of cooperation, but first you need to bail him? Electronically ankle-cuff him and bail him? We'll see.

If Melvin doesn't bite, what Debby's telling Cynthia? What Cynthia tells Mickie later in bed? Doesn't mean shit. Because, what rhymes with bed, that's going to apply to me and Mickie when WD learns we failed?

Dead. That's what.

CHAPTER TWENTY-THREE

Mickie and me meet Dumpy Brown in the lobby of the federal courthouse. Upstairs, past security, is where the United States Attorney's Office is located. Assistant U.S. Attorney Melvin Johnson's there waiting for us. Today's the day we go see if our end-of-the-line plan has any legs.

Dumpy and we exchange handshakes, he and Mickie already cold-eyeing each other as they shake, say, How you doin', I can see it. Shit, we haven't even begun yet and blood's already boiling between them. Then we three get in the elevator, a couple of guys we don't know looking like IRS agents, maybe FBI, their haircuts and suits dead giveaways, riding up in the car with us. These guys are probably here to meet with one of the other prosecutors, get themselves prepared for the testimony they're about to give in some other case. We all nod at each other. That's it. No words. We size them up. They size us. Cordial enemies riding together. Nods only, no need for words.

Melvin makes us sit for about fifteen minutes in the waiting area, the government receptionist behind the bulletproof Plexiglas giving us our good-for-one-day-only, time-stamped, stick-on paper passes, telling us, Mr. Johnson axe can you have a seat, he be out and get you soon as he can. She's heavyset, way too much makeup, her rust-tinted jerry-curl hair glued in place. But she's wordlessly flirting through the bulletproof with Dumpy, batting her cow eyes at him like they're at opposite ends of the bar, DJ music playing too loud in the club. Dumpy's reading it, sitting in the fake leather low-backed chair decked out in his Day-Glo suit, winking at her through the glass, Hey, baby, how you doin' this fine day? Old guy like that, his own pasted over kinky hair strands covering his shiny scalp, and she's finding him attractive. What do you know?

Then the inner door opens and Melvin's standing there, shirtsleeves and tie, no jacket. "Morning," he says, indicating we should follow him down to his office. The receptionist is on the phone, but I see her eyes following Dumpy as he and we get up and follow Melvin Johnson into the inner sanctum of the U.S. Attorney's Office.

We get to Melvin's office. He's going to meet with us alone, apparently. There's no agent, no other young prosecutor. He indicates we should sit. He goes behind his desk. Then he waits on me and Mickie. Melvin and Dumpy haven't said a word to each other and Melvin's waiting for me or Mickie to explain Dumpy's presence. Mickie sees this too.

He motions his head toward Dumpy, puts on his best this-is-just-routine smile, and says, "Me and Junne have associated our colleague Harold Brown with us on the case."

That's it. Mickie's not about to explain that Dumpy's not wanting to be listed as co-counsel on the court docket. That he's here for this one meeting. Period. I watch Melvin and Dumpy eyeball each other.

And I'm looking for what? Some sort of black recognition thing? If it's there I can't see it. Fact is, I can't read shit between them as Mickie starts in to spelling out for Melvin, like WD Smith wants, all this crap how Rodrigo's thinking seriously about Melvin's plea-bargain offer, but first he needs to get some electronic-braceleted, home-detention bail here. Melvin's in his cheap white shirt and JC Penney tie, the outlines of his skinny black arms peeking through. He listens patiently to Mickie as I try and see, Is Melvin buying any of this? I notice something in Dumpy's eyes. He's way ahead of me here.

Mickie finishes. We wait for Melvin.

"That's it?" Melvin asks.

Mickie shrugs that's it, then pointedly looks over at Dumpy, silently telling him, Your turn. But Dumpy doesn't say a word. He sucks his teeth like he does, but he doesn't utter a single word. I see he and Melvin silently exchange glances, then Melvin looks away, back to Mickie. Waiting.

Melvin just stares at Mickie. Dumpy he is now ignoring. How many times throughout all the years he's been stuck in this job has Melvin Johnson sat at this same government-issue desk, listening to bullshit like this from some defense lawyer's got next to nothing to work with?

Mickie's eyes are now imploring Dumpy, Say something, for Christ sake, they're telling him. Dumpy looks at Mickie, then looks away. What's the point? he's thinking. This meeting's over.

"If that's it," Melvin tells Mickie, "I need to get ready for court." Meaning, Time for you guys to leave. Nothing more to talk about here.

Mickie's thinking, I can tell, should he try and press it some more. Is there any chance here? Even a sliver of daylight he can head for? Then Mickie looks over to me, signaling, Let's go. What's the point?

Down in the lobby, Dumpy's on the way out the door, Mickie grabs his arm. Dumpy turns and faces Mickie.

"Thanks for all your help," Mickie says to Dumpy, sarcasm dripping from every word.

"What you want, you got," Dumpy tells Mickie.

Mickie just stares at Dumpy. He doesn't want to hear what Dumpy's about to say. Neither do I.

"You wanted a rent-a-nigger. That's what you got," Dumpy says. "Didn't work, is all."

This stops Mickie cold. Look, not only is Dumpy right, that's what me and Mickie paid him for; Mickie's enough of a lawyer to know that if there had been any point in Dumpy chiming in up there with Melvin, he would have done it. We paid Dumpy—rented him, like he said—and Dumpy would have done more than sat there if there had been any reason to. He wasn't paid to make some shuck-and-jive comment to Melvin when there was no value whatsoever in his doing so. We didn't pay him to belittle himself, only to help if there was any point in it. There wasn't.

Dumpy waits to see, does Mickie have any more here. He doesn't. Dumpy nods at me, turns, and walks out of the lobby. I can't look at Mickie. He can't look at me. We're embarrassed, I guess. Because Dumpy's right.

So me and Mickie leave as well. Once out on the street we see the car. WD's boys are keeping an eye on me and Mickie again. Now at a distance, not like before, when Mickie confronted them outside of the courthouse and we thought those gangbangers worked for Rodrigo. No, those thugs are there, we can see them, but they're at a distance. Mickie and I understand. WD told them, Watch them. That's it. I mean, if WD wanted us dead, we'd be dead. Like Mumbles. Mumbles was our warning. WD's waiting. Keeping his options open.

Mickie says to me, Don't fucking tell Debby about this, about those shit heads in the car, about any of this. Okay? Yeah, Yeah, I got it, I tell him. Mickie doesn't want Debby telling Cynthia. He doesn't want Cynthia to freak out again. He's not ready for her to leave. Not yet, anyway. He wants to hold on to what he's got. I'm telling Mickie, Yeah, I understand. Don't worry, I'm not telling Debby. But I'm thinking, Did Debby tell Cynthia the other night they're whispering in the kitchen at Mickie's about me and her? What's really what? And did Cynthia then morning after tell Mickie? Can't tell from Mickie. In fairness, his mind's on something else right now. And so should mine be.

And since then?

Nothing.

It's been three weeks, just about. Me and Mickie have been going about our business. Our lives. As best we can. Every time the phone rings we're expecting it to be WD. But it isn't. Both of us noticing the gangbangers in the car, at a safe distance, keeping tabs on us. Everyone's waiting, it seems.

I've been seeing Slippery Williams at the jail. Been going over there regularly. As a lawyer I can see him pretty much whenever I want. And more and more with each visit I'm telling him about all this shit with Rodrigo. About WD Smith. Look, it's helping me somehow. Gets it off my chest. You know, I like Slippery. He's one smart guy. And yeah, I guess in a way he's kind of a friend. In a way. But I don't tell him anything about my private life. That I keep off-limits, strictly to myself. So maybe Slippery's not what you'd call a real friend. I don't know. It just helps me to talk about Rodrigo with him. So I do it.

And so me and Mickie wait, trying as best we can to keep our anxiety at bay. I mean, who knows? Maybe something will break, some lucky something will fall out of the sky. Land in our laps.

Something breaks, all right.

CHAPTER TWENTY-FOUR

I'm in my office and Janice tells me, Line one, the court's on hold, pick up, Junne.

On the line's the judge's secretary. "Mr. Salerno?" she says.

"Yes, I say," thinking, Which judge?

"The judge wants to see you and your co-counsel, Mr. Mezzonatti, in his chambers in one hour." She says this the way judges' secretaries speak to lawyers. Why? Because they know they can.

No way can you say to a judge's secretary, Hold on, there. How about you ask if can I make it? If my schedule is open? How about a Good morning, Counselor? Maybe a "please" thrown in there somewhere? Nope. Not all judges' secretaries are bitches. More than their fair share are, though.

I'm not even sure at this point which fucking judge she works for. I'm about to ask when she says, "*United States versus Rodrigo Gonzáles*. Can I tell the judge you and co-counsel will be in attendance as he has instructed?"

Like, what choice do I have here? Rodrigo's judge? I'm thinking. In chambers, not court? What the hell's this all about?

"Yes, ma'am," I say.

"And you will inform co-counsel, Mr. Mezzonatti?"

"Yes, ma'am," I say again.

"Very well, then," she says, and hangs up.

I realize I got the call first since on the court docket my name appears before Mickie's because back when this case started, I was the one Rodrigo chose as his lawyer. I brought Mickie into the case. So the judge tells his secretary, Call defense counsel, tell them my chambers one hour. Yes, Judge, she says. She calls me.

When me and Mickie get there, the secretary says, Go in, they're waiting.

They're waiting? Mickie and me exchange glances, then enter the judge's inner sanctum.

The judge is in his suit jacket. No robes. He's behind his desk, not on the bench, so, sure, he's in a suit. And who's sitting there on the side sofa, waiting on us? None other than Assistant DA Melvin Johnson. Both men have somber faces on.

"Please be seated, Counsel," the judge instructs, motioning us to the two chairs in front of his big square green-blottered desk.

This is the same judge told me I was smoking dope the first time I asked for bail in Rodrigo's case. He's this nondescript middle-aged white guy, would blend into the furniture if his name didn't begin with "Judge." There's not much to tell about him, really. He's somewhere around sixty, slight build, milquetoast pallid features, thinning gray hair. Nothing special in the appearance department. But he's been on the bench a long while. And I'll give him this. He knows his job. No matter what they tell you, most judges in the criminal courts know they need to move the perps from the courtroom to the prisons. They've got a kind of partnership with the DAs. Make sure the perps get their constitutional rights, at least enough of their rights that their defense lawyers can't convince the appellate court their clients were fucked over below. Then ship them out and get to the next perp. That's the only way they believe they can keep the system moving. Keep it unclogged. Like your toilet, so it won't overflow its shit contents.

Mickie and me take the seats we're offered. Melvin's looking at us, but there's no hello coming from him. He waits for the judge to speak.

"Counsel," the judge tells us. "You represent Mr. Rodrigo Gonzáles?"

He knows we do, else why the hell would we be sitting here, present at his orders? There's no court stenographer taking down what's being said. That's strange, I'm thinking. In criminal cases, rarely do you see that. Most everything's recorded. Mickie looks at me, letting me know I can answer the judge if I want to.

"Yes, Your Honor," I say.

"Yes," the judge says. "Well, then, Counsel. The court wants to inform you that your client has chosen to accept the plea agreement offered by the government when we were last in court."

Meaning? I want to ask. Last time I checked, me and Mickie were still Rodrigo's lawyers and Rodrigo—our client—never said anything like that to us.

"He has chosen to accept the assistant United States attorney's offer of cooperation," the judge tells us. "Correct, Mr. Johnson?" he asks Melvin, who now is busy studying his shoe shine. He can't look at us. That is not good.

What the fuck's this all about? me and Mickie are signaling each other.

Melvin opens the file that's lying on the sofa beside him, extracts a piece of paper, and hands it over to the judge. The judge glances at it, clear to me this is not the first time he's seen it, then pushes it across his desk in my direction, indicating, Pick that up, Counsel, read it.

I do. Then I pass it to Mickie. It's a statement, signed by Rodrigo. It says he understands that he has the right to have his lawyers present before he speaks with Assistant United States Attorney Melvin R. Johnson, and that he freely, knowingly, and voluntarily waives that right. Now I get it. I look over at Mickie. Yup, so does Mickie.

We made a tactical mistake when we met with Melvin and tried to sell him on WD's nonstarter idea that Rodrigo was favorably considering Melvin's cooperation deal but he needed bail first. That was a blunder. What we did was signal Melvin that Rodrigo was inclined to accept his deal. Of course, Melvin knows nothing about WD Smith. What he heard Mickie say in that meeting was that Rodrigo's ready to go for the deal. Forget the crap about bail and ankle bracelets at home, Melvin's thinking. That's lawyer posturing. Means nothing. The man wants to take the deal. And that deal is what's going to net Melvin some major goddamn drug smugglers. Some big noteworthy cases, Rodrigo his star witness against these guys Rodrigo knows, maybe some he's working for right now. And the notoriety of that's Melvin's ticket out of this dead-end DA's job he's been stuck in too long now. This is his ticket to the bench. Soon he gets to wear the robes, go home at four-thirty P.M., make the lawyers before him do the work, treat them like judges do. Only problem here, the only impediment, is the lawyers. He needs to bypass them.

Now, it's improper for a prosecutor to simply approach a defendant without his lawyer present. So what does Melvin do? I mean, he's not a bad guy, doesn't have a reputation for cutting corners. Melvin's problem? He does this by the book? He's got no chance Rodrigo takes the deal. Melvin's convinced me and Mickie are just too dumb to figure out what needs doing here. Melvin knows nothing, like I said, about WD Smith. Nothing about how WD's on top of this. About how WD will have me and Mickie assassinated if and when Rodrigo rolls over and agrees, yeah, he'll cooperate with the DA. So Melvin cuts this corner. Just this once, he tells himself.

How he does it, approaches Rodrigo, gets him to sign that paper and meet with him one-on-one, is anyone's guess. Maybe through some other inmate Melvin gets to approach Rodrigo on the cell block, makes it worth that inmate's while. Maybe through a guard. Slips the word to Rodrigo, tells him, You be smart, son, don't need no lawyers, see, the DA, he's good people. However he did it, he did it. And what Melvin's done, though he doesn't know it, is sign Mickie's and my death warrants.

"Your client's been moved to solitary," the judge is telling us. Letting us know that he and Melvin have thought of everything here. They're thinking that once it gets out in the cell block that Rodrigo's a snitch, he's done for; some other con shoving a prison-made shank between his ribs while he's standing in line for chow.

"Yeah," Melvin adds from the sofa. Now he's going to show poor dumb Mickie and me how thoughtful he's been, how he's covered everything. "We let the word out that Rodrigo's been moved to another facility, is in the regular prison population there. Just some routine inmate shuffling."

Yeah, right. It'll take about a day and a half for the entire Camden County Jail to learn that Rodrigo's still there, hiding out in solitary. How fucking long does Melvin really believe it will take? Of course, that's just a show for us. Melvin doesn't give a shit what the other cons think at this point. All he needs is for Rodrigo to stay alive so he can cooperate and testify when the time comes. And when WD goes to the jail to see Rodrigo, take his temperature? And he's told, Mr. Gonzáles has been moved to another facility? And he says, Yeah, which one? And they say, Can we get back to you on that? What happens then?

What can Mickie and me say here? Oh, hey, Judge, Melvin, listen, can we just tell you something? See, there's this guy whose name we don't know. Don't know where he works or lives, but we kind of think that he's Rodrigo's drug-baron boss. We call him WD Smith because . . . well, never mind that. But see, when this man learns that Rodrigo is in solitary confinement, out of his reach so he won't be able to kill him while he's out on bail and prevent him from cooperating against him? Well, then this man goes to plan B. Plan B? Right, Your Honor and Melvin, plan B has me and Mickie killed. See, WD makes it look like your boy Rodrigo ordered the hit, so then no way will you be able to use him as a cooperating witness after the papers get through with this story about how two former-cop, local-boy lawyers got wiped out by this Salvadoran scumbag drug dealer. I mean, how are you going to make a deal with him then? Offer him leniency and use him after that, right?

And what will the judge and Melvin say to Mickie and me if we say this? Well, you boys need to go to the police. Get them to protect you. And how are they going to do that? Rodrigo wants us dead, the police going to prevent that? How? Well, then, they'll say. You both be really careful.

Yeah, right.

The judge asks us, Any questions, Counsel? Me and Mickie just shake our heads no. I mean, we are speechless. Okay, the judge says. Nothing further, then. As we walk past the secretary, now busy on the phone laying the law down to some other poor son-of-a-bitch lawyer the judge wants for something or other, Melvin walks silently behind us. We get to the door to chambers, Mickie and me turn right, down the hall. Melvin turns left. His office is to the right, but he's pretending he's got business down the hall to the left. He doesn't say, See you, guys. Just turns and walks away. He knows he's done wrong. He just doesn't know how wrong.

I follow Mickie to the elevator. While we're waiting he tells me he's going home, fuck the office. I look at him. I mean, what can I say? Mickie repeats, Fuck the office. Cynthia's back on nights at the bar, he says. Might as well go home and get laid before I get killed.

We get to the lobby, Mickie just walks away. Yeah, sure, he's dispirited. Me too. It looks like there is no way out for us here. Our goose is cooked. What do I do? See Slippery. Why not?

CHAPTER TWENTY-FIVE

I'm in with Slippery. I tell him all about what just happened in the judge's chambers. How me and Mickie are fucked, no two ways about it. I am so dispirited. I say, "Slip. We are checkmated, boxed in. No fucking way out."

Here's Slippery Williams, sitting in the can, his bony self evaporating into his orange jumpsuit, his future up for grabs. And what's he doing? Sitting patiently across from me in the lawyers' interview room, listening to me.

What the hell am I doing here? What's the point? This is way too selfish, I'm thinking. Time to go.

"Slip," I say. "This may be the last time you see me."

Then Slippery says to me, "You want some help with this?"

Yeah, sure, I'm thinking. I mean, what can he do, where he is? Then I see he's deadly serious.

"I take care a this for you," Slippery says.

I really don't want to go there. Look, I ask Slippery for help (how he can help with Rodrigo locked away in solitary confinement is beside the point), I know right off the bat two things: One, the law will be broken. Two, there's a price to pay. The price? Could be anything, runs the gamut from money to things even more precious.

"Slip," I tell him. "You know I can't ask you."

Slippery knows that me and Mickie, for all our faults, are by-the-book guys. To ask Slippery for the kind of assistance he's offering would put us over that line we don't cross.

Slippery shrugs, waits because he's reading me. He can see that, despite everything I just told you, I'm thinking about it. We are probably being recorded here, I know that, and I'm still talking with him about this.

Mickie's home, in the rack with Cynthia, no doubt. Blocking this out as best he can. He's not telling her a thing. Cynthia's working nights at the bar, so she's home for him, giving him what he wants. Needs. Tonight, later, when Debby's back at my place from the spa she works at, me and her will be in the kitchen, having dinner she made. All we'll be doing is small talk. How was your day? Fine, yours? Like I said before, even without this Rodrigo business, things with me and her are strained. Really strained. I'm sitting here at the jail and all this is swimming through my mind like some whirlpool I'm getting pulled toward.

Slippery says, Think about it, Junne, talk to Mickie. Slippery's not about to do anything without me and Mickie green-lighting him. Slippery knows, he does something? Like I said, there's a price. Part of what's motivating him is friendship. I know that. But part's business too. It's how it is.

I don't tell him I will or I won't. I don't know myself what I'm going to do. I leave the jail, tell Slippery take care. Nothing more.

That night I'm in my apartment, in bed. It's late. Debby's asleep on the sofa. She hasn't made her crawl-into-bed-beside-me appearance. Maybe she won't tonight, I'm thinking. I'm lying there and every fucking little sound, every crack, every snap of a floorboard, every goddamn night noise is making me think it's WD or his goons. Plan B's in play, I'm convincing myself. It's too soon. WD couldn't have learned about Rodrigo. Or has he? Am I first, or have they already been out to Cherry Hill? Is Mickie already dead? His blood-soaked twisted body strewn over his bed, spent shotgun shell casings lying on the hardwood floor? Oh, come on, Junne, I try and tell myself. It's only fucking night noises. Get a fucking grip. And I'm thinking maybe Debby comes in tonight wouldn't be such a bad thing. Let me fall asleep.

The next day, midmorning, WD Smith makes another unannounced visit. I'm in Mickie's office with the two of them, WD's inquiring about our progress with Melvin Johnson. Has the DA reacted to our proposal (meaning WD's)? he's asking Mickie.

WD doesn't know yet. (Like I tried telling myself last night.) He apparently hasn't made another trip to see Rodrigo at the jail. Hasn't heard anything yet on the grapevine. So he's asking Mickie, Any news?

Mickie shoots me a quick glance.

"The DA's considering the offer," he lies to WD. "Should be hearing from him any day now." Mickie shrugs, cocks his head, like to tell WD, We may indeed have a shot here. Just give it a little more time. "The longer it takes," he tells WD, "the more encouraging a sign that is."

Like on his prior visits, WD considers what Mickie has just said, then gets up and walks out of his office and down to the street where his boys are waiting in the car.

Mickie and me look at each other. Mickie did what he had to do. I mean, what else could he say to WD? Tell him, Well, as a matter of fact, Mr. Smith, you'll never guess what happened? No, Mickie did the needful. Try and buy time.

But know what? There is no time. This fucking clock has stopped.

★

Later, past lunchtime, Mickie and me are still seated at a back table in the courthouse café, our uneaten sandwiches crusting on their plates. Tamara's eyeing us from a distance, seeing should she clean up, then deciding best leave us be right now.

I've been telling Mickie about Slippery's offer. First thing he says, "The man's in solitary, Junne. For Christ sake, what the hell can Slippery do with Rodrigo locked away twenty-four/seven?"

I'm sitting across from Mickie wondering, Do I look as bad as he does right now? Worse, probably, if getting even half that sandwich down, as hard as it was, is any indication.

Sure, Mickie's asking what can Slippery do with Rodrigo in lockup. Because, like me, Mickie doesn't want to really think about what Slippery's offering. Like I said, it's over the line we don't cross. And if we do, then we pay. Like I said, could be money, more likely something more important than money.

So we sit there, Tamara now in the kitchen, we hear her yukking it up with the Spanish guys in there washing the dishes, getting things ready for tomorrow's early morning breakfast crowd. The café's now empty out here. Just me and Mickie and our stale sandwiches, our cold coffee. Shit.

I mean, what can me and Mickie do? Leave town, just pull up stakes and disappear somewhere? How? Our homes are here, our families. Our identities. And anyway, we're licensed to practice law in New Jersey. We disappear, and what happens to all the cases we are listed as counsel of record in? Including Rodrigo's? The cases are called and we start not showing up for court, how long you think it will take before me and Mickie get disbarred? And if we lose our ticket in New Jersey, you think we're going to get licensed anywhere else in the country? Sure, we can run away. And then be what? It's out of the question. Okay, I'm sitting here with Mickie and I'm thinking about it. But shit, I couldn't do it. Neither could Mickie.

Mickie's staring at me. He shakes his head. "Christ, Junne," he says.

Red light? Green light?

★

Rodrigo's lunch is fed in his cell. Only time he's now allowed out is once every other day, twenty minutes for a shower, and then back in solitary. He gets his lunch tray handed through a slot in the steel door. He puts the tray on his knee and examines what they've given him this time. Beef stew. Maybe beef stew, Rodrigo thinks as he examines his meal, hunger just barely beating out revulsion. In a Styrofoam bowl there are some cut-up potatoes swimming in a brown fat-flecked watery gravy. He sees what could be shards of meat, some kind of brown stringy fleshlike substances swimming in among the potatoes, and what could be aged peas and maybe carrot chippings. On a paper plate there is one ultrathin slice of dry white bread, next to it a small carton of sugary fruit punch, and behind it a cloudy green-tinted Jell-O. Rodrigo sighs, then retrieves the plastic spoon and eats as much of it as he can get down. Twenty minutes later, Rodrigo's on the floor, writhing in pain. The guards eventually hear him, open the door, and see him, curled up on the floor, screaming in agony.

Later, after Mickie and me finally leave the courthouse café, I'm in my office, Mickie's on the other side of the wall, in his. My feet are up on the desk, I'm nervously chewing on a pencil. I should be thinking about what me and Mickie should be telling Slippery. I can't. Mickie's in there probably wall-staring like me. Thinking about anything but that. I know it's not helpful. Worse. It's pointless, but my feeble mind keeps drawing my thoughts back to how all this shit started. I'm like some kind of cheap magnet on a refrigerator door. Stuck on how could me and Mickie have been so stupid to get ourselves into this horrible mess. Okay, forget Mickie. How could I have been so fucking dumb? I'm going to die for a legal fee? I'm dwelling on this, all the while telling myself, Forget about it. Think about now, not then. But I can't. Why? I don't know. Maybe if I keep beating myself up on what I did, I can't think about what's going to happen to me. And to Mickie. Okay. I admit it. I'm scared. Shitless. Okay? You think Mickie isn't?

The guards now in his cell cuff Rodrigo despite he's immobile, and drag him to the prison infirmary. No doctor on call, just a male nurse. He looks at Rodrigo, still screaming and clutching his belly, the nurse tells the guards, Better take this man to the hospital. They say, Can't. Man's in solitary, strict instructions on him, can't be moved. Besides, they tell the nurse, he's a federal prisoner, we can't do shit unless the Feds say so. Call the Feds, then, the nurse says. Don't know what's wrong with him, but do know he'll be dead soon you do nothing. Then what are you going to tell the Feds?

The guards call the Feds. Two U.S. marshals just happen to be hanging around on their day off, say, We'll go. Aint' no thing. Can use the overtime. One's white, his partner's black. They've been a team for a few years now. Okay, the officer in charge tells them, but don't be using no heavy pencil when you're putting in your extra hours, those lunches you boys be eating, laughing as the two marshals, winking at him, say, Sure thing, you bet.

Slippery Williams is standing on the tier outside his open cell. It's late afternoon, all the cell doors are slid back, inmates milling around, visiting, scoring what's available from other prisoners, in some instances guards. He's with some of his boys, his co-defendants arrested and charged when he was. The others are from his crew doing time for earlier takedowns, here now on the tier for Slippery, watching his back. Slippery's leaning on the railing; he sees who he's looking for down below. The guy sees Slippery up there. Their eyes meet and the other guy nods up at him, letting Slippery know. Done. Slippery stares at the guard been on his payroll for years in case. Not a word, nothing, but he's gotten the message. Both know that. Slippery walks back into his cell, his boys following in behind. The guard down below goes about his business.

The two U.S. marshals, now on overtime duty, go to the jail, pick up Rodrigo who's now near-delirious with pain. He's all bunched up, mumbling things in Spanish how it hurts, calling for his mother. They put him in their car, tell the male nurse, Be faster than waiting for an ambulance, looks like this man's got no time left. They take him to Our Lady of Lourdes Medical Center, the closest hospital, just down on Haddon Avenue from the jail. Rodrigo's rushed through admissions, now more dead than alive. He's put in a private room, the marshals telling the hospital staff, Sorry, but we gotta cuff this guy to the bed, we'll both be outside the door.

The doctors do the tests, order Rodrigo's stomach pumped, put him on IV solutions, blood transfusions also. Easy to tell what this is, they tell the marshals. Tests will confirm, but this man's been poisoned. Rat poison's the best guess. Major dose, lethal it's not caught in time, one of the doctors says. Probably mixed into his lunch we just pumped from his stomach. Stuff's odorless, tasteless. Any of that in the prison commissary, you think? The marshals shrug. They tell the doctor, We don't work there, we're Feds. The doctor stares at them a beat too long, then says, Your prisoner'll be all right now.

It's suppertime and I'm at the kitchen table in my apartment. Until a minute ago Debby was here seated across from me. Now she's in my bedroom, the door's shut, and I'm out here alone. Whatever it was she asked me, I don't know, I guess my mind was elsewhere and I just ignored her. Didn't mean to. So I look over to my closed bedroom door, thinking, Screw it, I'll sleep out here on the sofa, use her sheets and pillow she daytime keeps in the hall closest. But I've got to get her out of here, I'm thinking, not wanting to think that maybe soon this apartment's going to be empty of the both of us.

And while I'm sitting here, Mickie's in his bathroom, leaning over the sink, staring back at himself in the mirror. He rubs his hand through his shaggy hair, examines his tired eyes, while Cynthia in the bedroom finally gets dressed for work. She told him no more, I can't anymore, I'm sore, please, baby, I've got to get to work. Mickie realizing that he can't really completely lose himself, make it all disappear by all afternoon and evening fucking her past exhaustion. He's ignoring Cynthia as she finishes dressing, lost now in the very thoughts he's kept away.

Later that night, both marshals still at the hospital calling in, telling the agent on duty, We'll stay here, work the night through, money's good. Up to you, the duty agent says, I'll stick it in the computer. He doesn't think to ask, You call the perp's lawyers? Let them know? The two marshals don't mention anything either. An oversight, they will later say. So they both stay outside the room. Rodrigo's sedated, hooked up to his IVs. The way they tell it later, one of the marshals, the white one, tells his partner, I'll go down for coffee, want some? Yeah, sure, he says. Not ten minutes after he's gone, the black marshal hears Rodrigo inside the room calling to him. He goes in to see what Rodrigo wants.

Around that same time I'm trying to sleep on the sofa, Debby still behind the shut bedroom door, her smell strong on the sheets and pillow I'm using. I'm wide awake, my mind's loop-de-looping like a roller coaster without brakes. Mickie's at his place alone, Cynthia at work, calling him now and then, saying sorry, baby, but you wore me out. Mickie's telling her don't worry about it. She can hear the distance in his voice, his mind miles away.

The black marshal's in the room, Rodrigo's now awake, says, Please, can I use the bathroom? Use the bedpan, the marshal tells him, you're cuffed to the fucking bed, bro. The way he tells it later, Rodrigo pleads with him, saying, Come on, what can I do, man? I'm weak as shit (*week as sheet*), come on, give me some dignity, here. Don't make me go in no fucking little pan. The marshal's thinking, Okay, man's just had his stomach pumped, what can he do? I'll uncuff him, lead him to the bathroom by the arm, then after recuff him to the bed. Sure, I should wait for my partner, but the guy's weak as shit.

Way he tells it, when Rodrigo comes out of the bathroom he's a new man, strong as a bull. The marshal's leading him to the bed, holding the wheeled pole the IVs are on, Rodrigo grabs for the marshal's gun, there's a struggle. Each man's using all his available strength, both have their hands tight on the gun, one pushing it this way, the other that. It's touch and go. The marshal later says he's not sure exactly whose finger was on the trigger when it went off, aimed point-blank at Rodrigo's face. Put a hole right through it, what a mess.

At the internal affairs hearing both men say, We should have known better. But what can you do? I mean, we thought the guy was half-dead weak. Had we known, then of course we would have behaved differently. We feel terrible about this, not so much for the perp, but for the procedure we fucked up on.

In the end, nothing happens. They both get four weeks' suspension, full pay, full benefits. They're told, This will have to go in your file, guys. Could affect something careerwise in the future. Sure, we understand, they say. But these marshals no longer need a career. They won't leave the marshals service right away. They know better than that. They'll wait two years, maybe three, then both will take early retirement. With their pension, and what they earned that night at the hospital, that part in cash, no taxes due, they're fixed up fine. Maybe one will buy a small house on the Jersey shore, or one will open a small business, repairing lawn mowers, something like that. These guys are done.

The genius of Slippery, when you think about it, is the thoroughness of his thinking. Did he expect the rat poison to get Rodrigo, or was that part of the setup? Were the two off-duty marshals there, hanging around the office just then, for insurance, in case? Or were they going to be the ones to take care of things from the get-go? And the black-white thing? It's the white marshal goes for coffee, leaving his partner without backup. The black one does the shooting. Harder for the papers to make a race thing out of it when it's the black marshal shoots the Hispanic prisoner. And Melvin Johnson, black himself, is not likely to do much of anything about Rodrigo's killing. Sure, he lost his star witness. But what's he going to do? Start a new grand jury investigation, probe into the black marshal killing a badass drug dealer to save his own life? Not a good career move, Melvin will quickly realize, not good press. Won't help with anything Melvin wants or needs. No, Melvin will read the papers about the incident, sigh, then go back to his regular caseload. I mean, what other realistic options does he have?

But what you've got to admire is Slippery's thinking on me and Mickie. We never said yes. We just didn't say no. But Slippery knew. He saw what this would mean for us. And for him. Slippery saw through our weakness. Our wanting to cling to the outer edge of respectability like some guy on a high-up floor. But without help we'd never get back inside to safety. Just not smart enough, I guess. So we never said no. To Slippery that was all the green light he needed.

Slippery isn't going to ask us for any money for his handling of the Rodrigo problem. Not a penny. Whatever those two marshals got comes out of Slippery's pocket. Not a dollar will change hands between Slippery and us. Slippery's upcoming trial we'll handle on the house. Anyone asks, we'll say we did that on account of Slippery's been such a good client in the past and his assets are frozen by the court. The man needs representation, we'll say. What we don't charge him for our work may or may not be roughly equal to Slippery's out-of-pocket for the Rodrigo thing. But here's the genius of what he's done. When Slippery told me in the jail go and talk with Mickie first, he wanted to make certain both of us understood fully the potential price Slippery was charging us in exchange for our lives.

Slippery goes to trial and he's acquitted of all charges, that's the end of the matter. He gets our representation free of charge, he's back on the street. That's that. But if he's convicted by the jury, and if he gets a sentence from the judge that puts him away effectively forever, well, then Slippery now has something to trade with. Think about it. He's got two local criminal lawyers asked him to off their client. Yeah, he did it, he might tell the district attorney. I mean, what could he do? he might tell the prosecutor. His assets were frozen, he needed their help with the trial. He arranged it. Cut me some slack, he might tell the DA, reduce my time, say to five years instead of what I got. I'll give you two members of the New Jersey bar and, for good measure, I'll throw in a couple of dirty U.S. marshals actually did the killing. If it comes to it and Slippery's convicted and sentenced to long hard time, will he give us up?

What do you think? Why wouldn't he? Yeah, we're friends. But a lifetime behind bars . . . Think about it.

But look at it our way. Mickie and me are alive. Can we live with it? So to speak. Yeah. I can. Mickie too. What does all this say about us? Nothing much good, I guess. We could have played it straight. Went to the cops. Done it by the book. With the best of intentions, what could the cops have done? WD Smith's plan B was plan B. Chances are we'd be dead by now. Two dead defense lawyers. Rodrigo the supposed killer, now effectively untouchable as a government witness. Me and Mickie would be pitied, well remembered in our obituaries. But dead.

And WD Smith is gone.

Me and Mickie have to appear in court for the dismissal of dead Rodrigo's case. A formality. The guy's stone-cold dead, but the docket needs to be closed. So me and Mickie are in court, standing in front of counsel's table, the judge up on the bench. Assistant U.S. Attorney Melvin Johnson's across the aisle from us, on his feet too.

"Mr. Johnson," the judge says matter-of-factly, like we're dealing with a request for a routine postponement here. Like he doesn't know what's coming. "Does the government wish to bring on a motion for the court's consideration?"

"Yes, Your Honor," Melvin says, with not even a glance in our direction. When we walked into the courtroom this morning, me and Mickie shook hands with Melvin. He smiled, said, Morning, and that was it. Not a word out of him about what happened to Rodrigo. We will shake hands with him when this proceeding ends. We will walk one way down the hall, he the other. We won't talk about this with him. Ever.

"Very well," the judge says, meaning, Speak.

"Your Honor," Melvin continues. "At this time the government moves for the dismissal of the indictment against Mr. Rodrigo Gonzáles. The defendant is deceased."

That's it. The judge looks over to us. We need to put something on the record as well. All neat and tidy. Mickie nods to me, You do it.

I'm thinking, do I say to the court, No objection? I mean, what kind of objection could there be to the government's not being able to prosecute our dead fucking client?

"That is correct," I opt for, meaning, Yeah, Judge, Rodrigo's dead, can we please go now?

"Very well," the judge says. "So ordered." Then he nods to the bailiff, who rises and announces that court stands in recess until further notice.

Three minutes later me and Mickie are out on the street down the steps in front of the courthouse. We are about to go to our car. Coming our way, heading up the street so that the front passenger side is closest to us, we see a car we recognize all too well. The car slows, then stops. We see WD Smith, window remaining up this time, looking at us. Our eyes meet. Then we see him turn to Carlos, his driver, and say let's go, or something like that, because the car starts moving and slowly drives down the street away from us. Me and Mickie can't help ourselves, we stand there frozen, silently watching as WD's car goes to the end of the block and then turns right and out of sight. Then we go to our car.

Because that's that.

Well, yeah, that's that, but we still have Slippery's upcoming trial. What are the chances me and Mickie will pull a rabbit out of the hat? Not good, you know that.

Still, as they say, in a courtroom anything can happen. Lightning can strike. At least me and Mickie will be around to give it a shot.

You never know.

FIVE MONTHS LATER

Spring has finally arrived in Camden. Gray is now blue. The trees have leaves, flowers are up. But me and Mickie are stuck inside the Camden County Courthouse and we will be here for a long while. Today is the first day of Slippery Williams's trial, not counting jury selection. That alone took two full days. The jury's in their room, not yet been called out here into the courtroom to hear opening statements from the lawyers. Judge Thurgood Rufus Brown hasn't yet taken the bench, he's late. Judges are almost always late; they take their sweet time before bouncing into the courtroom. Me and Mickie think that's their way of telling the lawyers waiting on them, Sure, you're making more money than me, but I have all the power here, so you wait until I'm good and ready to come out.

This trial is going to be a zoo. In addition to Slippery and his two lieutenants, including Lamont, the one Slippery's punk-ass nephew didn't bludgeon to death with the butt of his Glock pistol the night they got taken down, two more of Slippery's other thugs who were later charged and then added to the case are standing trial with him. That makes five defendants in all. The two thugs each have a lawyer. The two lieutenants have Dumpy Brown. The lawyers are all huddled around the defense counsel's table. I'm sandwiched in between Dumpy and Mickie, since to put them next to each other's inviting trouble. They are barely speaking, both hair-triggered. Hating each other, but doing their jobs. (Whether Dumpy knows about what went down between Rodrigo, Slippery, and us is anyone's guess.)

So Slippery and the other defendants are seated behind the defense table in a long row. All around them are guards, since all these defendants are in jail, no bond. And need I mention that they're lethal dangerous if left alone for even a minute? Across the aisle sit not one but three prosecutors. There's the black woman the DA forced into the courtroom to try and appease Judge Brown, who asked for the continuance when I represented Slippery's punk nephew a while back. With her are the two other assistant DAs from before, the white and the young Asian guys. Their part of the table's filled to the brim with files and other papers. They're loaded for bear here, ready to show their parents sitting in the gallery that all that money for college and law school was put to good use, look at us now, how about that.

Speaking of Alonzo the punk nephew, he's scheduled to be the first prosecution witness after opening statements have been made. Despite best efforts, Slippery never managed to get to the kid. He tried, I suppose, but the DA's office kept the kid safe somehow. Must have taken some doing, given Slippery's reach, inside the prison system as well as out. The courtroom is wired for sound, with speakers and other audio equipment everywhere so the jury and the rest of us can hear the surveillance wiretaps Judge Brown ruled can be played as evidence.

Speaking of witnesses, it's got nothing to do with this trial, but Little Chip didn't make it. Me and Mickie saw in the paper a few days after Christmas that her body had been found behind a strip club in Boston where she had been working. The article said her throat had been sliced with what appeared to be a razor-edged knife. Seems she was stripping under the name Rona Rosenberg—although it's doubtful that's how Buffalo found her. If it was Buffalo who did her. Shame, no matter who did it.

A lot has happened in these five months. Over Christmas I took Debby to my family. We did the seven fishes dinner and midnight mass together. My mother was so pleased to see me with a "girlfriend." Mickie and Cynthia came too, then they spent Christmas day with Mickie's family. I felt good about inviting Debby. Still, after New Year's Eve Debby left, quit her job and went back home. She told me she just needed to go. I told her I understood. I hear from her every now and then. E-mails. She's engaged to her high school sweetheart, says she's already pregnant so the wedding date's being moved up, will I come? You bet, I e-mailed back.

Cynthia died. It was really tragic. She was leaving the bar she worked at very late after closing. A kid in a car struck her as she crossed the street against the light not in the crosswalk. Like Mumbles died, but different. The kid was loaded, he had just dropped his girl off and was lost trying to find his way back to the Philadelphia suburbs. It really wasn't his fault, but maybe if he wasn't loaded he might have stopped in time. When the police arrived the kid was on his knees, cradling Cynthia in his arms, rocking her, begging her not to die, please don't die. He and his parents took full responsibility for what happened. Mickie was devastated. I have never seen him so torn up. He went about his life, but for the longest time he just grieved for her. He lost some of that excess weight he's been lugging around, worked harder than I've seen him work in a while. Like I said, first Mumbles, then her. Different, but still tragic.

Mickie's got a new woman now. Although I can see that he still misses Cynthia. Not that they were likely to last, but the circumstances of her death, her life cut so senselessly, so prematurely short, has just affected him. But that lesson we all think we learn when a tragedy like that happens; you know, life is fleeting, enjoy what you got while you can? It doesn't seem to stay learned. Right? Anyway, he's got a new woman.

She's Arty Bernstein's secretary. Ex-secretary now. Like most of Mickie's women, she's good- not great-looking, but has a body that more than makes up for any minor deficiencies in the beauty department. And like Mickie seems to want them, she's smart enough, not more. I like her. She's moved in with Mickie. First Monday night I'm over for football, she's already walking around in her halfway open robe, her underwear showing. What can you do?

And like I said, she's no longer Arty Bernstein's secretary. Arty had to let that go, her quitting after she hooked up with Mickie. You see, his entire firm, all of Bernstein, Smulkin, is under grand jury investigation for bribing insurance adjusters, and paying off cops and ambulance drivers to steer accident victims to their offices. Arty asked me and Mickie will we represent them. Here's the deal, he tells us, free rent in exchange for your help with the grand jury, we didn't do shit the other plaintiffs' law firms in Camden don't do, he's telling us. What a defense that will be. We agree to the free rent.

Then Mickie and me see how much trouble these guys are really in. All the paperwork needs to be reviewed that's been subpoenaed to the grand jury, all the potential witnesses need interviewing. Mickie says to me, That son of a bitch Arty's got the better of the deal, here. Free fucking rent isn't going to come near what we'd make we charged him by the hour *and* paid his goddamn rent, including the dollar-whatever for the coffee. I know where he's going with this. Don't say it, I tell him. Arty's just smarter than us, that's all. Look, I tell Mickie, we go with this deal for a while, see if him and the others in the firm get indicted. They do, we renegotiate the deal. What are they going to do at that point? I tell him. We'll know the case; it'll cost too much for Arty and his partners to retain new lawyers and pay for them to get up to speed where we're already at. We'll make it on the back end, I tell Mickie. You're right, he says. But he's grumbling about that fucking Arty anyway.

And I met somebody. After Debby went back home, Mickie losing that weight, it looking like we're both going to live after all, I decide it's time for me to go back to the gym. I'm doing a bench press and this guy who's working out on one of the machines says, Want a spot? Yeah, sure, thanks, I say. He's leaning over me on the bench, his hands on the bar in case I need help, I see he's wearing a wedding ring. I thank him for the spot. That's it.

Later, I'm in the locker room taking off my workout clothes for the showers, I see the guy walk by. He's got a towel tightly wrapped around his waist. Remember how I said mostly the fags do that in here? Not all who do that are fags, of course. I don't think much of it. Then, when I'm back from the showers (un-towel-wrapped), I'm sitting on the bench in my underpants, about to put my socks on, the guy's now fully dressed, his gym bag slung over his shoulder, he walks by on his way out, says, Take care. Yeah, I say, see you, hey, and thanks for the spot out there. No problem, he says. You new here? he asks. Nope, I say, just been skipping coming. I know how that is, he says. We keep talking as I finish getting dressed, then he says, Got time for a beer? Yeah, sure, I say.

We have a beer. Go our separate ways. The next time I'm at the gym he's out on the floor too. I get a spot from him on the bench press. I spot him when it's his turn. After the gym we go for another beer. Like I said, the guy's wearing a wedding ring. Still, I see something in his eyes; not all the time, but I see it when we're in the bar, across from each other at the table. Saw it the first time too. At least I thought I did. Then, midway through our conversation that second time out, we're just shooting the shit the way guys do in a bar, he says to me, I'm not gay, in case you were thinking. I don't know what to say, because that is what I was thinking, but no fucking way am I going to tell him that. So I don't say a thing.

I'm bisexual, he tells me. Tells me his wife knows, that they've come to an understanding on account of she doesn't want to lose him. She lets it go, his nights out, as he calls them. He assures her he's careful—real careful, and discreet. It's working so far, he tells me. I still don't say a word. I don't know what to say. He's a good-looking guy, about my age, kind of rugged-looking with graying hair, good build, nothing limp-wristed at all about him. So, he says. You?

What am I going to say? Me what? I know what he's asking. My mind says, Junnie, this is Camden. Where you live. You don't need to overreact here, don't need to act annoyed he even asked, say fuck no, like you're pissed he would even ask. All you do is shrug, tell him, Me? No. Hey, thanks for the beer, I gotta go. What I say is, Yeah, with an explanation.

I don't know. All this stuff with Rodrigo. Cynthia dying like she did. Even Little Chip. I don't know, I guess I told my hesitating mind, What the fuck, tell him. And I did, about how I've been hiding it all these years. How I don't want to be like I am, and why. I even told him about my thing for heterosexual men. Maybe when I came out that night in bed with Debby, it broke my cherry, so to speak. Maybe it's just easier now for me. Whatever. I told him. The guy smiles, says,

Sounds like a solid foundation for a relationship. A married bisexual guy and a semi-closet gay. I chuckle. Yeah, I say. Real solid.

We see each other off and on. I took him to dinner at Gallo Nero, the place Mickie's not ever going to again. He says he wants me to meet his wife, his kids. Says he spoke to his wife, she says she'd like that. Me? I'm not too sure how I feel about that, but I told him, Yeah, sure, be great.

Anyway, Judge Brown's due in the courtroom any minute. Me and Mickie may have more riding on the outcome of this case than even Slippery. We'll see. Dumpy's sucking his teeth, nervous like everyone else in here. I'm feeling okay, I guess. My life's far from in order. But at least I'm making some progress. And about my new friend? I'm not saying a word to Mickie about that, I've decided.

Of course, I will.

Mickie's my best friend.

ACKNOWLEDGMENTS

On occasion, when I am in New York on legal business, I escape my comrades-in-arms so that my publisher, David Rosenthal, and I can have lunch at one of our favorite restaurants. A two-minute walk from Simon & Schuster, turn left on 47th Street, and smack in the middle of the diamond district sits this foreboding Kosher style deli, more in style with the late 1950s than the here and now. On one of those occasions, over to-die-for (or from) briskets on rye with slopped-on mustard, and an endless supply of pucker-sour pickles, I told David I had with me the few pages I had written of what became *Death by Rodrigo*. (Truth is I forgot to hand him the pages, as he reminded me back out on the street before parting company, each in search of our own antacid tablets.)

I have known David a long time. He has always encouraged me to write. Sometimes it works; sometimes, well . . . I had a lot of fun with *DBR* and without David's encouragement I would have missed out on it. He assigned Marysue Rucci as my editor, and said she would make *DBR* a better book. He was more than right. Our collaboration was challenging, insightful, and immensely enjoyable. Marysue's assistant Virginia (Ginny) Smith was there twenty-four/seven with whatever needed doing, from matters of substance to those of mere form—never missing a beat.

My New York agent, Leigh Feldman, is my champion. She is the best; I could not ask for anyone better. Ditto my Hollywood agent, Lynn Pleshette.

Jane Daley, my legal secretary/assistant/reminder-of-all-things-pushed-to-the-side-of-my-desk, was there from the first word written. Jane is a reader, and her feedback guided me through to *DBR*'s concluding paragraphs.

Finally, my family: my wife, Simma, our two daughters, Shana and Margot, and Shana's husband, Michael. Without them there is no me. How does one express that level of gratitude?

—RL

ABOUT THE AUTHOR

Ron Liebman is a senior partner in the Washington, DC, office of one of America's top law firms. He specializes in litigation, both domestic and international. He is the author of the novel *Grand Jury* and the nonfiction *Shark Tales*. He is married to the artist Simma Liebman. Their two daughters live and work in New York.